The Ridge Walker

Written by,

Jack Hemphill

Published by
Willow Oak Publishing

Library of Congress Control Number: 2016907609
ISBN: 978-0-9899516-2-3
Printed in the United States of America

CHAPTER 1

JESS

My family lived on a little scrap of land between the Redbriar River and the Black Mountains of North Carolina. Besides Mama, I was the only girl in our family. I shared a bedroom with my two older brothers. To them I was just another guy and we fought like hungry dogs. I wanted the same things all girls wanted, and when I grew up, I needed what all women need, but I never dreamed I would live alone as the last Celtic medicine woman in these mountains.

I was fourteen when my two great-aunts, Aunt Reese and Aunt Brusie, told me I was ready. They were known all over the mountains for their healin' work, and many families depended on them just as they had depended on women in my family for almost two hundred years. With Mama and Dad's approval, I dropped out of school and moved in with Aunt Reese who lived at the base of Stumpy Ridge. At first, I helped with chores like carryin' her herb and medicine satchels as she climbed the mountain trails to her patients' houses. When we weren't takin' care of patients, I worked in her herb garden.

I've never had a single regret. Aunt Reese took good care of me. From the general store she purchased food, clothin', and just about everythin' I ever needed. Every few weeks, she bought an old book or two for me and insisted I read at least one a month. That was my only education after I moved in with her.

By the time I reached eighteen, I was treatin' half her patients by myself. By twenty, I took care of all of 'em. She lived one more year after that and left it all to me, includin' her property and her practice.

I've treated every kind of ailment that anybody in those mountains could imagine. I knew every person in every family and they all knew me. I held 'em when they were born naked and warm from their mother's womb. I held 'em when they were old and givin' up their last breath in silence and turnin' cold. I made my rounds every week and met with friends or patients almost every day, but I was always by myself at night.

The people that lived on Stumpy Ridge liked to call themselves *Ridge People*. They were mostly small farmers and crafters, but some worked the quarry owned by the Burns family. When the Second World War broke out, it was harder to ship crafts and produce to stores, so the Ridge People started a roadside market at the base of the mountain. They laid out goods on tables and blankets the first Saturday every month except, of course, in winter. By the time the war was over, visitors from as far away as Ashville, and Tennessee, and the other side of the French Broad River came to buy our crafts, and produce, and my potions.

CHAPTER 2

McKENZIE

Between Indian tales and the ancient traditions of Scots-Irish settlers, there is a myth or legend associated with almost every hill and stream in the Blue Ridge Mountains. After six weeks of searching, I knew all there was to know about The Ghost of Hot Springs, the Brown Mountain Lights, the Siren of the French Broad River, and at least a dozen Indian spots considered sacred. That's when I discovered Dauber Higgins who lived in a shack built on a rock where the Redbriar River empties into the French Broad.

Getting directions to Dauber's house was easier than finding it, since he had no street address, but people along the river all told me the only way to find Dauber Higgins was to walk upstream on the south bank a clean mile past the Redbriar. When I finally found his house, I wasn't sure if it was real or my imagination. It was made almost entirely of river stone clothed with the same thick green moss that covered everything in sight. The moss, the dark rusted tin roof, and the trees that stretched their long branches over the house, made the structure almost invisible. There were only three windows on the front and one on the side. All the windows on the river side of the structure had heavy wood shutters. A cold April wind following the river bit into my neck. I hoped someone was home.

I banged on the door. Somewhere in the old house a voice muttered, "Come on in." The inside was dark, except a glow coming through the three windows behind me and from a lightbulb above the sink where Dauber was cleaning fish. His gray beard was streaked with a color as red as the river's bottom. He wore a gray flannel shirt with a faded plaid pattern. He looked as if he had been born from one of the ancient tales I had recorded I my notebooks.

"What can I do fer ya?" he asked.

"I'm Mac Davis. I was told you know every legend and tale that ever came out of this area."

"Yep, that's me."

"I've been digging up old stories to put in a magazine series. Can you help me? "

"Which stories you wanna know about?"

"The ones I haven't heard. I'd like to write things nobody knows."

Dauber washed his hands and joined me in the front room.

"Look yonder," he pointed out the window toward the river. "There's a woman, a devil, been livin' in that old river for a hundred years and draws men like you into the water and drowns 'em."

"Yes, I've heard about her."

"I've seen her four times in my life."

"How did you keep from getting sucked into her spell?"

"I'm too smart for her."

"Tell me some tales I've never heard."

"I know at least twenty Indian stories I'm sure you never heard."

"Like what?"

"Lots of legends of deer and bobcat spirits. Haunted rocks and caves. Got stories of Indian braves searchin' for their lost lovers."

"Like the one at Blowing Rock?"

"Yep, but I can tell you 'bout one right over there in Stumpy Ridge, I'll bet you don't know."

I was skeptical, but I asked him to tell me about it anyway.

He had a raspy, strong voice, but lowered it to a whisper as he said, "Indians don't like to talk about it and people who live on that ridge *never* talk about it."

"Why?"

"'Cause some of them families been up there for generations and they don't want to stir up nothin' they're scared of."

"I've driven around that mountain a bunch of times. Never even thought about climbing the ridge."

He walked to the window that faced west. "Can see only the top of it this time of year, but in dead winter you see most of the ridge. From here it looks like a giant tree stump made of stone."

"So what's the legend about?"

"The mountain sings."

"You mean like it has a real voice?" I joined him by the window and looked toward the mountain.

"Yes, but there're two voices. The legend says that an Indian couple is searching for their boy lost in a snowstorm. On windy days, you can hear 'em callin' for their child."

"Mr. Higgins, if the people won't talk about it, how

5

am I going to research it?"

"You're right. They won't talk about it to *strangers*. You gotta get to know at least one of 'em.

"Okay, any suggestions?"

"Yes, a woman who lives there named Jess. Her family was among the first settlers."

"How do you know her?"

"I go up to their market a few times every year and buy stuff from her."

"What kind of stuff?"

"Medicine; she's a healer, you know, what some call a granny witch."

"Oh, God."

"No, she's no hag or nothin'. Strong woman, mus' be around thirty. You jus' gotta find a way to get close to her 'cause she knows everything 'bout everybody up there. Walks that whole mountain every week distributin' her potions, so she's got the whole history and every story 'bout that mountain in her head."

"Mr. Higgins, if the legend is a secret, she's not going to talk to me, a stranger looking for something to write. She'll know what I'll do with it, and if this tale is as interesting as it sounds, and if it's published, lots of people will want to stomp around up there. From what you said, I don't think she's going to let that happen."

"You're right. If you want to get to know her, or get close enough for her to open up to you, you can never tell her what you're doin'. You understand what I'm sayin'?"

"Yes, but I don't know how I'm going to approach her."

"Mr. Davis…I'm sure you'll be able to figger it out. Why don't you buy some medicine from her."

"What kind of medicine?"

"She got somethin' for jus' 'bout everythin'."

"Does she have something for insomnia?"

"Got somethin' for everythin'."

"When do they have that Market?"

"One Saturday a month and this is the Saturday and they close the market at four o'clock. Better getagoin'."

"Well, thank you very much for your help," I said.

"Happy ya came to see me, Mr. Davis. Come back anytime. I'm always here, but next time plan on stayin' awhile."

I could have spent days talking with him, but when he told me about Stumpy Ridge, I knew I had to go.

By the time I got back to my car, it was five past three, and I had less than an hour to get there before she packed up her medicines and headed home.

I still couldn't believe I might have found a story to write. Even if I only got one article published, I could call myself a freelance writer. An Asheville magazine was interested in my proposal for a *Mountain Folktale* series that would include photographs. I love that word, *free-lance*. Anything with *free* in it is good, but *free-lance* sounds like your first day out of the cage, like you don't know where you're going but can't wait to get there. It means I get to do what I want to do. The word implies someone that travels everywhere fearlessly, like some kind of dragon slayer.

I was as tired as I was excited. The road forks at the edge of the little town of Redbriar. The left turn was a shortcut to my farm near Asheville, and the right led over the covered bridge and up to Stumpy Ridge. If I had turned left for home, I could have gotten back to work on some of the nagging, unfinished work on my orchard.

But if I turned right, I would have enough time to find the medicine woman before she left for the day.

My tires roared over the planks covering the Redbriar River Bridge and I sped through Weavertown and climbed the steep drive to Stumpy Ridge Road. Dauber told me the market was always held in a cleared field beside the road near a building used as a general store. I parked in a grassy spot and dashed along paths of about thirty-five or forty tables, in three straight rows, and past two dozen blankets spread on the ground, beside a line of white oaks. I ran past farmers standing behind tables with tin cans filled with black dirt and tiny sprouts, and jars of fish bait, hand tools, and small wood furniture. I passed women seated by displays of woven baskets, sweaters, sweet potatoes, canned fruit, and pies. At the end of the lot, under a tree, I saw a red quilt with sealed bottles and jars of different sizes. A tall woman with hair the color of September straw smiled at an old lady half her size, as she handed her two bottles in exchange for fifty cents and jar of jam.

The tall woman looked at me and nodded a greeting. I realized I had no idea what to say to her. I nodded back and surveyed the display of medicines.

"A man named Dauber Higgins told me about you," I said.

"What'd Dauber say?" she said with a soft voice.

"Said you could cure anything."

"Whatcha need?"

"Oh, something for insomnia," I was impressed with how convincing I sounded.

"Yes," she said as she quickly scooped up a package at the edge of her blanket. "This is the last box," she said.

"What is it?"

"Hops. You put a few in your pillow each night and use some for makin' hot potions." I paid her fifty cents.

"Got something for allergies?"

She bent down and picked up two jars, one large about a quart size and one small enough to hold in my palm. "One of these will do it," she said.

I took the small one and said, "What is it?"

"Rabbit tea."

I paid her another fifty cents. She smiled and nodded as if to say "good-bye."

I couldn't think of anything else to talk about, so I walked away and glanced back a few times. She carefully placed each of her jars in a canvas bag. When she started rolling up her quilt, I hurried back to the car and watched her walk toward me. I always kept my camera on the seat beside me and managed to fire off a shot before she was close enough to notice.

I had hundreds of photographs of Blue Ridge people, mostly of the families along the Redbriar River Valley. They differed from the rest of Appalachia and for some unknown reason, they fascinated me. I drove a twelve year old blue Chevrolet with enough dings, scrapes, and rust spots to feel and look like part of the backwoods crowd. It had taken me through the mountains so many times, people probably recognized my car long before they knew me.

While watching her in my mirror, I took a pinch of the dry ground leaves in the jar she said would cure allergies, but it tasted so bitter, exotic, grassy, and musty I almost sneezed.

With her medicine bag strapped over her left shoulder and her quilt rolled up and held like a rifle braced against her right shoulder, she climbed a small hill to the grassy spot behind my car. Her eyes were fixed on the dirt road ahead as she marched toward me. I stepped out of the car, held the bottle up, and said, "I need to ask a question." She slowed down, but did not stop. "I'm going to try this tonight. Should I just brew it like tea, and how often do I use it?"

"It's tea. Take it as often as you can stand it and as long as it takes to get well," she answered glancing my way only momentarily.

"And if I don't get well?"

"Come back and get more."

"I will, but does that mean it's going to take a while to get rid of my hay fever."

"That's up to you."

"What do you mean," I asked as she continued walking by without answering. I started my car and caught up with her. "Give you a ride?"

"Where you headed?" she asked.

"Back to my farm."

"Where's that?"

"Just this side of Asheville."

"You're head'n in the wrong direction."

She caught me in a lie, but I was proud of how fast I bounced back, "No," I said, "I always ride this dirt road along the river. I like it a lot better than that winding paved road through Weavertown." She stopped, looked at me, glanced over my banged up Chevy, then walked around the back side of the car and got in the rear seat.

"I'm goin' 'bout two miles," she said.

"No problem." For the next mile, neither of us spoke. I adjusted the mirror to get a better look at her face. She had dark-green eyes and soft, light skin over high cheekbones. Her expression never changed—serious, but not somber. I didn't want to look like I was staring at her, so I started a conversation.

"Why do you call it 'Rabbit' tea?" I asked.

"'Cause of what's in it."

"What's that?"

"You taste it yet?"

"Yes."

"Whadya taste?"

"Bitter, maybe a little mint, and a little musty."

"That's it. The musty. That's rabbit tobacco."

"You can eat that stuff?"

"Yep. Nothin' better to cure swellin'."

"I thought it cures hay fever."

"It does. Hay fever's all 'bout swellin' in the nose. Rabbit tea will knock it right out of ya."

The car bounced on a wooden bridge over a small stream. "This is where I get out," She said. "Thankya kindly for the ride."

"Thank you for the tea." She closed the door carefully without another word, and passed by the front of the car. Her sturdy, slender frame was well-hidden under a checkered flannel shirt, waist-length jacket, and corduroy pants. Her cuffs partly covered well-worn but comfortable looking boots. She had an unforgettable face, strong jawline, natural color. I'm sure she never in her life wore makeup. She disappeared around the curve in her drive.

Just above the tree line, the corner of a dark slate roof peeked out from behind a stone chimney. A small trail of black smoke rose slowly until it disappeared in the sky.

I drove another hundred feet and parked by a long

rising rock outcropping on the right side of the road. With a tight grip on my camera, I walked to the rock and inched my way up the steep granite slope. Lying flat on my stomach, I saw the streaked roof shingles and porch that ran across the front. A young dark-haired woman sat in a chair in the shade of the porch, asleep, with the back of her head against the house.

Most of the cleared land behind the house was covered by a garden, laid out in neat rows running from the back of the house all the way to the stream. A chicken pen extended from the back of the house to a woodshed in one corner of the yard. I didn't see the medicine lady until she slipped out of the house into the garden, picked some plants, and returned inside. I fired off a couple of pictures of her. First time I had used my new telephoto lens. After a little more black smoke floated from the chimney, she tiptoed out the front door and across the porch to the sleeping lady. With a gentle stroke of her hand on the lady's shoulder, she woke her. They talked for a minute, but I was too far away to hear. With her arm around the back of the large woman, she helped her stand and guided her into the house. The woman walked with a limp and carried a stout wood cane. That was when I saw the sleepy guest was quite pregnant.

I was alone on the rock for twenty minutes or so while the wind hummed through the oaks around me. Of course, I felt guilty spying on those two women. Just when I finally decided it was time to go home, a burst of feathers flew from the back of the chicken pen. All I saw of the fox who had just snatched his lunch, dragged it under the fence, and dashed out of sight, was a flash of rusty red streaking behind the fence. The medicine lady ran outside clutching a long, black rifle. Halfway to the rock, she snapped the rifle to her chin and fired off a shot into the woods. She stood motionless, scanning the forest and the outcropping along its craggy top. Her search stopped at me. I fell on my chest and tried to blend with the granite below me. I peeked over the ledge and heard another blast from her rifle. The rock in front of me exploded, peppering my face with pieces of stone. Out of pure reflex, I rolled over two full turns before planting my hands and pushing my way to my feet. One more shot popped from her rifle. I remember my feet rising into the air, but I don't remember my head cracking on the stone below. The world around me sank into soft blackness.

Jack Hemphill

CHAPTER 3

McKENZIE

Warm broth trickled down my throat. The sound of my swallowing echoed in my head. Something slid into my mouth. Another warm flow crossed my tongue. I heard two women talking in the darkness around me. I heard my name whispered, "McKenzie." Another spoonful came in and more bitter broth. "McKenzie, open your eyes," the voice said. I cracked my lids and light sunk into my eyes like railroad spikes. I heard myself moan. She started again," McKenzie, open your eyes." Slowly I let the glare in and turned my head down, away from the windows and the blurred face in front of me.

"You're comin' back now and you're goin' to be all right, understand?"

"Yes," I said obediently. The room was quiet for a minute while I gained my focus. The medicine lady was sitting in a chair beside me. I lay on a long, soft couch. The pregnant woman sat at a table.

"What happened?" I asked.

"I'm not surprised you don't remember."

"Why?'

"Concussions erase it right out of your head."

"Concussions?"

"You've been out a day and a half."

"How did you know my name?"

"From your driver's license."

"You took my wallet?"

"And your pants and your camera equipment."

I lifted the green wool blanket covering me. I was in my underwear. "Yike!" I cried, followed by a thick pounding in my head. I fell back to the pillow.

"You've been asleep but your body needed to breathe and to be cleaned so I took off your clothes."

"Cleaned?"

"Yep. My job."

I groaned again, then said, "Where's my car?"

"I drove it up to the side of the house."

"I've got to go home."

"Anybody I need to call?"

"No. I live alone. Why?"

"'Cuz it's gonna to be a couple more days before you gonna be ready to go."

I wanted to argue, but I knew she was right. "I've got to get up for a minute."

"You probably need to go to the bathroom."

"That's right."

"It's outside. I'll walk you as far as the outhouse door, but you take care of your business from there."

I eased my way to a sitting position on the couch. The medicine lady wrapped her arm under my shoulder. I was surprised how easily she pulled me to a standing position. We clomped our way out the back door, then about seventy-five feet to a small brick building tucked under a clump of elms. She closed the door behind me. The inside was bigger and cleaner than I had imagined.

A cool natural breeze blew through the screens. I started shivering and by the time I opened the door, the shaking was uncontrollable. She guided me back to the couch, covered me again with the green blanket and walked back into her kitchen. I shook so hard the couch rattled. Thought I was going to pass out again until I felt a warm cloth gliding over my face.

"Gonna give ya somethin' strong," she said.

"What?"

"Jus' swallow it. It's a strong medicine. Understand?"

"Yes," I said. I had no choice. She sat by me on an armless chair. Beside her was a long, narrow cart holding a large bottle of liquid and a collection of small bottles, clear empty vials, and blue jars. From the large bottle, she poured something into a glass.

"This is pure cleaned water," she said. "Brewed it myself on the stove." She then measured out and dropped a teaspoonful full from each of three blue jars into the water, using a different spoon for each one. My eyes were too blurred to read the words she had scribbled on the side of the jars, but I did see that one of the three medicines was dark, almost black, and as it hit the water, it turned it murky gray.

"You gonna help do this," she said quietly, but with a demand in her voice as if she were the chief surgeon at a major hospital. After stirring the mixture with another spoon, she poured the concoction into a small glass container and sealed it tightly with a cork.

"Okay I'm gonna to shake this one hundred times in front of you while you count."

She held the little jar in her fist in front of my face and shook it so hard her hand was a blur. As soon as I counted one hundred shakes, she placed the vial in my hand, closed my fingers around it and said, "Feel how warm it is."

The vial wasn't just warm, it was almost hot. I held it to the light. The liquid was clear. I then closed my hands around it and gave it back to her. She filled another glass with distilled water and took a teaspoonful of the warm shaken water and dumped the spoonful into the glass of distilled water. She stirred the concoction with another clean spoon, then poured the liquid into another small bottle and sealed it with a cork. We went through the same routine as she did with the smaller bottle, but two hundred shakes this time.

"Feel the heat," she said again, handing it to me.

The vial was hotter than the first one. We did the whole thing one more time, but after shaking the last jar of medicine three hundred times, she poured it into another glass of pure water and scooped from it a single spoonful, cupped her hand under my chin like a mother feeding her child, and eased the spoon into my mouth letting it trickle slowly over my tongue. It burned all the way down. A single drop rolled over my chin. She blotted it immediately with a small red towel placed over her knee.

"Rest," she said. She gave me the same tonic at half-hour intervals for the next four hours then reduced the frequency to once per hour throughout the night waking me each time from a deep, comfortable sleep. I was awake each time long enough to open my mouth and swallow before my mind drifted back into sweet slumber.

The sun was shining in my face when I finally woke on my own. For the first time, I saw the room clearly. It was bigger than I realized and filled the full width of the house. I counted six doors around the room including the rear and front porch doors. A stone fireplace was directly opposite the couch. The house was flavored with the fragrance of a century of burning oak logs in the fireplace.

It was beautifully quiet that morning except for the constant murmur of wind through the trees and the sizzle of frying bacon. That's when I realized I was starving. The medicine woman was in the kitchen. There was no door between the two rooms, just a framed opening. She stood where she could watch me on the couch and keep her eye on the kitchen stove at the same time. "What are you cooking?" I asked.

"Eggs, bacon, and cream corn. If you eat solid food, maybe tonight you go home."

"Okay, if I can have my pants back."

"Yep, if you gonna eat at my table, you gonna have pants on. Look under the couch. All your stuff's under there."

"I should know your name." I said.

"Why?"

Because I'm having breakfast with you and you've seen me in my underwear."

"Before I tell you my name, you gotta tell me why you were on the rocks, spyin' on me."

I drew a deep breath and exhaled. I had almost forgotten about it. "I like to photograph people. I've been taking pictures of the people in these mountains around here most of this year. After watching you sell your medicine in the market, I wanted to shoot you…I mean photograph you." I stopped talking. It wasn't like me to be so open to people I didn't know.

She leaned on the door frame and said, "You can't just sneak up and take pictures of me without askin' my permission."

"I didn't know how to ask."

"If you been around these here mountains like you say you have, you'd know people here aren't shy. You want to know somethin', jus' speak up."

"Okay, would you let me take some pictures of you?"

"Hell, no! Nobody wants to see a picture of me."

"I would."

"The answer's *hell, no!*" She stood still long enough to see my surprised face before she walked back to the kitchen counter, clanked her wooden spoon against a glass bowl, and whipped hot butter into her corn.

I dressed myself and walked to the kitchen door, leaned my shoulder on the frame, and watched her work. Even though I only saw the side of her face, I could tell she was trying to hide a smile.

"So what's your name?" I asked again.

"Jess."

"That's your real name or is it short for Jessie?"

"It's just Jess. Jess Shew."

"You can call me Mac. Do you usually have patients staying here?"

"Nope, over the last twenty years, maybe four or five, but never more than one at a time."

"Any of them men?"

"No...No men but you."

That's when I realized that all the pain in my head and body had gone. Only the slightest lump remained on the back of my scalp. Completely rested, full of energy, relaxed, I said, "What did you give me last night? What kind of medicine, or herb, or whatever it was?"

"Somethin' stronger than the pain," she said.

I reached up and felt my head again wondering what the hell she was talking about. I asked her if I could help with anything.

"Light a fire," she said.

"Sure." I must have sounded a little surprised.

"We got to warm it up in here. It's too cold for Viola."

"Viola?" I asked, before I realized that was the pregnant girl's name. "Is she awake?"

"Probably, but I don't want her to come out until breakfast is ready. She needs a lot of rest. She should start labor pretty soon."

"How can you tell?"

"I feel it."

"But how?"

She put her spoon down, closed her eyes, and said, "I've seen seventy babies born and I always felt the same way just before it happened." Her cheeks flushed; she closed her eyes and continued, "I don't know how to explain... It's like hearin' things in the wind."

"Like what?"

She looked at me, again and said, "Listen."

I lowered my head. The long steady wind moaned softly over the roof, withdrew into silence, then returned. Leaves flew against the front door, the rafters creaked, the front door slammed. Both of us jumped, startled and embarrassed. The bedroom door opened and Viola walked into the living room, clutching the front of a white robe.

"How you doin' this mornin'?" Jess asked.

"I don't know. Been awake a long time though," Viola said.

"Couldn't sleep?" Jess asked.

"He's kicking. I think he's ready."

Jess flashed a knowing look at me. "We'll see," she said. "I got a big chair for you at the end of the table. Can you eat?"

"I'll try," Viola said.

Jess waived a spatula at me and said, "Now that he's got his pants on, Mac's gonna join us for breakfast."

"Glad to see you're feeling better," Viola said.

"Thanks, I can't believe it. Don't know how she did it," I replied.

"I know, she's been takin' care of me two weeks now." Viola stared at her hands folded over the bulge under her robe. The morning sun streamed through the front window, lit an oval hooked rug on the floor, while the smell of bacon and coffee almost overwhelmed me.

Jess served breakfast and I ate like I hadn't had a bite in a month. The two women talked, but I don't remember what they said. After breakfast, I excused myself long enough to go to the outhouse. When I returned, the dishes were still on the table, and the women were talking in the front bedroom. I cleared the dishes, put them in the sink, then walked to the front porch, and leaned on a post. A puffy cloud sailed by.

Viola screamed from her bedroom with a voice that hit me in the stomach like a brick fist. Men feel helpless when women go into labor. My instinct was to stay on the front porch, out of the way. Jess dashed back and forth between the kitchen and the bedroom. I guess two hours is not a long time to give birth, but still, I was relieved when I heard the baby cry—it was more of a loud, screeching protest, definitely a boy. Jess opened the door and signaled for me to come in. Still in bed, Viola held the child with both arms as it gazed into her face and listened to her voice.

Jess said, "Stay with her for a few minutes while I walk to a phone down the road and call the doctor. He'll be up here as soon as he can."

"As soon as he can? What does that mean?" I asked.

"As soon as he gets finished with his schedule and follows my directions how to get up here."

"So, it could take hours," I said.

"It usually does. That's why we don't even bother to call him 'til after the birth."

"So why is he coming at all?"

"Check out the baby and mother and give her a birth certificate."

It took the doctor six and a half hours to find us and park his car directly in front of the porch steps. I walked out to greet him, but he sat in the car writing for a good five minutes. I resumed my position, leaning against the post. He looked at me a couple of times but didn't acknowledge my presence until he got out and retrieved his bag from the back seat.

"Doctor Clayton?" I said, as if I didn't know who he was.

"Yep."

"Come in. They are all in the front bedroom."

"They?"

Yes, the mother and child and the...the nurse."

"You have a nurse?"

"Yes, sort of."

He was directly beside me by then, stopped and looked at me and said in a voice so low I barely heard him, "I hope the baby wasn't delivered by one of your people's midwives." I opened the door without answering and he followed me into house.

"Thankya doctor for comin'," Jess said as he entered the bedroom and walked past her. He asked Viola a few questions and she responded. I was standing in the living room where I could see them, but all I heard was a mumble of words. He slid his hands under the baby and eased him away from his mother, laid him on the bed beside her, and carefully examined every part of his little body. Viola never took her eyes off her child. The doctor made a brushing motion with his hand, telling Jess to leave.

"I think I should stay," said Jess.

"I want to examine the mother now and I want be alone with her," said the doctor.

"I've been takin' care of her. You may need me."

"I need to be alone with both of them now," he said with the exact same tone as before.

"Doctor," Viola said. "Please let her stay." He didn't answer but walked past Jess and closed the door, preventing me from hearing anything. They were all quiet for about a half hour when I heard Jess's voice—angry. It was getting louder, but it was an old house with solid, thick wood doors and I couldn't understand what they were saying. The doctor's deep voice was nothing more than a muted hum. I walked closer and laid my head against the door. I was able to make out a few words from the doctor who said things like "Unsanitary," and "No medication, no pain killer." I caressed the door handle just enough to unlatch and crack the door about an inch. I heard Clayton say, "What if it had been breach?"

Jess snapped back, "I made certain that it was turned right."

"How?" he asked but she didn't answer. Neither of them spoke for a couple of minutes while he fiddled with something in his bag.

"What are you doin'?" asked Jess.

"I'm going to give her a simple injection of an antibiotic."

"A what?"

"It's a new medicine. She has a low grade fever."

"She just gave birth! You can't give her that stuff."

"Why?"

"Cause, she's never had a drop of any kind of hospital medicine in her life. All she's ever had has been natural remedies. I mean, in her whole life nobody's ever stuck any of that chemical stuff into her. It'll be too hard for her. Can you understand that?"

"Too *hard*? God only knows what she's ingested from your so-called medicines under contaminated, unsupervised conditions by a mountain witch doctor."

"Why don't you just write the birth certificate and go?"

The door suddenly opened and the doctor, without seeing me, poked his finger past my face barely missing my eye as he said to Jess, "Out of the room...now!" But, one second later, he was sailing headfirst into the living room making a crash, facedown, on the hooked rug. He rolled, got up, and started back toward Jess. I blocked his way.

Viola spoke up, "Jess, let him do it. I'm okay. I'm really okay and you know I gotta have that certificate. Just let him get it over with." Jess stomped out of the house into the garden. I called her name, but she didn't stop. By the time I ran out the back door and made it to the upper garden, she was already going past the lower garden and had turned upstream along the creek bank. I ran down to the edge of the water and called her name again. She didn't look back at me, but I know she heard because she immediately turned into the water, crossed the stream to the far bank, and took off again, thinking I was too much of a wimp to ford the chilled, rushing creek, especially in my clothes.

The thigh deep water plowed against me so hard I almost lost my balance. *God,* it was cold, so cold my legs were stiff by the time I reached the other side. She was still stomping along the bank about a hundred yards away. I had little hope of catching up and no clue what to do or say if I did. I lost sight of her.

Fifteen minutes later I found her sitting on a rock by a small waterfall. She saw me behind her, but didn't move. The falling water roared so loud she couldn't hear me call her name again. I left her alone and found another boulder downstream close enough for her to know I was watching, but far enough away to clear my mind. I wondered why she ran out like that. I couldn't understand what was so wrong with letting the doctor care for Viola the way he was trained. I looked down at the blue, and green, and white patterns flowing across the dark water below. Wished I had my camera. The stream took my mind away for a few moments. When I looked up again she was sitting on the rock beside me.

"We should go back. I need to be with her," she said.

The water wasn't as cold going back. She held my elbow to be sure I didn't fall.

CHAPTER 4

JESS

By the time Mac and I reached the garden, Doctor Clayton was sitting on the back step rockin' and lookin' down at the baby wrapped in a blanket in his arms. When he saw us, he stood and handed the sleepin' child to me and said, "Take him for a while." The baby was light as a loaf of bread. I kissed his fuzzy head.

"How is Viola?" I asked. Clayton didn't answer my question, but walked back inside.

We followed him in, but he done disappeared into the bedroom and closed the door.

"What the hell's going on?" Mac asked. I shrugged and opened the bedroom door. The doctor was leanin' over her. I couldn't see what he was doin'. He heard the door creak, marched toward me, and slammed it in my face. I had just enough patience left in me to hand the baby to Mac.

"What are we going to do?" he asked.

"I'm going back in and check on my patient."

"What about the birth certificate?"

"Forget it!" I was steamin' under my sweater that I pulled off and threw on the couch.

Clayton came out of the bedroom, closed the door

behind him. He didn't look toward us, but muttered softly, "She had a reaction."

"What do you mean?"

"To the medicine...I think." He didn't look at us.

"I need to see her."

"It's too late!" he said.

"Dear God, what are you talking about?"

"I'm afraid she died. Just stopped breathing. I have no explanation why, other than a reaction to medicine."

I ran into the bedroom. The blankets were off the bed and she was covered with a sheet. I pulled it back. I couldn't believe she was dead. She looked asleep. Still had traces of a smile at the corners of her lips. I called her name and stroked her head, but she was already turnin' cold. I don't remember walkin' out of the bedroom or what I said. I only remember the doctor's face had turned a buttermilk white.

"You killed her!" I said.

"In my opinion, her heart stopped from a reaction to medicine," he said in a voice desperately calm and professional.

"It was the stuff you stuck in her."

"We don't know if it was my injection or the garbage you call medicine she took for the last two weeks," he shot back.

Paralyzed, I was too angry to speak and too much in shock to think.

"Let's all sit down for a minute," Mac said. Clayton sat in a wood chair by the fireplace. Mac and I sat on the couch. I don't know how long it was before anybody talked, but the doctor broke the awkward silence by suggestin' that he fill out a birth certificate and a death certificate at the same time. I nodded. He went to this car and returned with two copies of the printed forms. Sittin' again by the fireplace, he scribbled on the papers.

"Okay, I need to ask a few questions," he said.

I nodded again.

"First, the birth certificate. What was the mother's name?"

I looked at Mac, then back at the doctor and said, "Her name was Jess Shew. I looked straight at Clayton, but out of the corner of my eye, I saw Mac's head snap toward me, knowin' that was my name, but he didn't move or say nothin'.

Doctor Clayton, also knowin' my name, stared at me with a little squint in his eyes.

"The child's mother is named Jess Shew, Doctor," I repeated.

He looked at me for one more moment, put his pen to the form, hesitated, then scribbled in the name. He looked at Mac and said, "I presume you are the father."

"Yes," I said before Mac had a chance to answer.

Mac was sitting with his arms around the child who had, by then, nestled the side of his face into Mac's chest. Mac said, "Well, actually . . ."

"Actually," I jumped in again, "we *think* he's the father."

"Are you willing to be named on the certificate?" said Doctor Clayton to Mac.

"What happens if I say no?" Mac asked.

"Then I have to take the child," said Clayton.

Lookin' away from me to the doctor and, without emotion, MaKenzie said, "My name is Mac Davis. I'm the father."

"*You* are the father?" he asked again.

"Yes," Mac said.

He wrote it down on the certificate, then he asked, "What are you going to name the child?"

Surprised at the question, Mac looked down, then at me, then at the tiny boy. "Write down Robb with two b's. His name is Robb," he repeated. "It's my mother's maiden name."

"No middle name?"

"No," said Mac.

"Okay," said the doctor, "and what should I write down as his last name?"

Mac looked at me again, but said nothing.

"Shew," I said.

Mac agreed, "Yes, Robb Shew."

"Okay."

"Next, I have to fill out the death certificate. The only thing I need is the *cause of death* line. I'm going to write *unsanitary conditions*."

"The only thing unsanitary was the garbage you injected into her. We all agree she was fine before that point, right?" I said.

"She had a low-grade fever." Said Clayton.

"Did you think she was dyin' when you got here?" I said.

"Well, I wouldn't know. No telling what transpired before I came."

"Is it your medical opinion when you got here that there was anythin' seriously wrong with her other than just havin' given birth to a heathy boy?" I asked.

Clayton placed his hand behind his neck as he rolled his eyes and head upward, let out a short burst of breath and said, "The patient died during childbirth. That's what will go on the certificate."

"Do you have an undertaker to take care of her remains?"

"Yes," Mac said.

Doctor Clayton finished making three copies of all the documents, gave two copies to Mac, and left through the front door. The death certificate said simply that the mother had died during childbirth.

Clayton's car disappeared down the rocky drive long before the rumble of his tires faded away. Mac and I sat in silence for a while before I went to my room, closed the door, and gave in to a long, secret cry. I'm sure he knew what I was doin', but when I returned, he was still in his place on the couch, starin' at the empty fireplace and holdin' the baby stirrin' in his arms.

I picked out the softest, cleanest towel in my kitchen, tied a knot close to one corner, and soaked the knot in a little bowl of goat's milk. Mac stood and carefully handed him to me, then sat on the couch beside me and watched. I brushed the wet tip of the towel across little Robb's lips. He knew what to do and started suckin' the milk from the towel. We took turns holdin' him. When it was Mac's turn, I spooned fresh milk into the knot. After ten minutes of nursin', the baby boy drifted back into sleep. We laid him in a little nest of folded blankets on the floor by the fireplace.

Again Mac sat still on the couch and watched. Earlier, when he and I were in the sunlight by the river, I noticed strands of red runnin' throughout his thick, straight brown hair, long enough to cover his ears. Now, on the couch, as he rested his chin on this palms, his hair fell across his soft blue eyes fixed on Robb.

"I guess you need to call the undertaker," he said. I covered my face with my hands, then pushed my hair back.

"No, I'll bury her," I said.

"You're not going to tell anybody what happened?"

"No, of course not. The only record of my death is in Clayton's car, and I doubt if he will ever file it."

"What about Viola's family or friends?"

"She doesn't have any real family. At least none that's gonna miss her."

"Well, eventually somebody will miss her."

"She grew up and lived in the same cabin most of her life. Her mother died when she was a teen and she never knew her dad. Lived alone ever since. Kind of like me. That's why she was okay about comin' here and stayin' with me."

"Jess, she was pregnant. Obviously she knew *somebody* pretty well. Do you know who?"

"Yes, she told me."

"Well, he's going to miss her and he's going to know something is wrong."

"She told me she was goin' to leave these here mountains and take the child far away."

"Where?"

"I don't know, but she told me to never let the father, the real one, know about the baby and to never let him get his hands on him if somethin' happened to her."

"So you're not going to tell him?"

"Nope. He can never know."

"Jess, this whole thing is insane. How many laws have we already broken? What do you think this guy is going to do if he finds out? And isn't he going to be a little suspicious when he discovers you have a new baby and Viola is gone?"

"I don't think he even knew she was pregnant."

"Why not?"

"After it happened, she never let him in the door of her house. I don't know what else to do, but I gotta tell ya this. I'm not gonna to let him get this here child."

"So how are you going to explain the baby?"

I walked around the couch to the front door, looked out, walked to the back door, then around the couch again, and sat down. I whispered quietly, almost without moving my lips, "I have a birth certificate that says I'm the mother and you are the dad." My heart was pounding and I knew if I spoke louder, my voice would quiver and I didn't want him to know how afraid I was. He didn't answer right away. I thought that was good.

"That doesn't explain anything." He finally said, "You can't sell medicine by the road one day, all trim and slim, and give birth to a baby the next. These people aren't stupid."

"I have to go away for a while, then come back with my baby," I said.

"Okay, do you have a friend or relative who will keep you that long?"

"No." My throat was tight and my voice sounded too high, like a young girl. I walked around again. Checked the child each time I passed him. His little hands clutched the corner of the blanket as if it was his mother. I walked behind Mac and said, "We could stay with you."

"Jess, this is not my problem. It's *yours*. I know this whole thing just kind of fell on top of you, and frankly,

I don't know what the hell you can do, but please don't involve me."

I went to the kitchen, poured two glasses of tea, returned, and handed one glass to him and said, "His name is *Robb*. You gave him a name from your family and you are listed as the father. The truth is, I can't stop takin' care of my patients. I'm gonna to need you to help me with my baby."

"Your patients?"

"Yes, on both sides of Stumpy Ridge and all the way into Weavertown."

"You give them your medicine?"

"They pay for medicine and treatment. Like I gave you."

He ran his fingers across the smooth place on the back of his head where the day before a lump the size of hickory nut HAD bulged into the air. He sat back in silence for a while, then said, "You're going to have to pad yourself to look like you are hiding a pregnancy for the next few months. Do you have clothes too big for you?"

I nodded.

"You already wear large flannel shirts. You could pretend to have been hiding it for four or five months already, but by six months, it's got to look like it's showing through lots of layers of clothes."

"That would work for a month, but by the time I'm supposed to look seven or eight months along, they're all gonna tell me to stay home and not come see them, cause some of these farms are hard to get to on foot, even if you aren't pregnant.

"Good, then pretend to have an eight-month pregnancy, don't show yourself or the baby around for a while, a month or so, and nobody will know the difference."

"Yes, 'cept that when I show my newborn, he's gonna look like a four-month child."

"I wish I knew what to tell you." His voice had changed into a sound almost comforting. He continued, "Wrap him in a big blanket or something, so they can't tell how old he is. But, you'll figure it out, if that's what you want to do."

"I need someone to deliver my medicine for about three months." I watched his face. He understood what I was askin' and avoided lookin' back at me, but I knew, even then, he was a kind man, and I knew I was gonna depend on him.

I circled the room three more times before decidin' to get some fresh air. I walked to the front door and reached for the knob. On the little table beside the door was a piece of paper placed upright, leaning against the wall. It was Doctor Clayton's only copy of the death certificate.

After closin' the door behind me, I sat on the porch steps. Any thought of cryin' over Viola was pushed aside by the feelin' that my life had suddenly changed. I had a man on my couch, a baby boy on my rug, and a dead woman in my bed.

Jack Hemphill

CHAPTER 5

McKENZIE

The chill, thin morning air blew through my sweater. For the third time that morning, squawking geese sailed across the sky in perfect formation before disappearing into the valley.

I walked to the edge of the porch and waited and listened for the next flock. Exactly like the other three, I heard them coming from far behind the tree line out of sight. It started with a soft, rhythmic, constant sound no louder than the breeze. I walked down the steps to watch for the flock, but by the time I reached the gravel drive, it didn't sound as much like geese as it did clanging pipes echoing up the winding driveway. In about a minute, two white goats pulling a cart, rounded the curve. A tall, thin young man with a long, clumsy stride tapped the animals with a bent stick nudging them up the rocky drive. The man brought his two goats to a full stop in front of me. Both goats were long-haired white animals with curved horns. The wagon they were pulling was a long wood container that narrowed in width from its leading edge to its toe making it look like a child-size coffin. It had two bicycle wheels on the wide leading side, and one wheel centered in the narrow trailing end. The two goats wore bells on their necks made of copper that constantly gave out a hollow clang as they walked in rhythm.

"I'm Theron," said the young man in baggy pants torn at the knee, and a large leather shirt partly unbuttoned exposing the top of his cream-colored long johns. His long hair bulged from under a sky-blue knit hat pulled down to his eyebrows.

"My name's Mac," I said.

"I'm called the Goat Man. Got goat stuff for Jess."

"Milk?"

"Yeah, and stuff," he said as he opened the hinged wood cover over his wagon and pulled three glass milk bottles and a package wrapped in cloth.

"I'll get Jess," I said.

"No, it's okay, it's okay, I usually jus' put them in her refrigerator."

Without another word, the lanky young man ran up the stairs and into the house. The two goats stood obediently where they were stopped. He returned to the cart carrying empty bottles and a package.

"This here package is some medicine from Jess," Theron said as he held the package momentarily in the air and placed it carefully in the back of the wagon. "She always leaves it in the refrigerator for me where the milk goes."

"You're sure it's for you?"

"It's part of my payment for milk and cheese and she puts a big X on it so I will know it's for me."

"That's an interesting wagon you've got," I said.

"Yep, works great! Thankya."

"Looks a little like…"

"Looks like a coffin, don't it? People tell me that," he

said.

"Yes, it does."

Theron raised the lid again and said, "Works great. See how the milk bottles fit up here layin' in that bed of cotton at the wide top and how cheese packages go at the skinny bottom end. This here lid keeps everything cool."

"Why does it have just three wheels?"

"Cause the goats gotta pull it all over the place, some of it's steep and rocky. Three wheels ain't goin to turn over like four would."

I nodded. "Where do you live?"

"I live on the farm around the other side of the mountain, but Jess lets me take the shortcut right down the back of her property to get me home. Only takes a little while for me and the goats."

"Anything on your farm besides goats?"

"Jus' goats. And lots of things to feed them. I sell my goat stuff all over this here mountain."

"Well, these are two nice looking animals pulling your cart."

"Thankya kindly. This one's called *Nanny* and this other one's called *Billy*."

"Nanny and Billy?" I thought he was kidding.

"Yep," he said and he closed the lid again and fastened the latch with a stick, then pulled two small apples from his jacket pocket and gave one to each goat.

"Tell me somthin'," he said, scratching the top of his head. "What happened to Viola?"

"Viola?"

"Yeah, I saw her here several times, but I'z afraid to get close to her."

"Why?"

"I swear she looked like she was gonna pop. I knowed she was gonna have herself a baby and all that, but I didn't want to be anywhere around when it happened. Anyway where'd she go? Did her baby come out?"

"Yes."

"Well, where is she and the little thing?"

Overhearing the conversation, Jess said, as she walked out the door, "Theron, I'm need'n your help."

"Sure, Jess. What is it?" Jess placed her hand on Theron's shoulder.

"Viola died." Theron gasped so hard he coughed and then bowed his head so low we couldn't see his face.

"The baby boy is okay. He's sleeping inside the house now, but we gotta bury his mama and we can use your help."

"Okay, surenuf. How?" he said without lifting his head.

"You know some folks are buried back of the woods goin' towards your farm?"

"Yep."

"Doesn't seem right to jus' carry her back there. Besides, she's bigger than me. Hope'n you could put her on top of your cart."

He looked at the cart and back at her. "Both of you gonna have to hold on to her and push!"

It took fifteen minutes to carry her from the bedroom to the wagon and, even with Jess and me holding her on and pushing, it took another fifteen minutes to get her to the grave site. Jess had sewn a clean white sheet tightly around her, but it started to rip as all three of us lowered her from the cart. Theron screamed and dropped his side of her body that twisted and flipped to the ground face down.

"Oh, I'm sorry, Miss Jess! Sorry. Dead people scare…" Theron said as he walked away shaking his head, repeating, "They scare me. Scare me."

"It's okay, Theron. We got her here. Couldn't have done it without you," she said.

"I can't stay while you diggin'."

"I know. You've done enough. Thank you."

"What's gonna happen to the baby, Miss Jess?"

She put her arm around him and said, "Theron, you can't talk to others 'bout Viola ever bein' here and we can't talk about her baby. We don't want people from Asheville or somewhere like that comin' up here and takin' him away. Understand?"

"Yes, Miss Jess, but what's gonna happen to him?"

"He's gonna be my baby from now on. I'll take good care of him and you can help me with him 'cause I'm gonna need lots a milk."

"I got all the milk you need, Miss Jess." She kissed him on the cheek. Not knowing what to say, he looked down for a minute then tapped his goats with his stick and led them down the path toward his farm.

"Will he keep the secret?" I asked.

"Yes."

"How do you know?"

"'Cause I asked him to."

"He's a nice young man, but a little . . ."

"Yes," she said cutting me off. "He's a little slow. Born that way. His parents are dead now, but they taught him everything he needs to run the farm."

"He's doing all the milking and making cheese?"

"Yes. His parents taught him how to do it clean and

sanitary."

"How about the money?"

"Well, I give him a little advice sometimes, but he makes do."

"You knew his parents?"

"His mama and my dad were first cousins."

We dug about five feet into the ground before we hit stone. I climbed into the hole and eased Viola down. I laid her on her back, still wrapped in the sheet. We packed the dirt hard around her and over the grave, and we spread some stones and leaves on top. Jess made a small cross from sticks and twine and pushed it into the earth.

Exhausted and covered in dirt and clay, we returned to the house. Jess heated water for me to take a bath in a steel tub in a little room beyond the kitchen. She fed Robb and we rested until late afternoon. Robb was hungry again. I rocked him and waited for Jess to heat some fresh milk.

She returned carrying a bowl of warm milk and a dish towel knotted at one end. She dragged her only rocking chair from its usual spot by the fireplace to the front window. The chair had a cushion covering the back and seat which she had made from an old blue blanket. She also moved the small table from a spot beside the front door to a location beside the left arm of the rocker and she put the bowl of milk on the table. Once she was seated, I placed Robb in her arms with his head embraced by the inside of her left elbow. Jess had only one piece of real silverware. It was a spoon she inherited from her aunt. She said it dated back to the time when her family lived on the west coast of Scotland. She had already soaked the knot with goat's milk, but she wanted to use the family's spoon to resupply the milk into the knot as fast as Robb sucked it out.

She sat with her right shoulder under the window. Robb was wrapped in a soft blanket with his face and one hand free. His fingers moved up and down with every gulp of milk. Jess rocked slowly and hummed melodies I had never heard. Her face was silhouetted in shadow against her hair lit by the setting sun behind her.

She became so absorbed in the child that I think all awareness of me disappeared. I pulled my camera out of its case and started snapping pictures of them from different angles. She never noticed what I was doing or heard the quiet clicking of the shutter.

When Robb had enough milk, she put the towel on the table and continued humming and singing. I couldn't understand most of the words, but she had such a beautiful clear voice that it didn't matter. His dark eyes were fixed on his mother's face looking down at him.

She stopped singing and lowered her head until, for one moment, her nose touched his nose while strands of her hair drooped around his face. I shot my final picture. She sang a few more songs much more quietly as his little eyes slowly closed into sleep and the room grew dark.

Jack Hemphill

CHAPTER 6

McKENZIE

First morning light bounced off the high mountain ridge beyond my farm. The moist air around me shined. I didn't mind the cold September morning's bite. With my back against a tree, I sat motionless, watching the big buck glide from the forest into my orchard. He knew I was there. As he had done every morning for the last two weeks and every September for the last two years, he walked a cautious semicircular inspection no closer than twenty yards around me. I placed one knee on the ground and one knee against my chest to steady my arms as I shot pictures of him strolling past, standing tall with his crown of ivory horns held high in the air. After his inspection, he disappeared back into the trees, then two dozen deer appeared and slid by in slow motion, grazing on fallen fruit scattered across the twelve acres beside my barn.

That early in the morning, I had to use a very slow shutter speed to gather enough light to take sharp, clear images. Some of the animals, without taking their eyes off me for more than a few seconds, crept as close as fifteen feet as they gobbled up the sweet fruit. After about an hour, all at once, they turned as if called by a secret voice, and drifted back into the forest.

45

I had recently finished converting my barn into a living space, darkroom and photo studio. The old structure always felt more like home to me than any other place on the farm, including the house. Two of the four sides were made of field stone granite and it had a high and massive wood timber structure with more room than I would ever needed, but I loved it. Maybe it was because the barn felt as if it would last forever and was stained with a hundred years of my family. I built a stone fireplace with a chimney that towered the full twenty-five feet from the floor through the roof ridge

One of the gable ends faced the house and the other end faced part of the orchard. The big barn doors were on the orchard side where I made a room to store farm equipment and to use as a garage for my car and truck. I kept the old dirt floor in that area, but throughout the rest of the barn I installed pine flooring over a concrete slab.

On one side of the big room, I built two bedrooms and a small office. On the other side, behind the stone fireplace I built a darkroom tucked under what was originally a hayloft. I installed hot and cold water, racks and files for prints and negatives, and a separate closet for chemicals.

Across one wall of the darkroom, I strung wire for hanging prints to dry. A row of spotlights were mounted on a drop ceiling to review new photographs before filing them.

The farm was always my home and I never thought about living anywhere else. Both my two brothers, however, announced to the family back when they were still teenagers that they wanted no part of the orchard business. Their opportunity for escape came with the war. They volunteered to fight the Germans and I followed them soon after.

I had started my sophomore year studying literature at UNC when Pearl Harbor was bombed. Dad died one week later, Mama didn't last much longer. I always knew she wouldn't last long after my Dad passed away.

The following spring, I dropped out of school and joined the Army. How I got into the Signal Corps, I don't really remember, but I was trained to be a combat photographer and eventually found myself landing in France with the 3908th Signal Battalion, 12th Signal Photographic Company with the mission of supporting the 82nd Airborne Division. My mission was to make a visual record of the attack on the German army, how well our troops performed and survived, and the effects of the war on the German soldiers and the civilian population. Our entire photo lab and darkroom were in the back of a 2½ ton Army truck covered in dark olive drab canvas. Sometimes, because of steep terrain or snow, I left the truck behind and walked with the infantry. I needed to stay with the leading edge of penetrations into new territory, photograph the villages as we found them, and record how we left them. Every seventh day I had to be resupplied, and sometimes it required hikes ten miles back to wherever our truck had stopped.

Although the Army was primarily interested in historical military documentations of the war, I was more fascinated with the faces we encountered as we plowed our way across France and through the Ardennes Forest in Belgium, and eventually across to Brussels. I photographed American troops, outnumbered, charging into places and towns they never had heard of before. I recorded the faces of flocks of families escaping on foot with no place to go. I gathered pictures of German soldiers being dragged away from their homeland and other German infantrymen with lifeless bodies lying beside fallen American soldiers, half buried in the snow — their eyes frozen and fixed on the sky. Even though I photographed all the places, and territories, and events the Army required, the military had no interest in the hundreds of pictures I had taken of the people and faces in our path and I was allowed to keep the prints and negatives and bring them home.

Whatever was filling the minds of the people I photographed was unmistakably molded on their faces. Fear, joy, anger, despair, love, and so on, oozed from every pore regardless of whether they were men or women, old or young, alive or dead.

No one ever had to say what they were thinking. It was all displayed for everyone to see. The thickened or tightened lips, the drooping or craned neck, the bright or unforgiving eyes peeking from the shadows of crinkled brows, all sang and cried out louder and more honestly than anyone could ever think or say, but the most memorable were faces of the dying, gazing into the infinite.

Good war photographers forever hold in their minds every image they have captured with their cameras — the full gamut from peace, to death, to deliverance. I never threw any pictures away, but even if I had, they would still float in my memory. Growing up the youngest of three farm boys, I never admitted to anybody that I was afraid. That is, I never admitted it to anybody but myself. I lost forty pounds that year, along with my ability to sleep and laugh.

We crossed the line back into France when VE day finally exploded over the country. My company was ordered back to southern France to be shipped home, but we couldn't resist driving our truck into Paris to see the entire city flooding into the streets in unanimous, uncontrolled celebration. Some of my favorite pictures were taken that day when we were surrounded by endless Parisian faces glowing as if each had suddenly been reborn.

My brothers returned to Asheville after the war, and together they started a construction business. I went back to the farm. My parents left all their savings and their stocks to my brothers, but they left the farm to me. So it was just me there with the Stinsons, the married couple my mother hired to take care of the two hundred acres, manage the migrant workers, harvest the apples, and preserve the five buildings including my house and barn, a few other farm structures, and a caretaker's house. My boyhood dreams of running the farm died somewhere in Belgium and I let the Stinsons continue to stay on to manage the property and the workers.

The Army taught me to shoot with a Graflex Speed Graphics camera, but when I got home, I bought an Ektra camera by Kodak that was one of the first cameras with interchangeable lenses. It was smaller and lighter, but perfect for me to explore the mountains. From the summer to the following spring, I combed the lower Blue Ridge all the way into the Great Smokies.

The latest pictures of Hot Springs, the French Broad River, and my time with Jess and her place on the bottom of Stumpy Ridge, were still hanging in the darkroom. The Hot Springs and French Broad shots were good pictures, but I couldn't stop looking at the prints of Jess.

Beside the darkroom, under the hayloft, I had set up an office/studio with a desk, chair, a typewriter, file cabinets, and a flat work table. I took notes constantly. In my studio, I converted my scribbled notes into descriptions and thoughts by typing them on paper which I stored chronologically in cardboard boxes.

The first thing I learned about Jess was that she was an extraordinarily independent woman and cherished her privacy. I had already thought of at least a dozen ways of telling her about my writing, but nothing seemed right. No thinking person could know her and not respect her, and I never wanted to mislead her or disappoint her either.

Late one afternoon, Sidney Smith, editor for *Great Smokey Mountains Magazine,* came to my barn. We had talked on the phone twice and he had agreed to look at a rough outline and pictures for a proposed article I wanted to name, *Last Celtic Healer.* My idea was to spend a whole year with Jess, recording and photographing her unusual life. He was encouraging, but didn't want to be strung out more than a year.

That night I cooked dinner in the little kitchen in my barn. Whenever I cooked for myself, which was most of the time, I liked to make simple dinners. Within ten minutes, I was enjoying a pile of canned Italian spaghetti, slices of French bread, and a large cup of Brazilian coffee. For dessert, I had another cup of coffee. I went to bed early without the slightest hope of sleeping, not just because of the coffee, but because I had not enjoyed a normal night's sleep since the day we invaded Belgium. I was used to lying awake most of the night, and that evening I wanted to roll over in my mind thoughts about working with Sidney Smith and finishing the article. After ten minutes, however, I started thinking about Jess and Robb. Two hours later I remembered Jess' package of hops that I had stuffed into my camera bag. Returning to the kitchen, I made a large pot of strong hops tea with sugar, and I crumbled some of the leaves inside my pillow case as Jess suggested.

The mild fragrance was pleasant, but I felt a little ridiculous. It was too simple, but nothing else had relieved my insomnia, and I was looking for any kind of relief. Just an hour of normal sleep.

All old heavy timber structures give off noises at night. In my bed, I listened to its constant music. As it continued, it seemed to soften into a lullaby and I slowly faded into sweet slumber.

A beam of light bounced under my door and against my eyelids. When I finally remembered I was still in my bed, I shuffled to the door and stuck my head out into the big room. The blinding morning sunshine blasted through the barn windows. The clock beside the fireplace said it was nine. The last time I had slept until nine in the morning, I was still in college.

After telling Stinson I would be gone a few more days, I jumped into my car and headed for Stumpy Ridge.

Jack Hemphill

CHAPTER 7

McKENZIE

Jess's old couch and I quickly became good friends. The couch was long and deep with lumps and valleys in just the right places. Even with my sleep problem, I still thought of myself as an early riser, but I never got up before Jess. Sometimes she quietly slipped out the front door and sat on the porch until dawn, but on most mornings, she arose, turned on a light in her bedroom so early that I woke up, but I always went back to sleep until she came out to make breakfast. I never had trouble sleeping at her house. I couldn't understand why.

One morning Jess wanted to pick dandelion greens in the clearing beyond the garden behind the house. I had Robb all to myself for about an hour. With Robb on the blanket spread over the floor in front of the couch, I let myself be as silly as I felt.

I think I may have been a little afraid I would do something wrong, like hold him upside down or something. But, I had to learn—no choice. Soon, Robb began recognizing me and he made noises as if he were trying to talk. I returned the affection with endless rhetorical questions like, "You know you're so smart don't you? Huh? Huh? Aren't you my smart little boy? Huh?"

It actually felt good to act like a fool when no one but my little friend could hear me.

I left the front door open to let in the morning light and some fresh air. Robb squealed like a baby bird every time I made a face or tickled his ribs. What a voice for such a tiny guy. I laid him across my arms and kissed his neck. His lips tugged at my sweater as if he wanted to nurse.

"Can't help you there, big guy."

After feeding him goat's milk, I washed him with a warm rag and changed his diaper. I laid him down on the little nest made with pillows sewn inside old blankets and I sat back on the couch to say a few more brilliant, childish things. The front door was behind me and I didn't hear the man walking into the house.

"Where's Jess?" he blurted.

He startled me and I jumped so hard I almost fell over. I bolted to my feet.

"Who are you?" I said.

"I'm looking for Jess."

"You mind telling me who you are?"

"Helms. I'm Helms. Where's Jess?"

"She's resting," I lied.

"I need to see her."

"You need to go," I said as I walked around the couch and grabbed his arm.

"Whoes baby?"

"Time to go, Helms." I gave him a nudge.

He walked toward the door, stopped, turned toward me, then said, "Tell her I'll be back." He glanced again at Robb, then walked halfway through the open door, but he stopped again and dropped his head as if he suddenly thought of something. He then picked up a cane that was leaning against the door frame and rubbed his thumb across something carved on the grip.

"This is Viola's," he said, before placing the cane back against the frame.

I didn't know what to say, but my awkwardness was hidden by Robb who was starting to cry. I picked him up and bounced him for a moment in my arms before looking back toward the door. By the time I looked back, Helms was gone. I walked to the door as Helms finished turning his car around. He gave me and Robb one last stare before driving away fast enough to spit gravel on the steps.

After walking around the room for a few minutes with Robb in my arms, I put him down again in his floor-bed. He went to sleep as I knew he would after eating his lunch and enjoying a little snuggle with his daddy. Jess lifted her reed basket in the air as she came through the back door, as if she wanted me to see her dandelions. I put a finger to my lips to let her know that Robb was down.

"How'd the feeding go?" she asked.

"He took it all. I think maybe he wanted more, but I've got to tell you, we had a visitor."

"Oh, God. Who?"

"A strange man. Husky build with scrubby beard. Said his name was Helms."

Jess rolled her eyes without saying a word. "Do you know him?" I asked.

"Yes, I'm afraid so."

"What's the matter?"

Jess turned away from me, took a couple of long breaths, knelt beside Robb and watched him sleep, then stood and faced me."

"Tell me what he said," she asked.

"I had the front door open and he just walked in."

"Oh, Mac. Wish you hadn't done that."

Her voice was high and soft. Her head was down. For the first time she looked vulnerable. We stood awkwardly facing each other.

"You're right," I finally groaned, "I should have closed the door, but I wanted to let some sunlight and fresh air in. Thought it would be good for Robb. Anyway, he saw Robb and asked for you. I told him you were resting. He started to leave when he spotted Viola's cane, then asked where Viola was."

"Oh, great," Jess grumbled as she went into the kitchen. "Whad'ya tell him?"

"I told him to get out and he left. So who is he?"

"That's Doug Helms. He's Robb's real father."

I walked into the kitchen and stood beside her until she looked at me. "I'm sorry, I didn't know," I said.

Jess pulled a chair out from the table, sat, and looked down at her hands folded on the table. I sat beside her.

"When did Viola tell you about him?"

"Jus' a day or so before you came."

"I'm sure he put together the baby and Viola's cane."

"He's a wise ol' weasel."

"I can't picture her being with somebody like him at all. How did it happen?"

Jess thought about it for a moment, raised her eyes at me and said softly, "She, of course, never talked about that with me, but I know she was lonely."

"What do you think he's gonna do?"

"Don't know, but he can hold a grudge…for years. I've seen him do it."

"Is he going to get violent?"

"Can't say, but I know he don't mind a fight."

"You think he'll call the sheriff?"

"No, not right away, but he'll try somthin'. Maybe somthin' on his own first."

"Jess, maybe we should . . ." I stopped. I felt anything I said would be wrong. We sat for a while.

"I've been away from the ridge almost a month now," she said. "Let's try another way. Next two weeks you make my deliveries for me. Then we'll go to church and take Robb. Let everybody see him, then I'll start making the rounds up the ridge a few days later."

"I'll do the deliveries for two more weeks by myself, then we'll deliver together for a while. That's what they would expect me to do if they thought I was the dad and you recently gave birth. We don't know what Helms is saying to them — don't know what to expect — so we'll just plow on. Do you know if anybody else knew that Viola was pregnant?"

"No, she said she told nobody about it and she was a big woman so she covered it and carried it well. Mountain women do that, ya know. That's why they're gonna to believe me — they'll think I covered it up and kept my baby secret too."

"Does Helms go to church?"

"Every Sunday."

"What's the preacher going to think about us bringing Robb to church when we're not married?"

"Won't be the first time somebody did it. Besides, he and half the congregation already think I'm some kind of a witch and I'm going to hell for sure, but Preacher Ron will be worried about the baby's soul and maybe yours too. You watch 'n see," she said.

She bathed Robb that night and put him down in his nest. We sat on the couch and talked in whispers. The light was low, but I could see her eyes, stretched wide, looking straight at me, asking for comfort. She was afraid, but not for herself. She was afraid for Robb. I wanted to hold her close and tell her whatever magic words she needed. Her strong face became as delicate as reflections on a pond. But underneath that face and the quiet voice, I felt the rage of a mama bear.

"Okay, one change," I said. "Let's go to church *next* Sunday, so the first place they see us will be in church, then I continue deliveries."

The house was warm enough, but Jess started a small fire in the fireplace and used Viola's cane as kindling.

CHAPTER 8

McKENZIE

Jess wanted to be a little late for church so we wouldn't have to talk with anyone as we walked in. She said there were always empty chairs in the back of the room where we could sit. It was a sunny but cool Sunday morning and that day was the first time I had seen Jess in a dress, the only one she had. A lavender cotton print with a matching cloth belt around the waist. The dress was long and covered her legs all the way to her shins. That day was also the first time she saw me with a tie, and I wore my corduroy jacket which I hadn't put on since college. It almost fit. With the rocking of the car, Robb fell sound asleep long before we got there. Jess had him bundled in white blankets and insisted on holding him the whole time we were in church.

The bright morning sun on the white clapboards of the old meeting hall made it look like a real church. The large assembly room was above the General Store, but because the building was built on the side of the mountain, there was an entrance directly into the General Store from the lower side of the slope and another entrance directly into the Hall on the upper side of the slope, without needing steps. The parking lot was nearly full. The two front doors of the Meeting Hall stood open, letting a breeze blow through the hall and out the side windows. We waited at the door until they started singing. We then slid in, hoping to find seats at the back. The closest empty seats were on the outside aisle almost all the way down the right side of the room. We looked down as we made our way up the aisle. The enthusiastic billow of singing voices deflated as the crowd saw us walking toward the two empty seats. I picked up a songbook and nervously tried to find the hymn, but by the time I found it, the song was over and Preacher Ron said with authority to everyone, "Be seated."

Two ladies beside Jess and one in the seat in front of her turned and smiled at Jess and looked at Robb who was still sound asleep. Others nearby shot an unwelcome look at us as if we had forgotten to scrape manure from our boots or were carrying our pet pig instead of a beautiful child. Several women continued to stand, leaning forward and backward to get a glimpse of Robb. The preacher gave a second command to be seated. All three tall windows on the right side of the hall and the three on the left side were open. The walls were painted wood, and the roof trusses were exposed timber revealing a high ceiling that made the music and singing reverberate and sound alive and powerful as if it were coming from a big congregation.

Preacher Ron read the usual announcements about the calendar of events and gave thanks to volunteers for various unremarkable tasks. He sat down and a young, thin girl, maybe sixteen, with long, brown, well-combed hair that fell straight down her back, stood in front of the room with piano music accompanying her solo. She had a pretty voice. Not strong, but she found most of her notes and sang with sincerity the old song, "I'm a Pilgrim, I'm a Stranger." I took some comfort in the mere fact that I remembered the hymn.

After the soloist found her seat, Preacher Ron stood and lifted a large Bible onto a wooded pulpit made from a chest of drawers. He took a few moments to move paper markers in the book to different locations as if he had decided to change his scriptural readings. The minor break in his ordinary routine gave some of the crowd the opportunity to shift in their seats for a fresh look at Jess and her new baby. The men kept their thoughts hidden behind their stone eyes and leather skin, while some of the women wrinkled their faces with soft, kind smiles and others puckered their lips like they were hiding a sour taste fermenting in their mouths.

Preacher Ron raised his head and said, "You probably saw me moving the scriptural selection markers. When I stood up, all the thoughts I had gathered for what I felt was the sermon for this week, were replaced in my mind with things I feel need to be read, and things I think you need to hear today. I will start with the book of Deuteronomy, Chapter 18." He raised his hand as his powerful voice instantly filled the room. He read a passage that described superstition and witchcraft as an *abomination* in the eyes of the Lord. I doubted whether three people in the room, other than the preacher and me, understood exactly the Biblical meaning of the word *abomination*, but Preacher Ron seemed pleased with his citations.

Chairs squeaked from each side of the room as some of the women turned to take another half concealed peek to see Jess' reaction to the first scriptural selection, but she sat without expression with her eyes fixed on her baby, giving the women no satisfaction.

Wondering what he would read next, the crowd sat still. The piano player sat in a straight ladder-back chair against the front wall. Her hands were folded in her lap and her head faced us, but her eyes were cast toward the preacher. Something the size of child's hand moved along the top of the chair rail behind the piano before disappearing in the shadows. But it reappeared on the other side of the piano, creeping along the rail attached to the front wall and moving silently behind the young woman in the ladder-back chair. After another minute or two, it inched its way out from behind her, along the rail into full view. It was a white-footed mouse. I think because of the preacher's location and the pulpit in front of him, only people seated near the front on the right side of the center aisle saw it. Gaining its confidence, the mouse made short little bursts along the rail toward the communion table behind the preacher. Watching the little critter, all heads in front of me moved together like weathervanes blown by the wind.

Perched above the baskets, the mouse sniffed at the mountain of food below him before making a nose dive and disappearing into the pile of communion wafers. The people around me exhaled in a chorus of disbelief. Two ladies on the front row leaned forward as if they needed a closer look. The man in front of me looked at this wife and rolled his eyes.

Oblivious to what was going on behind him, Preacher Ron lowered his hand and his voice and said, "Now we'll go to Exodus and look at another important lesson." He read about the sin of a man who lies with a woman he has not married and how the Old Testament says that all men like that should be punished by stoning.

Feeling cold stares behind me, I turned and saw eyes

quickly dart away from me, back to the Preacher. I saw a man and two women slipping out the door, unseen by all except me and Preacher Ron who raised his hand again with his palm forward and said, "I know this is hard language from the Old Testament. Of course, no one should be *stoned*, but remember, it is written for a purpose, and that purpose is to wake us up to the fact that disobedience to God is a serious crime and there are consequences to anyone who turns his back on Him. But, now listen to our next scriptural reading from the New Testament, Romans Chapter 2."

Unlike the two passages in the Old Testament, the passage from Romans said that judging others is also a sin and that those who do it are condemning themselves.

The preacher talked about it for a few minutes, but I didn't hear most of it because while he was speaking, a second white-footed thief scurried along the rail behind the piano player and, without hesitation, plunged into the communion basket with the other mouse. The preacher read and talked for another twenty minutes, then he announced another hymn. The moment the pianist stood to play, the two mice scrambled out of the basket, jumped to the floor and scooted behind the piano. Again, only those sitting in front on the right of the room could see what was going on.

After the hymn, we sat down again and Preacher Ron remained standing. He changed his voice one more time and spoke in a fatherly tone. "Once a year, we celebrate communion. No one here needs to be told why we do this, but I do want to say, especially this year, that by taking communion, you participate in the fundamental purpose of this event that allows you to be reminded of the sacrifice that it implies and the pureness it achieves in you. Each of you who take communion with us today should be prepared to find personal sacrifice—giving up the thing you most need to surrender. No one but you can discover what it will be, but every right step is always divinely driven, even if you are living in sin." He looked to our left then scanned the room back toward us, then continued, "As these baskets are being passed, think about the things you need to give up."

Chairs creaked and groaned from all sides of the room. One man in front of me carried his son in one arm and pulled his wife with the other and stomped out of the church.

The preacher closed his books and waited until the noise from shuffling feet and from grumbling old men leaving through the door, stopped. He looked over the faces of those still seated as they stared back at him.

Preacher Ron nodded at two men who then picked up the baskets and carried them to the congregation, while the piano played softly. The first basket contained the wafers. It was passed down each row from left to right, then to the next row, from right to left, and so on. Preacher Ron stood in front of us, leaned on his book, watching each person's decision whether to take communion or not. Jess and I refused to reach inside the basket. Just as I had anticipated, the bottom was covered with gnawed wafers, crumbs of all sizes, and a wide distribution of little black dots undoubtedly left by the mice. From what I could see, no one in front of us and no one on my row, ate a single wafer or crumb. Having no idea what was causing us to abstain, Preacher Ron's face broadcasted his surprise and deep concern over Jess, me, and all those who sat near us and around us who couldn't make themselves eat even the smallest piece from the basket. The preacher didn't hide his delight for all the others in the back and on the left side of the hall who ignorantly gobbled down the contaminated wafers.

After the basket of wine glasses was passed around, Preacher Ron, with a voice that sounded like God himself said, "For those of you who chose to participate in the communion, I'm certain you will taste the sweet purity of this sacrament for a long time to come. My sermon today will be quite short and simple. Our Father, our Creator, our Day-Maker forgives those that repent, even those who are dead in sins. But, for those who do not repent, I can only pray for God's mercy to guide you out of your temptations."

He paused. No heads turned. No chairs squeaked or creaked. No sound, except the flutter of birds in the rafters. Preacher Ron continued, "But, He, our heavenly Father, will require every one of us to make sacrifices. Some of the things we'll have to sacrifice will be precious. Remember the story of Abraham and Isaac. Others will be deep inside the secret places of our minds. Things we were born with and came to us from our ancestors, or things we picked up along the way. Some of these may be things we have believed in and loved our whole lives, but remember, sacrifice is the mother of purity and purity is one of the keys to the Kingdom, which means that without personal sacrifice, there will be no salvation for any one of us." The room remained silent. No one dared look around. No one moved.

He searched again the faces in front of him from front to back and from left to right until his eyes stopped and fixed on me, and Jess, and Robb. The moment his gaze landed on us, Robb shuddered violently in Jess' arms and kicked his legs as if he were falling. His little body remained extended and rigid until his mother kissed the top of his head and rocked him and whispered in his ear. The child answered with a small cry so soft, many thought it was the cooing of doves in the rafters, but when it stopped, the people realized that it was the sound of Jess' baby who had suddenly awakened, frightened, and reached out instinctively for his mother whose arms encircled him and who quieted him with a kiss.

Reverend Ron raised his right hand again, closed his eyes, and gave his final benediction. The congregation rose and sang the Doxology. I stood with the crowd, but Jess remained seated and pulled Robb's blankets a little tighter around him. The preacher marched down the center aisle and stepped outside the door.

When the music stopped, there was a moment while the reverberation drifted out the windows and then the room, once again, filled with silence and the standing crowd turned toward Jess. She was still seated and only those near her saw Jess rocking her boy side to side. He was wrapped so completely in white blankets that only his face was showing. The congregation melted into groups of families either making their way to the exit or flocking with friends to exchange greetings and gossip. Several women and a few men gathered around Jess and smiled at Robb who knew nothing more than the fact that he was safe with his mother. I noticed several men, however, pushing their way down the side aisle to get closer. They said nothing, but their straight tight lips and bunched dark eyebrows scowled at all three of us.

The service had finished early and most of the crowd regrouped in front of the Meeting Hall. The bald spot on the back of the head of the last man in line in front of us glowed red, and it wasn't until he turned his ear, trying hear someone whispering to him, that I recognized it was Doug Helms. Doug then joined a group of men in the yard standing in a circle, lighting cigarettes, and blowing smoke from their nostrils.

People from both sides of the ridge were there. Some nodded, some gave me a hearty hand shake, others darted away from me and started their climb up the ridge toward their homes or scuttled across the lot to their cars. By the time Jess and I left the building, Doug was leaning against a sycamore tree waiting for Jess and me to walk by. He waited until she passed him before he spoke.

"Fine-looking baby you got there, Jess," he announced.

Jess, recognizing his deep barking voice, stopped, and pulled the corner of the blanket over Robb's face.

"Lemme take a look," Doug said, gesturing with his thumb as he walked toward her.

Jess pulled the edge of the blanket down far enough to show Robb's face. The bright sunlight startled the baby who shivered and opened his eyes as Doug Helms leaned his lumpy face over him. Robb screamed as loud as a screech owl. People in the yard rushed to see what was going on. Jess quickly covered Robb's face and tried to push past Doug who raised his hand to stop her.

Doug turned his head toward the crowd and bellowed. "Well, Jess, he sure is a bigon'."

The crowd returned an awkward laugh.

Jess didn't answer. Doug bent forward again and pulled back the blanket for a longer look which triggered another scream from Robb.

"Well, look at them giant dark eyes! They look like a couple of big ol' brown sausage patties," Doug said, raising his voice again for the crowd to hear.

I stepped between Jess and Doug and gave him a shove with the back of my right hand. Doug swung his left arm around and grabbed the shoulder of my coat. I lunged forward and grabbed Doug's collar. Both of us yanked each other forward so hard that our foreheads nearly touched as our eyes locked in visual combat. We held our positions frozen in place for exactly five seconds as if in obedience to some natural animal instinct or unwritten male code. We then pushed away from each other, simultaneously, with a short jabbing motion.

I continued to stand between Jess and Doug, giving her time to walk by. Once she was well beyond reach, I joined her without another word to Doug. We walked to my car and drove away. Once again, the rocking of the car lulled Robb to sleep. We were halfway back to Jess's house before either of us spoke.

"I never even thought about it...not once," I said.

"What do you mean?"

"Robb has brown eyes."

"So what?"

"You've got green and I've got blue. Don't you see, it's considered very unlikely we would have a brown-eyed baby. Doug knows it. That's why he blasted out that Robb has big dark eyes, and if they didn't get the hint, he's going to tell them later."

"So what do we do?" she asked, but neither of us spoke again until we pulled into her driveway.

"Don't change a thing." I said. "You're the mother; I'm

the dad. We've got a birth certificate for Robb that says so." We both nodded and carried Robb into the house.

We talked until we reassured ourselves we were doing the right thing. October was only a day away and we were already burning logs in the fireplace. By midnight, Jess went to bed. I stayed up two more hours recording in my notebook.

Jack Hemphill

CHAPTER 9

JESS

Gettin' used to a newborn son was easier than havin' a man stay with me, even if it was only a few days at a time. Mac always went back to his farm on Monday mornin's and returned to us by 10:00 AM on Friday, but I still had not gotten over the feelin' each time he left, that he might never come back, and I had to remind myself to expect nothin' and conceal my emotions when he returned on Friday mornin's. I never lived with a man and, before then, I never let no man or anybody else know so much about my personal life.

A shiver and a little fear ran through me as I sketched a map with a soft pencil on a large piece of brown wrappin' paper. I drew the windin' path along Stumpy Ridge showin' landmarks and every hidden trail leadin' to each farm and house scattered around the mountains.

I knew every boulder, every bush, every tree, and every animal. All the dogs remembered my scent and the sound of my footsteps crunchin' along the trails.

I couldn't believe I was doing it — turnin' so much over to Mac. I never trusted anyone like this before. It was hard for me since I done everythin' for myself since I was a teen.

Six of the houses on the south side of Stumpy Ridge

were filled with direct relatives of Doug Helms. They all knew what kind of character Doug was, but I was sure he was already tryin' to convince them that I stole his baby boy, and I would have to be careful whenever I walked that side of the mountain. I hated the thought of fibbin' to my friends up there, but for Robb's sake I needed the Ridge People to believe he was my child—that I bore him. So far, Mac seemed to understand how important that was to me.

I had no idea what he thought of me, but he agreed to make my rounds.

That alone said something. Before he got there, I ran a brush through my hair and changed into a blue cotton blouse that matched the bowl of wild violets on the shelf by the front door.

We sat side by side at the kitchen table. Like most Scottish descendants, he had strong cheek bones makin' light shadows fall across both sides of his face. I'm sure I told him too much, but lettin' him take my place and make my deliveries, even if for a short time, was like givin' my baby to a stranger, not that Mac was a stranger, but he knew nothin' about the Ridge People and next to nothin' about me. I sketched while I talked. He listened without movin' with his eyes fixed on the map as if he were tryin' to memorize it.

I wanted to tell it all right away, but somebody done told me that when people like Mac, who go off to a big college for a while, sometimes get a little foggy on real life kind of matters. I gave him just enough to chew on, and just enough to think about and keep him out of danger.

I described every family that used my services and medicines, how they lived, and what they grew or raised on their farms. I told him what their children were like, and what they feared.

"I'm gonna' to walk you through it, startin' at the General Store," I said to him.

"Yes," he said, "I see where you drew it on the map."

"Okay, that's where we start. You'll first pick up any mail or messages for me at the store. I'll give you a note to prove to the manager, Mr. Wallace, you're helping me. Hope you're a good walker 'cause it's two miles to the upper end of the ridge."

"I can walk all day," he shrugged.

"But that doesn't count climbin' the mountain slopes on both sides of the main trail to find the houses and farms. You can't see any of 'em from the spine and some are as much as a quarter mile down the slope." That's when I started sketching more landmarks, trees, stumps, big rocks, whatever I remembered as clues to keep him from gettin' lost or confused about whose farm he was on.

Just to make a point, I lifted my pencil slightly in the air, placed it on the table between us, folded my hands in front of me and said, "Now, there are a few things you really need to know before you go kickin' around up there."

"Oh, God," he said, "That sounds serious."

"Mac, they're good people…most of 'em. Presbyterians and Baptist, mostly. You told me you've been pokin' around these mountains for years so you know what these people are like."

"I do, and one of them shot me off a rock just a few months ago."

The gleam in his eye threw a little jab at me, but I kept on talkin'. "I'm glad you mentioned it," I said, "but, you gotta remember I'm not like anyone you ever met. Do you

think I would have shot at you that day if you were walkin'
on the drive up to my house instead of spyin' from that
rock where you didn't have no business? If you do that
kind of stuff up there on that mountain, you gonna have a
bullet cleanin' out both your ears at the same time."

"So what should I do?"

"Walk straight up to 'em. Tell it right out. Let 'em get
to know you first and if they want to, they'll let you get
to know them, and their children, and their parents livin'
with them, and their dogs, and by the way, most of 'em
got dogs."

"What kind of dogs?"

"Some got big dogs and others got really big dogs. If
the people decide they like you, the dogs will like you
too."

With tight lips and wrinkled forehead, he stared at the
map, then said, "Show me where the really big dogs are."

I didn't answer, but instead drew two kinds of circles
scattered around the map. One circle had pointed ears and
one with a little stub nose.

"What are those?" he asked.

"Pointed ears are dogs and stub noses are mean sows."

"Pigs?"

"Yeah, big and ornery."

"But they're in pens, right?"

"No, none of the animals up there got pens."

"Why not?"

"Cause there's not enough flat land up there for
pastures and big barnyards and all that, so they jus' let
'em roam, but they put some of 'em in barns at night."

"Okay, besides dogs and pigs, what other kind of
animals are we talking about?"

"Oh, jus' chickens, and mules, and some horses, and goats, and a few cows."

"Bulls?"

"Oh yeah, I forgot to mention the bull."

He looked at me for a moment without movin', then said, "Show me the bull on the map."

I sketched a circle with horns. He studied it for a minute then said, "Why did you draw almost all the mean dogs and sows on the south side of the mountain?"

"Well, I was hopin' you'd find that out for yourself."

"Find out? No surprises, Jess!"

"The oldest families live on the north side. My Great Aunt Brusie lives in the last house on the north side."

"Why?"

"Lots of reasons. They came here first and picked the north side. They say it's 'cause things grow there that won't grow on the other side."

"Why? It's the same mountain, same weather, and same air. What's the difference?"

"All I know is what they tell me and what I've seen for the last twenty years. Almost all the weather comes from the Gulf, jumps over Alabama, Mississippi, and Tennessee, and dumps its load on the mountains, but because of the winds, more falls on the northwest side.

"So you can actually see the difference?"

"You'd have to be blinder than a salamander not to see or even feel the difference between the two sides. The first settlers, including some of my ancestors, were all good farmers and I'm sure looked carefully at the soil and what was under the soil before they picked a spot to farm." He leaned forward and placed his chin on his hands and elbows on the table and kept his eyes fixed on me. I continued, "Ginseng, and ramps, and all kinds of roots just out of sight under a layer of dark leaves. They tell me there is no place in the entire Appalachian Mountains that grows those treasures like the north side of Stumpy. They started settlin' here more than 150 years ago and they never harvested more than what they needed for themselves and what they could sell. When it's the right season, they buy medicine from me, pay me in cash, and sometimes pay me with roots instead of money."

I still don't see the difference between the two sides."

"Well, one thing you're gonna figger out is that the old families on the north have grown up with women like me helpin' them."

"And why does that make a difference?"

"Some on the south side trust me, but a lot of 'em are scared of me, and always will be.

"Do you trust the south side people?"

"Some."

"So what side of the mountain is Doug on?"

"He owns all the land startin' from the General Store and wrappin' around the south base of the mountain for 'bout half a mile."

"So he's not really on the mountain"

"That's right but he's got a couple hundred acres of good land, owns the General Store, and he's got a bunch of money stashed away. He raised cows down there until his wife died, then he kinda gave 'em all away."

"He ever use your medicine?"

"No, he won't have nothin' to do with me as much as he can. He's always been afraid of me and my family."

"He didn't look like he was afraid of you in the churchyard."

"I know, and he's been here at my house a couple of times. He gets pretty riled up, but I noticed he almost never looks me in the face, even when we're talkin'."

"So he's like a toothless dog acting mean?"

"No, when he bites, he's got teeth. He's jus' afraid to bite *me*. Most of the men on the south side will believe anythin' he says and will do anythin' he wants. He can call together a pack of 'em as fast as a blink."

"You're saying I should stay away from him?"

"I'm sayin' he's got a permanent grudge against me, jus' like a bunch of 'em do. He's scared enough not to act on it, but Mac, Doug's not afraid of *you*."

Are these people going to believe me and my tale about how you suddenly had a baby?"

"Once you tell 'em you are helpin' me, you'll be okay — with most of 'em."

"So I tell them about the child right away?"

"Jus' put it out there."

"So, I should just tell 'em you had a baby, but no details."

"Yep, they'll assume the rest, you bein' the father and all that, but they won't ask nothin' except to know if I'm okay and the baby is okay."

"Either that or they'll just throw me out."

"Yep, you already saw a little of that at church. Some are gonna know us as good people, some'll know us as sinners, and some as agents of the devil. They'll want their medicines to keep acomin' and they may figger your walking the ridge ever' week for me is a sign of repentance…there is nothin' they love more than a sinner that's really sorry, so you need to act like a sinner seekin' salvation and forgiveness."

A red blush spread over his cheeks as he smiled at me. I told him a few more things to watch out for, but didn't tell him everythin'. Didn't want to scare him away. I couldn't tell him about the voices that sing out across the mountain when the winds blow. I'm sure that would have spooked him. I just hoped he didn't hear 'em on his first walk over the ridge.

CHAPTER 10

JESS

On my knees in the upper garden, I filled a basket of mint and almost finished fillin' another with rosemary. I must have been lost in my thoughts that day when Preacher Ron's voice popped out of nowhere.

"Jess," he said like thunder.

"Oh, Lord!" I screamed, startled.

"It's only me," he said with a puzzled, but serious voice.

I pushed the rosemary basket to one side, sat on the ground, and pulled my hair back with both hands to catch my breath. "Reverend, what brings you around here?" I said.

"I was hoping I could talk to you." He sat on the ground beside the mint basket.

"What about?"

"Well, Jess, I'm sure you know I'm concerned about you." He extended his hand as if he were giving me something.

"No, didn't know that, but I can't rightly say I'm surprised. Some of your people never cared for me and my family."

"I think you should know it's not just you I've been

thinking about. You have a child."

I braced myself for a sermon.

"How 'bout Mac, my boy's father," I asked.

"Oh, yes, of course. I'm concerned about him too."

"Reverend Ron." I rolled back to my knees. "Do you think we're sinners?"

He scratched his head. I don't know why men like to scratch the back of their scalp when they're tryin' to think of what to say.

"Well," he finally replied, "I think you, by no fault of your own, grew up with a kind of curse...I mean parts of your background...I think will eventually be dangerous for you — and your boy."

"You think I grew up with a curse?"

"I didn't come to talk about that, nobody can change the past. I want to talk to you about taking care of yourself and your child from now on. It's about where you're going."

"Well, that's mighty kind of you, but I think we're doin' jus' fine."

"I guess it's like walking around Stumpy Ridge. If you don't know the paths up here, you're either going to get lost or fall off a cliff. You know what I'm trying to say?"

"No, not sure. You think we're lost?"

"Sort of."

I stood and picked up the rosemary basket, and asked the preacher to carry the mint. He followed me down the path toward my house.

"Why do you think we're lost?" I asked.

"Because I know a lot about being lost," he said as he caught up with me.

"Have you ever been lost, Reverend?"

"No, but I learned all about it in seminary."

"What's that?"

"That's where I learned to be a minister."

"But why did you go there?"

"I had a calling?"

"Who called you?"

"Our Creator."

"He speaks to you?"

"Yes."

"If He speaks to you, why'd ya need a *seminary*?"

"It helps me hear Him better."

I broke off a rosemary leaf, folded it in half, and breathed its fragrance. "So ya haven't always heard Him clearly?"

"No, but I'm always getting better at it."

"So ya still got a distance to go?"

"Yes, like all of us."

"So maybe He's speakin' to me too! And maybe I've had one of them *callin's,* too."

He stopped for a moment and pointed his finger and said, "What you do, Jess, is *not* His work."

"Is it possible for me to hear Him talkin' to *you*?"

"*No*, what He says to me is in secret — you know, inside me. Understand?"

"Then, doesn't that mean you can't possibly know what He says to *me* in secret. Right?"

"No, I only know what He says to me, and He's saying you're working against Him and it's dangerous."

"Dangerous?"

"Yes. Let me ask you something, Jess. Do you think you're a God-fearing woman?"

"A *what*?"

"A God-fearing woman."

"No! Why should I fear God?"

"Because He's judging you."

"Judgin' me? No! I see Him more like a mother bird with her wings spread over her nestlin's, protectin' 'em."

"That's just what I'm talking about! You're still against Him—against His very word."

By then, we were outside my back door. He handed me the mint bucket and I placed both containers on the ground and said, "You know I never went to any seminary, or big school, or nothin' like that, but over the last twenty years in these mountains, I've seen 'bout every kind of sickness you can imagine and durin' that time, I discovered a few thin's," I said.

He dropped his head and replied as if he were talking to a child, "Okay, what did you discover?"

"Patients afraid of their ailments are always hard to heal."

"Okay, interesting," he said in the same tone.

"But, the only kind of patient more difficult to heal than that," I paused to be sure he was listenin', "the patient *most* difficult to heal is the patient who believes his sickness was sent from God to *punish* him."

"You see what I mean? You're working against God."

"Preacher Ron, do you have any real idea what I do?"

"Yes, I've heard plenty from people around the mountain."

"From my patients?

"No, but from others who knew about your family for generations."

"What'd they say to you?"

"They told me about incantations, and using spirits,

and other supernatural things."

"I grew up watchin' my Great Aunt Reese and my Great Aunt Brusie takin' care of these people."

"You learned from them?"

"Yes, but I don't do incantations and I don't call on spirits or any unnatural forces."

"Do you cast spells and interpret omens?"

"No! But I gotta tell ya, I don't *have* to do those things. I been healin' for over twenty years, seen lots a people get well, thousands of cases, and I know there's a kind of spiritual force at work in my healin'."

"Yes, that's what I'm talking about. What you do is all about *superstition*, but I want you to consider another way."

"Why do you call it superstition?"

"Because it's not from God. Simple as that."

"*How* do you know that?"

"Jess, let me say it again, I want you to consider another way."

"You mean you want me to give up the stuff I've been taught?"

"Yes, much of it anyway."

"Well, I think that's exactly what I just told you. I've been doin' lotsa things *different* from my family."

"You give potions, read tea leaves, and talk to the sick, and get them to shake vials, and stuff like that?"

"Yes — no. I don't read leaves. I heal."

"I got to tell you something."

I turned to him. He looked straight at me and talked slowly, extending his hand again as if he were giving me something. "It's going to be very difficult for you to realize that you've worked hard and think your family has blessed so many people for years, but you have actually hurt them and I've seen witnesses, right there in my church, that you have power over them."

"So you think it's all just some kind of evil?

"Yes. Whatever you call it, it's still a form of witchcraft."

"You need to talk to my patients, Reverend."

We were quiet for a moment. "Do you want us to stop acomin' to the services?" I asked.

"No! Of course not. Come and be changed. Bring your baby…and that boyfriend. You understand I'm here just to try to help you?"

"I know you are."

"I'll pray for you, Jess."

"Thank ya kindly, Preacher Ron. I'll pray for you too."

His mouth opened and quivered with a slight stammer, but no words came out. He raised his hand as a gesture of good-bye and walked away.

I had been expectin' a visit from the preacher for some time, but I knew he would never approve of me and my life, and all my hopes that I could soften his fears of me were crushed that mornin' when he described me as *dangerous*. I knew then he would look for ways to stop my healin' work.

CHAPTER 11

McKENZIE

Jess warned me that some people pay with produce rather than cash, so I walked to the top of the ridge to start delivering Jess' packages and worked my way down the spine toward the General Store where I had parked my car. That way I wouldn't have to carry the produce up the mountain, then back down.

My first delivery was on the north side to a man named Eli Williams. Jess told me he had been a widower two years and he still missed his wife so much he couldn't sleep at night. I was glad to find that his house was only about a hundred yards down the north slope. He lived in a simple, well-kept little structure with painted clapboards and a shingle roof. The front door was open and when I stepped onto the porch, I saw Mr. Williams sitting in the living room, asleep on his overstuffed chair with his white dog named Boney across his feet. A wood upright radio sat on the floor beside him, tuned to a faraway station playing as much static as music. I eased into the house and walked slowly toward him not wanting to wake him or the dog too fast. I recognized the song on the radio, *Make Believe* by Jo Stafford. It was one of my favorites. The song and the static were loud enough to muffle out the squeaking of the planks under my feet. I stopped and waited for a moment. They were both so deep in dreams, I didn't know whether to leave, or wait, or just drop off the package and go.

Mr. Williams was long and thin with faded red hair and ruddy skin. He must have been in his mid-seventies. Definitely came from Scots-Irish stock. The deep crisp lines on his face, had been etched in even rows over his forehead. They radiated from the outside corners of his eyes and down his cheeks like spider webs, but they were laugh lines, not lines from labor or worry. His boots were placed side by side on the floor against the radio. He wore a light-blue denim shirt with its left sleeve rolled halfway up and the other sleeve buttoned at this wrist. Both his hands were in his lap, one holding a book and one cradling a pipe with a tiny thread of smoke rising from its bowl.

The touch of Eli's wife was still on every inch of the house. I tiptoed into the dining room arranged with furniture in all the right places. Paintings of flowers and pictures of children hung on the walls. Against the far wall was a small round table. On the table sat a white vase filled with fresh wildflowers, mostly wild roses and white asters, undoubtedly placed there by Eli that day. On the wall, above the flowers, was a portrait of a lady I assume was Mrs. Williams.

Jess had carefully marked a name on each medicine package to be sure I gave out the right container to the right customer. I placed the small package on the dining-room table in the center of Mrs. Williams' lace tablecloth so the name *Eli Williams* was in plain view. A strong breeze flowed freely through the front door and pushed laced curtains out the open dining room window causing them to float and wave in the outside air. I watched them for a moment before discovering the view from that window overlooked the western valley all the way to the hazy blue mountains of Tennessee. I turned and took a single step toward the door when I was greeted by two small black holes at the end of Eli's shotgun, pointed at my face.

"Who are you?" Eli asked.

"I'm Mac, Jess Shew's friend. I'll be making her deliveries for a few weeks."

"Oh yes, heard she had a baby," he grunted as he lowered his rife.

"Yes, she had a fine boy."

"You the father?"

"Yes."

"How are they?"

"Doing great."

"Tell her I need some more sleep medicine."

"I just put some on the table for you, but…when I came in, you were doing a pretty good job of sleeping and I didn't want to disturb you."

"Well, I nap during the day, but don't sleep at night."

Eli turned and placed his rifle against the wall and walked back into the living room. "Sorry 'bout the weapon," Eli said." "Didn't know who you were. I take lots of naps in the daytime. My wife slept by my side every night for fifty-five years. Just can't sleep without her."

"Oh, I'm sorry, Mr. Williams."

I handed him the medicine package and said, "Hope this helps."

"Thanks." He clutched the package, looked at me and said, "You got yourself a good woman…What did you say your name was?"

"Mac."

"Mac. Before you go, pick some flowers for Jess outside the house. Wild roses grow everywhere around here. Take 'em to her. Ya hear me?"

"I will."

"Gotta show her you love her, you know?"

"I know. Thanks. I will, but let me ask you something," I needed to change the subject, and this was the first thing that popped into my mind, "Are there any shortcuts to some of these houses and farms without having to climb all the way back up to the Ridge each time? I gotta go to a farm owned by the Berryhill brothers next, and Jess warned me about a man named Mike Cobb whose property I have to cut through walking down from the ridge."

"Yes, I'll show you a great way to get the Berryhill farm, but you gotta follow me."

"Okay."

"Boney!" he clapped his hands, waking his dog who eased himself off the floor and followed Eli out the door.

I picked up my bag and caught up with Eli and his dog as they made their way through thick laurel and headed east. The walking was easy enough for the first two hundred yards, then trees and bushes became smaller, the slope became steeper, and the rocks grew much larger. Another two hundred yards and Eli and his dog were shuffling their way on a ledge around a solid granite bulge in the side of the mountain. Eli never slowed down or looked back while I slipped further behind. The old man and his dog disappeared around the stone corner. When I finally rounded the same turn, the narrow ledge stopped with no place to walk. I looked around and down to the bottom of the rock wall fifty feet below. I couldn't find Eli or the dog anywhere until I heard a halfhearted bark from

Boney. I looked up. Standing on a ledge thirty feet above, Eli grinned, waving his hand.

I put my shoes in my bag and strapped it across my back, then slid all twenty of my fingers and toes into fissures and crannies in the rock. I didn't look down. I didn't look up. Somehow I made my way to the higher ledge. "Eli," I said. "I know you must be twice my age so…you can understand how embarrassing it is for me to ask this, but will you please slow down?"

"Of course, I will, but I'm sure you know I'm *more* than twice your age."

I just nodded, put on my shoes, looked over the valley to catch my breath, and then said, "Okay, and I'll try to keep up with you, but you got to tell me how your dog climbed up here."

Eli laughed aloud. "It was easy. I carried him with one arm and climbed with the other. But, don't worry; the tough part is over, 'cause the Berryhill Farm is around the next corner."

Eli and Boney guided me another fifty yards beyond the limestone cliffs before we intersected the worn trail leading down from the Ridge to the farm owned by Tupper Berryhill, and his brother Lorne.

"That's where you want to go," Eli said as he pointed at the downward side of the trail.

"You're not going with me?"

"No, gotta go home and finish my nap. When will Jess be back?"

"A few weeks."

"Give her my love. But, Mac, you forgot the flowers."

All I could do was smile and shake his hand and say that we'd be back in a couple of weeks. "Hope you sleep well tonight, Mr. Williams."

CHAPTER 12

McKENZIE

The Berryhill brothers' houses were so close they looked like a single house. Through the small gap between the houses, I saw the brothers pushing a cart filled with bulging burlap bags into a root cellar. They stopped when they saw me. I immediately explained who I was and why I had to make deliveries for Jess.

"Well, she sure fooled us," said Lorne. The two men wished her and her baby well. Men are always happy to hear about the birth of children, but never comfortable with the details, which was fine with me because the less I had to explain, the safer I felt. I didn't know until then that the brothers were identical twins. I couldn't imagine how anyone ever told them apart except one wore a plaid green shirt and the other wore a plaid red shirt. Both wore blue jeans with cuffs rolled up to the ankles. As I talked, they nodded simultaneously and flashed the same gap-toothed smiles.

I had brought six different packages for the Berryhills and I had been looking forward to lightening my load, but I had forgotten the Berryhills were going to pay in roots and herbs and wild fruit from the north slope's underbrush and the produce was going to weigh more than the packages I was dropping off. "What's in the burlap bags?" I asked.

"Some stuff Jess needs like ramps, toothwort, nettle, black cohosh, ginseng, bloodroot, and mayapple."

"Mayapple?"

"Yeah, some people call it 'wild lemon', anyway, she'll use 'em all year long. I'll have these same packages ready for her every week for the next month. After that, we stop harvestin' for the winter."

I placed their medications, ointments, and tea on one of the porches and the two brothers loaded my bag with their payment.

"Tell Jess congratulations and we look forward to seein' her back," said Tupper.

"I'll tell her, thanks. I'm as anxious as you are for her return. But now I have to walk back to the ridge and cross some property belonging to a guy named Mike Cobb."

"Oh yes…Cobb," said Lorne.

"Jess warned me about him. What should I do?"

"We'll walk you back up the hill. He won't mess with ya."

"How does Jess get through when she comes?"

"Oh, Jess never has a problem with people like Cobb. He's plumb scared to death of her."

"Of Jess?"

"Yes, and her aunt right up the ridge."

"Why? Is he one of those who thinks she is a witch?"

"He knows she's one. He's been tellin' everybody for years how she knocked him off the mountain with a spell and broke his knee. Still walks with a stiff leg."

"I came here from Eli Williams' house and climbed a cliff with him that I'm never going to do again. So, how can I get past Cobb next time I come?"

"Easy, just be sure you come with Jess."

We climbed back to the ridge. My bag must have been ten pounds heavier, but no sign of Cobb. The next stop was the Crowder's farm on the south side of the ridge. A troop of kids, two boys and two girls, returning from school at the Assembly Hall, passed me as I started down the winding rocky slope to the Crowder farm, a quarter mile from the ridge. They laughed and giggled until they were out of sight. I didn't know whether they were laughing at me or their private jokes. The house faced due south with its back wall made entirely of stone. The dark reddish brown tin roof sloped from the mountain to the front edge of the porch. Bucket-sized rocks were scattered around the roof to hold it down during strong winds. The steep trail I was on curved around the west side of the house and disappeared in the front yard.

Two high steps greeted me at the porch. The first was a big flat slab of granite and the second was part of the wood deck. A mug of tea or coffee was balanced on the arm of a chair beside the front door. I touched the side of the mug. It was cold. The moment I knocked on the screen door, I was startled by something that sounded like a giant threshing machine gobbling the side of the house with a rhythmic pattern of banging and pounding, two short beats followed by one hard slam, over and over. The entire porch was shaking and vibrating so hard the ceramic mug fell off the chair arm and smashed into bits of clay and brown splatter.

I'm not sure I wanted to see what was making the sound, but I had no choice. I slunk across the porch and leaned around the corner of the house to see what force sounded like it was ripping the place into kindling wood.

The younger of the two girls that passed me on the trail, had changed from her school dress into jean coveralls and was kneeling beside an upside-down steel washtub on the side porch. With two sticks made from what looked like cut-off broom handles, she drummed a constant rhythm on the bottom of the tub. Her brother and older sister stood straight up with their arms by their side, clogging to their sister's drum beat. Their long hair whipped their foreheads keeping time with their dance. The sound was amplified by a clogging platform placed two inches above the porch floor, constructed from plywood and two-by-fours. They stomped their hard leather shoes with such strength the sound echoed off the hills surrounding the farm. Their lips were tight and pulled slightly upward in determination, pure joy, and celebration that took them so far away they lost themselves in the dance and never noticed me. The dancers stared across the valley at a hazy blue-green mountain and the younger girl never took her eyes off her steel drum. I stepped back to the front of the house, got my camera from its bag, and returned to the corner of the porch to snap some candid shots of the Crowder kids. While looking through the lens, I saw someone dressed in red outside a wood building near the lower trail. I slipped back to the front porch, cleaned up most of the broken cup and stacked the pieces on the chair.

Someone stepped onto the porch behind me. When I turned around, a woman wearing a red jacket was shaking a finger at me. Her lips were moving, but I couldn't hear anything she was saying because of the clogging.

I moved closer. "Mrs. Crowder?" I yelled. "I'm Mac Davis. I'm helping Jess deliver her medicine while she's nursing her baby."

Her intense face broke into a smile, not only because she was glad I was helping Jess, but also, as I found out, she needed the medication.

"Got your packages right here. Just tell me where to put them," I yelled.

She walked by, waving her hand for me to follow her into the house. I placed the packages on the kitchen table and waited while she unwrapped them. She then pumped the long black handle on the kitchen sink until she drew a kettle of water that she immediately placed on the stove.

She smiled, shook her head, then picked up one of the packages and said, "It makes a bitter tea. I add honey to it." She spooned some of the dried tea into the center of a soft cloth, gathered the ends of the cloth, and twisted it into a knot with the clump of tea inside. After placing the knot into a cup, she poured hot water over it and let it sit until the water turned dark. From a clay honey jar, she scooped a large spoonful of the thick golden liquid into her cup.

"We used up the last of her potion two weeks ago. Sometimes I don't need it and sometimes I do, but right about now, I do," she said as she sipped from the cup.

"Oh, I'm sorry. Are you in pain?"

"Oh, just a stomach thing. We almost had it cured when Jess stopped acomin'. That's why I'm so glad to see ya. My husband tells me he feels better jus' havin' Jess in the house. When's she comin' back?"

"Soon. Maybe a couple of weeks."

"Well, there's somethin' you need to tell her. Doug Helms is tryin' to get me and others to stop usin' her potions, and tea, and such, but I been tellin' him 'bout all the things we been healed of since she's been helpin' us. I told him 'bout me and my ailments she done took care of, and all the children's diseases she wiped out of our family, and I told him plenty 'bout my husband who had pneumonia bad. Thought he was gonna die. She came here and sat by his bed, in that room right over there, and that whole thing was gone in about three hours. Completely. It never came back."

"Where is Mr. Crowder now?"

"He works at the quarry."

"I know he works hard, and pneumonia could have put him out of work for a long time. Tell me how or what did she do to heal him?"

"She wouldn't let nobody else come into the room. I could see 'em from the kitchen and, far as I could see, she jus' gave him some medications and talked to him, but whatever it was, she knocked it out of him."

"Well, I know she will be glad to be back at work."

"Tell me 'bout how she's doin' with the baby and everything. I thought I noticed last time she was here that she was gettin' a little larger. Women can always tell, you know, when another woman's expectin'"

"I promise she's going to be here as soon as she can and take care of everythin'."

I hated to use the word "promise." It was apparent these people were dependent on Jess, and I wanted to do something for them even if it was simply giving them a little comfort, but I couldn't make promises for Jess, especially since most of what she did and how she did it were still mysteries.

CHAPTER 13

McKENZIE

I made about nine or ten deliveries before stopping at the Rook farm. Mr. and Mrs. Rook made lunch with ham biscuits and beans and cider. I couldn't believe how hungry I was and how tired my legs were. The afternoon deliveries went faster. By four o'clock, I had one delivery left, the Hollars Farm.

The medicine bag was lighter by then, but felt heaver with every step. I took a short rest, then continued down the spine. I heard a sound like several men stomping their feet behind me. I looked back and saw nothing, but the sound continued to get louder and closer. I looked again and saw someone leading a mule with a load of bags strapped across its back. I waited until they were within a few feet of me before I stepped aside to let them pass.

The man was tall with dark hair and, to my surprise, he stopped beside me.

"Looks like you're carryin' a load in that basket," he said.

"Yep, it's getting heavier, too"

"Lemme give you a hand".

"No, thanks. Looks like your mule's got enough on his back."

"Naw, he's the strongest one I got. He'll be fine. Com'on let him take it. He's happy to help."

I couldn't resist and my feet were killing me. "Okay, just a little way down the mountain."

As he walked toward me, I noticed his left leg was completely stiff, but he was strong and lifted the bag with one hand and wedged it between two cloth bundles on the animal's back. With a tug on a rope, the mule continued his march down the hill. I knew right away it was Mike Cobb and somehow I got the feeling that he already knew who I was.

"Whatcha got in the bag?" he asked.

"Medicine," I blurted out and was immediately sorry I did.

"Big bag for medicine. You a doctor?"

He was fishing. "Sort of," I replied.

"Whatcha got in the bag over your shoulder?"

"That's my camera bag. Much lighter."

We walked about another fifty feet. "That big poke on the mule looks to me like Jess Shew's bag," he said without looking at me.

I decided to just throw it back at him and see what he really wanted. "That's right, I'm working for her."

"Why is she not here herself?"

"Had a baby."

"Can't be!"

"What do you mean?"

"She's so damn strange, she couldn't have no baby!"

"Well, I think you're wrong about that. Maybe you don't really know her."

He stopped the mule, walked to the side of the trail, and picked up a stick the size of a baseball bat, then walked back to me and said, "Listen to this." With the stick, he tapped against his leg twice below and twice above his knee. It gave off a metal clanking sound. "Hear that?"

"Yes. What is it?"

"That's a steel brace holding my leg together so I can walk. I think about Jess every time I take a step."

"Why?"

"She did it. She did it with her witch stuff…with her spells and things."

"But how?"

"Happened years ago. I saw her comin' up the trail, like she always did, carrying that same bag. I stood on a rock, a big one the size of this here mule. I told her to turn around and go away and she pointed her finger at me. That's all she had to do and the rock beneath me crumbled into powder and rubble. I fell to the ground on my leg and then off the side of the mountain. She came after me. And gave me something to drink. She said it would help. I was in too much pain to argue. Don't remember much after that, but I passed out and my family picked me up and carried me all the way to Weavertown where they got somebody to drive me to the hospital in Asheville. When I woke up, I had steel bolts in my leg and this here steel brace."

"I know it must have been painful."

"The doctor said it wasn't the pain, it was whatever she gave me to drink that knocked me out. He asked me what it was and I told him I didn't know, but somebody named Jess Shew done gave me a potion. He said my leg would never bend again, but I was lucky to be alive after drinking that potion."

We started walking again. "Did he say what was wrong

with her medicine?" I asked.

"He said that somethin' in it sent me into such a deep sleep that, for a while, he didn't know if I would ever wake up. Jess knew I was against her and against what she was doin', and she poisoned me."

"I'm sorry that happened to you, Mr. Cobb, but I've talked to lots of others that don't agree with you about Jess."

"How do you know my name?"

"I just guessed."

"Of course." He leaned back and looked at me through the bottom of his eyes.

"Well anyway," I said. "I think you've got it wrong about her and I know there must be some other explanations about what happened to you."

"Like what?"

"Well, did you ever stand on that rock before?"

"No. Why?"

"How do you know that stone was not ready to crumble, just waiting for someone like you to stand on it?"

He shook his head and steamed a little, then said, "The only Stumpy people you're talkin' to are her patients, right?"

"Yes, except for you and a guy named Helms."

"You need to talk to some more people up here. Anyway, how did you get to know her and why are you working for her?"

"We're going to raise a child together."

"You the father of her baby, Mr. Davis?"

"Yes, I'm the father, but how did you know *my* name?"

"Doug told me all 'bout you, but listen here, Davis, we gonna run that woman off this mountain, understand? So ya better get away from her or we're gonna run you off too."

"I'm really sorry about your leg, Cobb, but you got her all wrong.

"Look, Davis, you're not from anywhere around here, are ya?"

"Born and brought up just this side of Ashville. Not more than twenty-five miles away."

"Well, I was born and raised 'bout a quarter mile from here. Growin' up, we never knew a doctor except what we called "kerosene doctors" who came by on horseback 'bout once a month. Ever hear of 'em?"

"Yes, they were itinerant doctors."

"Well, I don't know that word, but they'd all studied and were real doctors, and when I was a boy, I sometimes had stomachaches, and they always gave me a spoonful of kerosene. When I had swelling or fevers, they gave me sulfur and whiskey along with the kerosene. Sometimes it worked and sometimes it didn't. The only other kind of healin' up here was what Jess Shew's family was doin'. Don't you see, the people on this ridge never knew nothin' else? Maybe the treatments her family gave were as good as the kerosene doctor's, but that's not good enough now. This is the 1940's and we can go to city doctors and go to real hospitals when we need to, but the Ridge People, some of 'em, are still scared of that kind of stuff. Don't you see? Kerosene doctors are gone, so all they got is Jess and she's keepin' 'em from getting the help they never got before!"

"Okay, Cobb, but listen." He stopped walking. "Before now, I never knew *any* kind of treatment but *city* doctors and hospitals and things like that, then I met Jess, and

I've seen her do things no one else could do. Nobody in Asheville or anywhere else. How do you explain that?"

"I think it's like the kerosene doctors. Sometimes it works and sometimes it don't."

"Either she heals or she doesn't. I can only believe what I saw for myself and what others have told me they saw."

"Davis, I'm goin' to give you some advice." He took two steps toward me. I didn't move.

"Go talk to some other people on this here mountain, people who are not her patients, or even better, go see people who *stopped* being her patients for good reasons."

"Why?"

"I'll tell you why, 'cause I'm not gonna wait for her to kill somebody and I think you're gonna wanta get out of my way."

"It's time for me to get the medicine bag and make my last delivery."

Cobb stood still beside the mule and threw a cold glare at me. I said to him with an emotionless voice, "Mr. Cobb, if you will step aside, I'll get the bag now." He stood still another five seconds, then turned and yanked the bag off the mule so hard it flew out of his hands and crashed at my feet with a thud and the sound of breaking glass. Cobb gave the mule a yank and marched away. I watched them walk down the ridge. Then I headed to the north side of the mountain toward the Hollar's place.

I wondered if the Hollars' medicine jar had broken when Cobb threw the bag on the ground. I sat on a rock and carefully removed the broken glass from Jess' bag, but the only thing broken was an empty vial. The Hollars two packages were tucked safely between the zucchini and Berryhill's roots. I carefully removed the little cloth sack and a small jar wrapped in paper. Hollars' name was written on labels glued to each one.

In front of me was the old trail leading to the Hollars' farm. The trail was nothing more than a narrow path winding around tall oaks. The oaks cast heavy shadows over green ferns that covered the ground like a thick carpet from the base of the mountain all the way back up to the cluster of rocks where I was sitting.

The forest was beautiful in its simplicity. The Ridge people loved their isolation and that is why they chose to live and raise their families there. Cobb was right. Most of the people on that mountain grew up taking medications and remedies that came out of the ground around them or came to them by someone they trusted.

The jar had a metal screw lid and came off easily. Inside was a finely ground light-green powder. It had a sweet smell like honeysuckle. A note on the side of the jar said to *rub the powder directly onto the rash two times a day.*

I screwed the lid back on, returned the jar to the bag, and picked up the little cloth sack that contained a bottle full of dark liquid. Slowly I eased the cork off and smelled the bitter potion. I soaked the tip of my finger and licked it off. It made me shudder. I coughed and my chest heaved. I raised my arm to slam the bottle and its stinking contents against the stone boulder beside me when two dogs came running out of the woods. As soon as they saw me, they stopped and remained perfectly still and silent. They didn't look angry or vicious, but suspicious about why I was there.

I recorked the bottle, shoved it back into the bag and continued down the hill. The dogs followed me a hundred yards before disappearing into the woods. From a clearing beside the trail, I looked down on the Hollars' house. A woman was sitting on the front porch overlooking a muddy stream. I watched the woman for a moment. A baby was crawling around her feet. Something darted across the trail beside me. I turned just in time to jump out of the way of a charging black sow being chased by the two dogs. They almost knocked me down. The pig vanished in the underbrush and the dogs ran in circles, trying to regain the scent. The woman looked up. I gave her a friendly wave, but she just stared back.

I walked down the hill to her front steps and nodded to the woman before giving my usual introduction explaining, why I was there.

The woman continued husking her corn while the baby boy, naked from the waist down, peeked out from behind her chair. An orange cat chased loose corn silk swirling in the wind. I pulled one of the packages from my bag and read the name on top, "Mr. C. Hollars. Is that your husband?"

"Yep," said the woman.

"And that must be Mr. Hollars' son?" I said waving at the child who was reaching for the cat's tail.

"Yep, his son and my boy."

"Where's Mr. Hollars today?" I asked.

"My husband works the quarries; gone from dawn to sunset most days,"

"Well, I hope I meet him someday."

"If you want to meet him in the daytime, you need to go to the quarries."

"I guess this is his medicine, but can I leave it with you? Jess wrote the cost on the side."

The woman held out her hand. I walked to the porch

step, leaned over and stretched my arm to give her the two packages. She looked at them for a moment. "I'll take 'em inside and find the money. Please watch my boy for a minute." She stood and walked into the house with the medicine in one hand and the bowl in the other.

The child crawled toward me chanting something in baby talk while the cat tiptoed close behind.

"Hello, little guy," I said. The baby squealed and scuttled faster until he reached the edge of the step in front of me. I drew my camera from its bag and knelt to snap some shots of the boy who was fascinated with my every move. Holding on to the wood post, the toddler struggled to his feet. His cat circled behind and curled his neck and shoulders around the boy's cubby legs, joining him in constant admiration of me. The pair stood still and watched while I took pictures of them from different angles and heights. "Is this your friend?" I said, wiggling my finger at the cat. The baby laughed. "Is this your friend?" I said again with the same hand gesture but a little more exaggerated. The baby laughed harder.

"Is this your . . ."

"I'm sorry, whadjah say your name was?" interrupted Mrs. Hollars as the screen door slammed behind her.

The baby crawled back behind the chair and the cat shot to the far side of the porch, spun around, and then slunk his way back to a spot behind the boy.

"It's Mac," I said.

"Mr. Mac, I know we owe Jess some back money and then some more for today and it comes to almost two dollars, but all I can find now is ninety-four cents. I hate to make Jess wait for it, but nothin' I can do about it right now." She handed me an envelope full of change.

"I'm sure Jess will understand, Mrs. Hollars, but I have an idea. Just a minute ago, I was taking some pictures of your son and cat. If you will let me take pictures of you and your son together, I'll just give Jess a couple of dollars from my pocket to pay off your debt and you can keep your envelope with the change inside. Would that be okay?"

"Mr. Mac, I can't ask you to do that."

"You didn't. I asked you to let me take some pictures and I'll pay you two dollars. Okay?"

She reached down and scooped up her boy and placed him on her lap. "His name is Albert."

"Well, hello again, Albert. Let's take another picture," I said readjusting my camera, then took shots from all angles.

"Why would you or anyone want pictures of us," asked Mrs. Hollars.

"It's a picture of a mother and her child. It's actually very beautiful...anyway, photography is kind of a hobby for me. So how old is Albert?" I asked.

"He will pass his first birthday in a week."

"I know you and Mr. Hollars are proud of him."

"Yes." She paused, then said, "We're proud of him, and we're grateful for Jess, too...She ever tell you 'bout the first time I sent for her?"

"No, don't think so."

"Well, if you're Jess' husband now, you should know about it."

"I'm not exactly her husband...yet...I'm...I'm the father of her son."

"Okay, even more reason for you to know. When I was seven months pregnant, my husband got crazy drunk and knocked me down with his fist. I felt pain in my stomach so bad I had to stay in bed. I couldn't get up for more than a few minutes at a time. I got Jess to come and help me when Cal was at work — that's his name, Calvin."

I sat on the step and leaned my back against the white wood post. "Did he get drunk a lot?" I asked.

"I married him three years ago when he was thirty, but he didn't tell me until later that he'd been drinkin' ever since he was twelve years old."

"Twelve? How does a twelve-year-old get stuff like that?"

"His dad had his own still. Didn't sell the stuff or nothin' jus' made it for himself. His dad was a hopeless drunk. Drank himself to death. Cal always knew he inherited the taste for drinkin' from his dad and hated him for it.

"When he's not working in the quarries, Cal's always doin' work around the mountain. You know, helpin' somebody dig, or pickin' some crops, and things like that, and at times they paid him money, but they all knew he liked good *shine* more, and half the time he brought home his pay in a bottle."

"It must be difficult for you."

"It was, and when he hit me, it hurt, but I didn't care much about the pain so much; I was afraid I was goin' to lose my baby.'

"My God."

"Yes, but Jess helped me."

"Did she give you medication?"

"Yes, at first, but then she did more. She helped cook and clean the house and clean up after Cal. One day when he was gone, she found Cal's bottles hidden inside his tool box. She poured them out in the sink and left the empty bottles sittin' out for him to see as soon as he came home that night. Told me to tell him that *she* poured them out it, not *me*.

"What did he do?"

"He already had something to drink before he got home and he blew up when he got here. Because of the pain, I stayed in bed. Couldn't even sit up. I heard him open the closet door and load bullets into his rifle. I screamed for him to stop, but he wouldn't answer and slammed the door shut as he left.

"It was ten o'clock that night when he got back. He didn't say nothin' at first. Put away his rifle, and sat on the bed beside me. I asked him what happened and he was quiet for a little while longer, then said he went to her house and when she opened the door, he asked her if she had poured out his bottles and she said yes, walked back into the house, and asked him to come in and talk about it. I never heard Cal talk so soft to me. Didn't sound like him at all. Anyway, he said that Jess had already placed two cups and a hot teapot on the table in her kitchen as if she somehow knew he was acomin' or somethin', and that he placed his rifle right across the table between them, and they sat down to talk."

"What about?"

"Cal said she asked him right away about his dad, and I asked him how she knew about the troubles with his dad, and he jus' shook his head. Then, after listenin' to Cal's answers, she said things to him that he didn't exactly understand, and he couldn't remember the words, but he said listenin' to her was like when he was a little boy and got washed outside in the yard by his mama with buckets of steamin' hot water and lye soap."

Albert wiggled in Mrs. Hollars' lap and she lowered him to the floor. He immediately started crawling back to me.

"He didn't remember what she said?" I asked.

"No, but she left him a feelin' he never knew before. He walked home in the dark. Couldn't shake it. Couldn't describe it either.

"That was a Saturday night. We sat together in bed and talked 'til 'bout four in the morning when he fell asleep. Cal rose at eight o'clock, cooked breakfast for both of us. After breakfast, he sat by me in bed, held me, and cried for an hour, almost without making a sound, just breathin' hard and givin' up a flood of tears. Then, he went out and sat on the porch. That's when I discovered all the pain inside me was gone. It was gone—and never came back. I jumped up and joined him outside. First time I'd walked in days."

"*How?*"

"Don't know. Jess hadn't been there since the day before. I jus' remember that when he came home after bein' with her, I felt better inside. I gave birth to Albert two months later. That was twelve months ago. Cal hasn't allowed a drop of anything with alcohol in it into the house since then. Now, when he does extra work for folks, he gets paid in money or produce."

Mrs. Hollars kissed Albert who, by then, had crawled back into her lap. I rested my head on the post behind me and looked over the valley and the muddy stream flowing by. On the hill, the black sow was still forging his own zig-zag path toward the house.

Another minute or so, Mrs. Hollars said, "The last few weeks we've both missed Jess, so when is she gonna be able to come back?

"Whenever she's ready to climb the ridge."

"She goin' to bring her new boy?"

"Sooner or later she will." Another minute went by. The sow strolled through the yard and around the house.

"So, Mr. Mac, the one thing I can't figure out is why she never told me about *you* or about the baby comin' on and everything."

"Well, we met over a year ago and I'm sure she'll love for you to meet her little Robb...I mean, meet *our* little Robb. We'll both be back soon." I waved to Albert. "Nice to meet you and happy to get Mr. Hollars' medicine to him."

She nodded, then said, "My husband's gonna be glad to have it when he gets home tonight."

As I left, the same two dogs that greeted me earlier, sniffed and followed me all the way back to the ridge.

I delivered packages for Jess two more weeks—just enough time to feel I was beginning to know her patients. Most of them were always glad to see me and showed nothing but kindness. But they needed Jess and were becoming anxious for her return.

CHAPTER 14

Late afternoon sun washed across the white stone on the back side of Stumpy Ridge, casting long shadows. Theron pushed the cart while Billy and Nanny pulled it through the narrow gap of thick rhododendron. The deep-green trees concealed a small private grassy knoll near the foot of Stumpy Ridge's highest cliffs.

After untethering the goats to graze and drink from the nearby stream, Theron removed his knapsack and placed it gently on the ground allowing his half-grown orange cat, Pickles, to climb out of the bag, stretch her legs, and dash up the stone ramp to a long, thin horizontal opening in the rock. Flat on his stomach, Theron squeezed through the mountain's crack into the dark cave. Pickles had already scrambled out of sight as Theron started the ten-foot climb to a wide ledge in the shaft. He closed his eyes until they adjusted to the dim light. He then pulled a short candle from the bag and, with his fingers, felt the back of the ledge to find the little niche in the rock he always used to place a candle to protect the flame from the constant rush of air rising up the shaft. Once the candle was lit, he looked slowly around to greet each form and crevasse in the rock as if they were his friends. He was sitting in the same spot where his dad brought him each summer when he was a boy. It was their secret place. From the candlelight, Pickles' eyes shined like tiny headlights while the steady wind rippled across fur on her face and ears.

Theron picked up a photograph he kept under a rock beside the niche and held it close to his face. It was a picture of his mom and dad taken on the goat farm before he was born. The flickering light made them look as if they were moving — almost like they were alive. He recalled his mama singing when he was a boy and while looking at her picture, he hummed along from memory.

After replacing the photograph under the rock, he crawled to a spot at the back of the ledge directly under the towering shaft. The ledge was just wide enough for him to lay on his back. He looked into the tunnel above him rising out of sight into darkness. He continued to hum melodies that made no sense except from his enormous imagination.

As always in the spring, during the last five minutes before sunset, a column of light shined through an opening in the shaft somewhere far above him. The glow bounced its way down to the ledge. The rising wind increased as it often did around that time of day. Without taking his eyes off the dying glow on the rock above, he stopped humming and listened for his parents. The sound of wind slowly became a deep, soft voice singing a constant note. He always believed it sounded like his dad. The wind increased again and the low voice waned away, but minutes later another long, sustained note, much higher, made the whole cave vibrate. To Theron, it sounded like his mom, and he listened until it, too, faded away and the breeze slowed down to nothing more than a gentle breath.

Theron still missed his parents and had never really

understood death, but when his parents had died, Preacher Ron helped bury them on the farm, and tried to explain it to Theron. It didn't make any sense to him, and all he knew was his parents had gone to another place to live on. The voices and the few minutes of sunlight finding their way down the shaft were, to Theron, a message left by his parents to remember them.

Jack Hemphill

CHAPTER 15

Theron steered his goats into the shade of a tree in front of the general store and let them nibble on grass and weeds while he collected his mail and delivered milk and cheese to the manager.

Two boys sat on the front stoop and laughed at Theron's awkward, lanky movements as he wrestled with containers and bottles from his cart.

Most children on the Ridge knew Theron as part of the mountain—odd, quirky, but very gentle and quiet. Some of them, mostly quarry kids, enjoyed making jokes about everything he did. Theron had learned over the years to ignore them and to keep doing his work.

"Hey, Goat Man," said one of the boys, "Didja bring me some ice cream?" He pretended he didn't hear and walked past them into the building all the way to the two coolers behind the counter. The manager, Mr. Walton, had Theron's mail, along with notes from customers, stacked on the counter. The Ridge families always left messages to Theron requesting milk and cheese they needed for the following week. Theron opened the mail and Mr. Walton read each piece to him. He usually left some of the orders in Mr. Walton's cooler to be picked up by the customers and other orders he delivered the following trip to the

Ridge.

"You got another letter from the Redbriar Bank," said Mr. Walton. "Would you like me to read it to you?"

"Naw, Mr. Walton, but thankya kindly. I'm stoppin' by Jess' on my way home. She'll help me with it."

Carrying his empty containers in his arms, Theron left the store and took only a few steps when he noticed his goats were not under the tree. He dropped the containers in the shade and looked around the property. Couldn't see them. With his long fingers interlaced behind his head, he walked around the General Store up the slope to the higher side and the entrance to the Assembly Hall. After spinning a full circle, he looked around for someone to help him. The boys walked down the hill past him as they tried to contain their laughter.

"Didya see where my goats went?" he asked softly.

The boys didn't answer except with a burst of snorts and hisses through their teeth.

Theron put his hands behind his head one more time and started walking up the ridge. A series of large stone formations capped off the rising trail that made the ridge look like a human spine. After walking up the path about a hundred feet, he called out, "Nanny, Billy." Immediately they strolled from the back side of a boulder, chewing something green and pulling the cart behind them. He gave them a pat on the neck and they followed him back to the General Store where he gathered his containers. With a tap of his crooked stick, the two goats walked down the road beside Theron. Thirty minutes later they arrived at Jess' house. She had heard the clanging of the goat bells coming up the drive and was standing on the porch waiting for him. She gave him a hug and had two apples for the animals.

"Howya doin', Miss Jess," said Theron.

"I'm fine, Theron. What can I do for ya today?"

"Got some more mail from the bank."

"Let me read it to you."

'I'd appreciate it," he said as he handed her the unopened envelope. Jess walked up to the porch and sat on one of the chairs. Theron sat in the second chair.

Jess read the letter slowly to herself, then said, "Okay, they're still talkin' 'bout you paying back the loan they gave your parents. Honestly, I can't understand everythin' they're sayin' here, but they're talkin' 'bout dong somethin' to get their money back."

"What does that mean?"

"I'm not really sure, but Mac would know and maybe he'll go down to Redbriar and talk to them 'bout it for you."

"I'd sure appreciate it, if he would."

"I'm sure he'd be happy to help." She patted his arm. "Don't worry, he'll find some way to take care of it."

"Maybe he can tell them that Dad and Mama done died."

"I think they already know that."

"Then why they still writin' me letters? I didn't borrow no money from them."

"I know, but your parents did."

"But my parents can't pay it back 'cause they're dead."

"I think they want *you* to pay it back."

"But, why? Maybe when Mac's there, he'll tell 'em that I can't do that."

"Don't worry, Theron. He'll let 'em know. I'll keep the letter and give it to him as soon as he gets here on Friday."

Jack Hemphill

CHAPTER 16

McKENZIE

Jess and I were concerned about how the Ridge People would react when they first saw Robb and she had never told them she was pregnant. Also, we weren't sure how to explain why her pregnancy never showed, but it was typical of Jess to wear baggy clothes, bulky slacks, and flannel shirts in winter and summer.

I had learned by then that Jess doesn't talk when she's nervous. She was very quiet that morning, and I tried to hide the fact that I was probably more anxious than she was. I knew how important that day was to both of us. Originally she was going to do her deliveries by herself while I took care of Robb at her house, but I convinced her that for her first time back, we should all three go together as a family.

She carried Robb wrapped in a blanket, in a sling across her chest. It took until late morning for the mid-November sun to burn off the night chill. Some of the people on the north slope, kissed Jess and Robb and commented how much they thought he looked like her. One or two people said he looked more like me. I just smiled. Some of her patients on the south side seemed skeptical, but kept their thoughts to themselves.

We visited all her usual patients on both sides of the Ridge starting with farms and houses at the bottom, closest to the General Store. The last place we visited was John Curley Todd's house. Long before the farmhouse was in view, John Curley's dog caught our scent and started barking. I remembered how much the dog looked like his name, *Mudhound*, and how ferocious he sounded, but it was an act. The house was surrounded by a fence made of wild grapevines wound around posts driven into the ground. Mudhound ran loose inside the fence and jumped high enough to get a view of us and display his fangs. The house was covered with rough clapboards except the oldest part which was made of exposed logs with joints mortared full to keep the cold out.

The moment Jess lifted the latch on the gate, Mudhound ran away and disappeared behind the house. We never saw or heard him again until we left.

I never knew John Curley Todd's wife's first name. He called her, "Tiny" but it didn't feel right for me so I called her, "Mrs. Todd." The house was placed on a rock shelf that wrapped around part of the north side of the mountain. The shelf varied in width from about ninety to one hundred and fifty feet. On one side of the house, large stone steps led down to a heavy wood door under the structure. John Curley made extra money from wild harvesting and he stored his crop in the cool root cellar under the house.

Jess knocked on the front door and called out, "It's me, Jess." The door flew open and Mrs. Todd's face lit up as she threw her arms around Jess. The Todds had too many children for such a small place. Homemade toys of wood and paper for the small kids were strewn around the yard and house. The Todds were quiet people, but energetic and scampered around their home like nesting squirrels in fall. I followed Jess into the house, but before I entered, two cats ran out so fast they were nothing but a streak of yellow and black.

The living room was dark. Heavy blankets covered the three windows. A child with long curly hair toddled straight over to Jess and hugged her leg. She was about two years old. Her shaggy blond hair covered most of her face. The little girl squawked and giggled as Jess gave her a big hug. "How's my little Berry today? Feeling good?" Jess asked.

Berry nodded.

"I brought my baby boy. Do you wanna touch him?" Jess said.

The little girl nodded again. I wondered why she said "touch him" and not "see him." Jess carefully guided Berry's hand into the sling and over Robb's face. That's when I realized Berry was partially blind. I found out later the blankets over the windows were there because light bothered Berry's eyes.

"Ain't he cute?" said Mrs. Todd to Berry. "I think he's got Jess' nose." Berry reached out and Jess guided her hand back to Robb's nose then to her own.

"Where are the other children?" Jess said.

"Well, my other two girls are playin' outside, and the boys are workin' the crops for John Curley."

"Where is John? What's wrong?"

"He got a swollen foot."

"How?"

"It's his right foot. He thinks he stepped on a nail."

"Okay darlin', I got jus' the thing for him."

"Where is John Curley now?"

"He's lying down, back in the bedroom, but he told me he don't want to be disturbed for a while."

"Tiny, you go tell him I got to see him, and I got to talk with him, and I got to give him the first doses of medicine. After I leave, you can give 'em to him once or twice a day, but I gotta talk to him today."

Mrs. Todd went into her husband's bedroom, and Jess walked into the kitchen. I followed with her medicine bags. Jess and Mrs. Todd's oldest daughter, Eugena, who was washing dishes in the sink, exchanged waves. Jess handed me the baby, removed from her bag a half-dozen bottles, and carried two of them to the window to read her own writing scribbled on the sides. Jess mixed ingredients from one of her small containers into a larger vial, then poured the mixture into one of the glasses. Ten minutes later Mrs. Todd came out of the bedroom and said that John Curley was ready. Jess picked up the large vial and two glasses then marched to John Curley's bedroom.

"John Curley," Jess said with a soft, but deliberate voice. He opened his eyes and tightened his lips as if he were embarrassed. "Got somethin' that's gonna knock that pain and swellin' right out of you."

"Hope so," he said.

Jess pulled back the blanket covering the window to let in light, then carefully poured about a quarter glass full of medicine. "Now, sweetheart, you need to sit up for a minute. I'm giving you medicine, powerful medicine that you have never had before. It will taste very strong and will burn going down, but don't worry, nothin' can stop it from doin' its job."

John took the glass and sniffed the ingredients then

gagged. "Can't drink that stuff; it smells like a handful of stink bugs," he blurted.

"Okay, John, which is gonna be worse, the swellin' in your feet or the stink bug taste in that glass?"

"The taste!" he said.

"I know how bad it smells and it's gonna taste worse, but it'll all be over soon and you're gonna feel better. Now you can do it—drink it down, sweetheart."

He closed his eyes.

"Swallow it, please," she said.

John swung his legs over the side of the bed, shivered a bit, and after a deep breath, started pouring the thick dark-gray liquid into his mouth, but the moment it hit his tongue he threw his head back, let out a loud gasp, and smashed the glass against the wall. Mrs. Todd dashed in, but stopped when she saw broken glass and the dark medicine running down the wall.

"What happened?" she cried out through her fingers pressed against her mouth.

"Tiny, go back to the children," Jess said quietly as she turned her around and guided her to the door.

"That's it, Jess...not drinking that stuff!" John said as he fell back on the bed and yanked the covers over him.

Jess picked up the broken pieces of glass and wiped the wall with a towel. She then poured a small amount of the same foul smelling medication into the second glass. "Okay, time to get back up and drink this. It's not goin' to taste *any better*, but it's a smaller amount. Just enough for one big gulp. I know your foot hurts and I know you're afraid, but you're gettin' somethin' bigger, a whole bunch bigger than the pain and the fear."

John threw the covers off, rolled over far enough to sit

on the side of the bed, and rest his good foot on the floor. She handed him the second glass which he reluctantly took, and with a final brave motion, swallowed the whole glass of medicine. He handed the glass back to Jess and pounded his fist on the bed before placing his hands over his face.

"I know it tastes bad," she said, "but you're gonna start feelin' better very shortly. Now, just let it go and see how fast it'll all change."

He leaned back, rolled on his side, then put his head on the pillow. Jess carefully tucked his feet under the covers and pulled the blanket over him to his chest. After leaning toward him slightly, she said, "Okay, John Curley, now you can rest."

Back in the living room, Jess explained to Mrs. Todd that she was going to have to make him take two doses a day until the pain and swelling were completely gone. "I'll try," Mrs. Todd said.

"Tiny, don't worry. He's gonna start feelin' better and that'll continue until the problem's all gone." Mrs. Todd smiled and bit the nail on her thumb.

Changing the subject, Jess said, "I've got somethin' for Berry. A little sugar cookie."

"She's in the kitchen with Eugena," said Mrs. Todd.

Jess picked up a sealed masonry jar from the bottom of her bag, opened it, and pulled out a round cookie the size of a sunflower. Jess sat at the kitchen table and Mrs. Todd put Berry on her lap.

"My little Berry," said Jess, "I have to go now. I'm all finished with your dad and he's gonna feel better, but I want to give you a treat. It's a cookie just for you, darlin'." Jess placed the cookie in her fingers. She took a timid bite, then another.

Jess said, "Would you like me to come back next week?"

Berry nodded...still eating.

"I'll bring you another cookie."

Berry reached toward her and Jess bent forward until Berry's little fingers touched her face.

Eugena sat down at the table across from Jess.

"Hello again, Eugena," said Jess.

"You goin' home, Miss Jess?" she asked.

"Yeah, in a minute. Wish we could stay for lunch."

"Yeah, me too," Eugena smiled so wide, her cheeks dimpled and her eyes squinted almost shut. Her voice was high and so soft I had to listen carefully to hear what she was saying. Her stocky frame was topped off with medium brown hair that spilled over her shoulders. She had wide, slightly protruding eyes. A bright colored apron covered her thick neck down to the hem of her dress just below her shin.

Eugena asked Jess, "Have you seen Theron yet today?"

"No, not today, but he should be along soon."

"What's today?" asked Eugena.

"This is Friday. He'll be here."

Before we left, Mrs. Todd touched Jess' shoulder and spoke softly, like it was a secret. "Doug Helms is trying to convince people how you and your medicines are dangerous and un-Christian." Jess thanked her and said she knew what Helm's had been doing and told her not to worry.

We said good-bye to Mrs. Todd. I handed Robb back to Jess and we started back up the hill.

"Eugena does all the cooking," said Jess.

"I noticed she was not with the rest of the children and stayed in the kitchen," I said.

"John Curley and Tiny realized early-on that Eugena wasn't going to keep up with the other kids and needed to learn something she could do for the rest of her life."

"Why? "

"They jus' saw she needed special trainin'."

"She seemed very nice."

"Oh, she's a lamb, and very happy with what she's doin'."

Jess was unusually quiet on our trip back to the Ridge. She loved her privacy and sometimes sharing her thoughts was difficult. She was starting to trust me and beginning to let more of her mind trickle out. I never asked much about her medicines or about her healing work, but I noticed earlier that day, when her patients told her they had been healed, she fought to hide her smiles, and tears, and she held back any sign of emotion. I didn't know why. I thought at first it was simply her nature, but I think it may have been because she was selected to work with her great-aunt when she was only fourteen. She never finished her girlhood, and so she put it away in a high, safe place in her mind, and only on rare moments, in complete privacy, took it down for a brief look before lifting it back into her secret nook.

Jess pointed to a clump of maple trees that grew around and over three large boulders the size of buses. The largest rock rose out of the ground and rested on the other two. This made a perfect ramp into the thick branches of the trees — a natural tree house. We shuffled up the rock into the limbs. She needed a break, so I held Robb while she nestled in a corner of the rock and closed her eyes. A cool breeze swayed the trees. I think she may have dozed off for a few minutes. When she awoke, she extended her arms for Robb.

From her backpack, she pulled out a milk bottle wrapped with layers of paper to keep it cool. Robb enjoyed his lunch while Jess and I ate apples and cheese.

"I'm sorry about poor John Curley," I said. "He sounded like he was really hurting,"

Yes, I know," said Jess.

"He's got a serious injury."

"I gave him a tonic of yellow root and ginseng to help remove the poison."

"So why did he yell?"

"Ginseng's real bitter."

"He looked like he was in so much pain. Can't you do something about the taste to help him get it down?"

"Not much, but to tell you the truth, healin' isn't as much 'bout the medicine as it's about people learnin' to trust in somethin' besides themselves."

"Why?"

"'Cause we all got fears keepin' us from seein' or thinkin' 'bout anythin' but the pain, and we gotta have somethin' to soothe or take away our fears first, before anythin' else can happen."

"I watched you today. You did a lot more for them than soothe their fears."

"Oh, I jus' did what I was taught and the medication did what I was told it would do, but the final healin' isn't somethin' that comes from me or the medicine."

"Then, what is it?"

"The final healin' is somethin' we feel."

"Then tell me how it feels."

Jess closed her eyes as if she were searching her mind, listening for a way to explain it, then said, "I had nightmares when I was a little girl. I always cried for Mama who came to me, stroked my hair, patted my back, and watched over me until all my fears melted away and I went back to sleep…Healin' feels just like that…like Mama watchin' over me."

I closed my eyes, trying in vain to understand. Jess lay back against the tree with Robb in her arms and chest. They watched the branches above sway back and forth in the wind. We heard a clanging sound coming from the ridge. I walked across the top of the boulder and leaned over a tree limb. Only had to wait a moment before Theron and his two big goats walked by beneath us, heading down the trail toward John Curley Todd's house. Theron carried his stick loosely over his right shoulder and walked behind the wagon. Obviously, the goats had made the trip so many times they knew the way without prodding.

Jess packed her gear and placed Robb in the carrier. She said, "Mac, it's time for you to meet my Great Aunt Brusie."

CHAPTER 17

McKENZIE

At the top of the mountain, near the stone knob, the trail stops abruptly, towering about forty feet above the ridge. I was so fascinated by the giant chunk of granite that I didn't see Jess slip through the narrow stone passage and around two large outcroppings. When I turned around, she was gone. I had never been this close to the mountaintop before, but I found my way through the maze and caught up just as she made one more turn down an overgrown path. I don't think she ever realized I was not keeping up with her.

Great-Aunt Brusie's house was covered with cedar roof shingles and siding, all weathered to a dark gray matching the tree trunks surrounding it. The cottage was well kept, but so still and silent that I shivered as we walked up the steps. The front door was half open, letting out whiffs of baking bread. Jess walked in after a firm knock on the door.

"Aunt Brusie?" Jess called out. No answer. She walked straight to a round wood table near the kitchen. Three cups, a teapot, and a plate of honey shortbread covered with a cloth napkin were arranged on a calico tablecloth.

"My darlin' Jess!" Aunt Brusie said as she floated

through the back door. I jumped. Her voice was more wind than sound. She was five feet tall at most, and wore a loose cotton gown that flowed in slow motion like the curtains in the window. Her long hair was pure white. She moved effortlessly across the floor. She was so ethereal, she was frightening.

"This is my friend Mac," Jess said.

Aunt Brusie touched my hand and gave me a light kiss on my cheek.

"Jess!" she said, seeing Robb wrapped in his blankets and canvas sling around Jess' neck. "Who is this?"

"This is Robb," said Jess.

"Yours?"

Jess nodded.

"You didn't tell me. How could you keep a secret like that from me?"

"Aunt Brusie, Robb's my boy…our boy, but tell you the truth, one of my patients bore him shortly before she died. We decided to take care of him rather than tell the father what happened."

"Where was the father when she died?"

"Wasn't there. He didn't know anythin' about it. Didn't even know she was pregnant."

"Who is he?"

"Doug Helms."

"Oh, my goodness."

"Yes, I know," Jess said as she cuddled Robb a little closer.

"Doug has no idea?"

"Unfortunately, he knows. He figgered it out and he's not goin' to let it go."

"What's he gonna do?"

"Don't know. If I did, that would make it easy."

"My darlin', you know I'll help you."

"What can you do?"

Brusie sat at the table, placed both hands in her lap, and closed her eyes. She sat so straight and still that we didn't dare speak. Her skin was as white as a cloud. In spite of her age, she had only a few tiny wrinkles under her eyes. Her lips were slightly parted as if she were enjoying a peaceful sleep. Robb was beginning to stir so Jess tiptoed to the front porch with the baby, leaving me alone with her aunt. Aunt Brusie tilted her head back and started humming a soft melody while rocking to her own slow rhythm. When she opened her eyes, she looked straight at me, but I realized she was looking right through me.

"Jess," I whispered just loud enough for her to hear. Jess returned, holding Robb against her shoulder.

Aunt Brusie stood, walked to Jess, and signaled for her to follow, then she took me by the hand and led us out the back door and down a long set of stairs to the ground. We walked between a chicken coop tucked under the house and a woodpile stacked in a long row about twelve feet behind the house. We stopped at a shed forty feet down a steep hill. She swung the door against the outside of the shed revealing a waist high pile of logs stacked along an inside wall. From a shelf above the woodpile, she pulled down a stack of burlap bags, selected one, handed it to me, and returned the rest to the shelf. After lifting a log from the pile, she placed it on the dirt floor, then eased her fingers into a crack between two other logs on the pile. Her thin hand slid into the narrow dark slot well past her wrist. Her arm moved back and forth as if she were caressing something just out of sight, then she pulled out, by the neck, a four foot snake. Jess and I jumped back.

Holding the snake with one hand behind its neck and one around its belly, she turned to me and quietly said, "Open the bag, Mac."

I stretched open the mouth of the bag and held it at arm's length. "What kind is it?" I asked.

Observing my obvious fear, she said with a slight smile, "Copperhead." She continued, "They're all copperheads in this wood stack, but don't worry. They have already started their winter sleep. See how slowly he's moving." She slid it in the bag and said, "I'll get you another one."

"Another one? How many are out here?" I asked.

"Don't know. A bunch. Be ready to open the bag again." She went through the same slow process and handed me another snake identical to the first. With a piece of twine that had been hanging on the wall, she tied the opening of the bag and sealed up the two sleeping snakes.

She looked at me, then at Jess and said, "Number one rule—keep them in a dark, cool place so they stay asleep and give them a pan of water every day. They will eat nothing until spring. Second rule, keep them with you every place you go for the next month or so. Make yourself a big, dark, cloth bag as a carrier, but don't leave them in your house; it'd be too warm. And they'll wake up."

"How long will they sleep?"

"All winter."

"Aunt Brusie, what am I suppos' to do with two sleepin' snakes?" Jess asked.

"Don't worry, darling. Just keep 'em with you. They'll protect you from Doug—protect both of you. You'll know what to do with them."

"How? I don't even know what Doug's gonna to do

next."

"I can't tell ya, but I know this is what you'll need, at least for a while."

"And after that?"

"Jess, it's gonna take time, but there's one more thing I want you to do." She led us outside and closed the shed door behind her.

"Tell me something, Mac. What do you do for a living?"

"Well, I live on a farm. It's actually an apple orchard."

"Where?"

"Buncombe County, Just this side of Asheville."

Aunt Brusie looked at Jess and said, "Listen carefully, darlin'. I want you to plant an apple tree on Doug's farm."

"What?" said Jess.

"It must be big enough to bear full-sized apples within three years."

"Aunt Brusie, how can I do that? He's never goin' to let me plant anything on his property, especially somethin' the size of a tree, even a small one."

"Doug Helms has lots of property. Doesn't use half of it. You can find a spot—a sunny spot somewhere beyond his woods."

"But why?"

Aunt Brusie turned to me and said, "I'm sure you know how to plant apple trees, right?"

"Of course."

Jess wrapped her arms around her aunt to exchange good-byes. In her embrace, Aunt Brusie looked like a child's doll. "Before you go, dear…" Aunt Brusie paused.

"I know, Aunt Brusie. We'll go down and visit Mama and Dad," Jess said.

"That's a good girl, I'll take care of little Robb until you come back up," said Aunt Brusie.

I held her tiny hand in both of mine for a moment, then followed Jess down the narrow trail.

"Your Great-Aunt Brusie is a fascinating person," I said.

"But?" she replied.

"But, Jess, she gave us two poisonous snakes and asked us to plant a tree on Helms' property."

"Yes, I know that seems strange."

"It *is* strange. So why did you agree to do those things?"

"'Cause she's asked me to do lots of odd things over the years that I couldn't at first figger out, and eventually I saw good reasons for 'em."

"So you just trust what she says no matter how weird it is?"

"Yes, I trust her and I'm askin' you to trust me. Give it time."

I changed the subject. "Did I hear you say you were going to visit your parents?"

"Yes, my parents and their parents and all brothers and sisters are buried in a little yard down the hill. I stop by to see my aunt every week when I finish my deliveries, and Aunt Brusie never forgets to remind me to visit the graves."

"It's obviously important to her."

"I don't do it all for her, Mac. It's a beautiful spot with lots of memories."

We walked another quarter mile down the hill to a ring of thick mountain laurel ten feet high, placed in a circle with an inside space as big as a circus tent. The graves in the center, had single stones lying flat on the ground marking each resting place. Only dates and names were carved in the rough stone surfaces. A mason jar with two or three strands of golden rod in each had been carefully placed at the base of every marker. Jess strolled into the yard while I stood at the entrance made of nothing more than an opening in the mountain laurel just wide enough to allow pallbearers through. I don't know why I hesitated. I didn't belong there. Of course, I never believed in ghosts or anything like that, but I just felt safer at the edge of the circle. Jess came back to me and took my hand. I followed.

"My mama," she said, pointing with her free hand, then motioned to the left and said, "Dad's over there."

"Very peaceful," I whispered, not knowing what else to say.

"I often came here with my family when I was young.

"Do you feel close to them when you're here?"

"No, I'm closer to my memories here, but I never thought of my family as actually being buried under this soil."

"Where are they buried?"

"Oh, we buried their bodies here. That's all we knew of them then, but now I think they go on."

I looked at a few of the names and dates. Some died young. I wondered if they had been soldiers. "Where do they go?" I asked.

"I don't know, but I think it is like...like fallin' asleep and wakin' to some place new."

"But where would that be?"

"Like I said, I don't rightly know, but wherever they are, I think they see each other there."

She continued to hold my hand as we walked past dozens of chipped flat granite slabs with carefully chiseled names. We didn't talk any more until we were halfway back up the hill. A long gust rolled from the ridge down the mountain. The blast was followed by another one lasting a little longer and then another after that. Wind picked leaves from the limbs and threw them straight into the air as they mingled with the scatterings of other trees before falling like yellow snow into the valley below.

"Beautiful," I said.

"Yes," she said approvingly, then her voice changed as suddenly as the wind. "Sometimes when it blows like this, it makes the mountain sing."

"What do you mean?" I said, hoping it had something to do with the legend that I heard from Dauber Higgins. I never had the courage to ask Jess about it.

"The wind sometimes blows through crannies in the mountain and makes noises like voices singin' or like people callin'," she said.

"How many people?"

"Two."

"Two people?"

"Sometimes it's just one, but when the wind keeps ablowin' and changin' like it's doin' today, it makes a low sound like the yawn of a big man, and later when the wind blows even harder, it sounds like a high note of a woman singin'." For fifteen or twenty minutes, we listened to nothing but waves of wind and leaves clapping together.

"I've heard of something out west they call 'wind caves' , but never heard of anything like that in North Carolina," I said.

"There is a cave jus' below the top, on the steep side. It starts as a big long crack that widens as you climb around the stone wall. 'Bout half way to the back side the crack gets wide enough to crawl inside."

"Is that where the sound comes from?"

"That's what they tell me. I hear the sound on days like this, even sometimes in winter at my house, but I've never been up there, at the top, when it happens. Actually, I've never been in the cave. Only peeked inside once, through the cave's mouth."

"I haven't heard anybody around here talking about it, but when I was a kid, I loved to explore caves."

"Nobody goes into the cave here."

"Why?"

"Because the Ridge People can't get to it without walkin' past Aunt Brusie's house, and most of 'em, especially those on the south side, are so afraid of her, they won't even look in her direction or come near her house, and the children are forbidden to go near this part of the mountain."

"I guess, when I first saw her, I was a little afraid, but that feeling went away after I met her."

"Sometimes I walk with her down to the General Store and people who see us comin', hide until she's gone. But they've got other fears besides that. People 'round here remember old stories from their ancestors and from the Indians 'bout those voices bein' the sounds of an Indian couple searchin' for their lost child."

We walked up the steep hill to the woodshed. That's when I heard a long, low, somber moan fill the air, continue for a good minute, then stop as if it were breathing in before billowing another moan. I closed my eyes, trying to remember everything about that moment, afraid I would never hear it again. The deep one-note song floated through the forest one more time, then ended .

"There was nothing spooky about that voice. It was

almost like a real person," I said.

"I know, but some people claim the voices are castin' spells. Over the years, some men have fallen off the mountain after listenin' to 'em and things like that have happened."

Who owns that part of the mountain?"

"Aunt Brusie not only owns this house and all the property around us, but she also owns the top of the mountain includin' the caves, the cliffs, and the stone face."

A feeling inside me was crying out to hear the sound one more time. Jess slipped her hand into mine as we listened another minute. Everything momentarily vanished from my mind, but I didn't hear another sound except from the trees.

Aunt Brusie made sure we didn't forget our burlap bag and reminded me again about keeping it cool. She kissed Jess then, still smiling, lifted her head to me. I leaned down and she kissed my cheek. After promising to bring Robb back the following week, we walked back to the ridge.

CHAPTER 18

JESS

I was surprised at how seriously Mac took my request to follow Aunt Brusie's instructions. The apple tree in the back of his truck must have already been ten feet tall, all burlapped and tied up. The sun had not yet peeked over the hills. I had Robb well- wrapped in his warm clothes. The air was cool and wet. Nobody was at the Meetin' House as we slipped by it down to the stream. Mac drove a short way along the bank 'til he found a shallow, rocky part where he easily forded across the creek onto Doug's property.

"Perfect spot, right here," he said as he stopped the truck. "Just above the stream, in an open area, and I can already tell it's good soil. I'll have a hole dug in minutes."

I stayed in the truck, but had just enough light to watch him dig. The mornin' mist made his thick hair curl. He looked like a little boy with ruffled hair and a new shovel in his sand box. He quickly had the tree righted in the hole and back filled. He had a five-gallon bucket of water and another bucket filled with manure that he mixed with the soil and covered the roots.

"That's it," he said, jumping back into the truck.

"When's it gonna bear fruit?"

"Well, she's already four years old and should be bearing fruit next fall, and in another three years there'll be apples all over the ground."

"Perfect!" I said.

"So can you tell me why Aunt Brusie asked me to do this?"

"No. I don't even think about it."

"You're not curious?"

"Yeah, but it doesn't do no good," I said, "According to her, we're suppos' to plant it and jus' wait."

We drove home. Mac fed Robb, rocked him, then put him to bed.

After flap jacks and coffee, we sat on the couch, made up crazy stories about why Aunt Brusie told us to plant the tree, and watched the fire in the fireplace.

"Mac, how many people have told us that Doug's been talkin' 'bout me," I asked.

"At least three or four. Mrs. Todd seemed very concerned."

"I need to borrow your car tomorrow."

"Why?"

"I need to go see Doug."

"Are you sure about this?"

"Yes, very."

"Want me to go with you?"

"No, I need to talk to him alone."

"Will you please tell me why?"

"He has to understand why he needs to let me be."

"Jess, do you even know how to drive?

"Oh yes, I did it a couple of times."

"How long ago?"

"Before I moved in with Aunt Reese."

CHAPTER 19

JESS

I had driven a car maybe a half dozen times in my life…but had not done it since I was fourteen. Mac's truck billowed red dust high into the air as I ran over the dirt road to Doug's house.

Except for his meanness, Doug Helms was completely forgettable. His hard face and cleft chin were always partly hidden under a week-old stubble. He was short, had round but heavy shoulders, and small, stubby hands—too small for a farmer's son.

I knew Doug would be in the garden; it was time to harvest his gourds before winter. I stopped beside the cook's house. My dust trail drifted across his garden and gobbled him up. He ignored me, so I made myself comfortable on the porch swing, sittin' in the spot the cook used to save for little Douglas, Doug's first son. After enough time had passed for him to be perfectly rude, Doug strolled to the porch, pressed his shoulder against a flakin' post, pulled a stick and a knife from nowhere, and began to whittle.

"What do ya want, Jess?" he asked.

"We gotta talk," I replied.

"'Bout what?"

"My patients."

"You wanna know why I'm talking to 'em?"

"Tell me."

"They need to know about you."

"They already know me. You're not gonna change their minds."

"A few months ago I came to your house lookin' for Viola and I think I found somethin' else," he said with his eyes still fixed on his whittlin'.

"What?"

"Somethin' that belongs to me."

"What would I have that belongs to you?"

"Viola's baby." He scowled at me for a few seconds, as if he demanded an answer then said, "I want *my boy.*"

"And you think I got him?"

"I know you do."

"You must be talkin' about *my* boy," I said.

"You know I'm gonna get him back."

"Back? You never *had* him."

"He's mine with Viola."

"Doug yur goin' down the wrong holler."

"So tell me where's Viola?"

"She's dead." I watched his face to see if that stirred the slightest ripple in his mind. Doug stopped whittlin', didn't look up at first, but folded his arms loosely across his chest and then fired a brief, brave glare at me and said, "I guess you want me to ask what happened to her, but why don't you jus' tell me whatever it is you came to say."

"She died right after childbirth."

"After childbirth?"

"Yep."

"Well…I guess I'm not really surprised."

"Why?"

"I shoulda known. She could never be no mother—too weak. Anyway, what did you do with her?"

"Doug, there is one thing you should know. Somethin' I haven't told anybody...yet. Before she gave birth, she made me promise that if somethin' happened to her, I would never let you get her baby."

His eyes were fixed, gazing at nothin', like an old goat that never looks straight at anythin'.

I continued, "I buried her with her stillborn child."

"Where?"

"On Stumpy Ridge."

He shook his head almost like he was goin' to laugh, then said, "And so, you jus' happened to have a baby boy right at the same time as Viola."

"Not quite. Mine's a little older."

"Got a birth certificate?"

"Yep."

"Did ya bring it?"

I pulled the folded paper from a pocket inside my jacket and handed it to him.

"Who wrote it?" He asked.

"Doctor Clayton from Asheville."

Without readin' it, he crumpled the paper in his hand and squeezed it into a tight ball before throwin' it at my feet.

"If you think I believe this, you must think I'm stupid." he said. "You obviously know I'm the father. One way or another, I'm gonna get my son."

I glanced around the porch, then to the gourd garden with its green and yellow rows, and beyond to the big maple filled with orange leaves embracin' an empty treehouse swayin' in the wind. He put his knife away and watched a strong wind blow leaves into the garden. A few more flakes of paint flew from the wood column by Doug's head. A piece of brown cardboard rattled in the window beside me. The fadin' pencil lines on the door frame marched upward with a mark showin' how much his first son had grown each year of his short life, six in all, stoppin' right before his wife, Ivy, died.

He walked toward the garden, looked back long enough to see me pick up the crumpled piece of paper and drive away leavin' another cloud of red dust big enough to swallow him.

CHAPTER 20

Jess was half way down the front steps before the screen door slammed behind her. On her knees, she slowly slid the burlap bag from under the porch, placed it in front of her on the ground, untied the cord and looked inside for a moment. She then retied the cord around the bag. Theron walked down the steps and stood beside her.

Jess stood, picked up the bag, and asked, "Can you think of anything else they said?"

"No, that's all," said Theron. "I was way back in the rear of the store puttin' up my cheese and I heard Mr. Doug talkin' with some folks, but I done told you all I could remember."

"Theron…the things you told me about what they said…do you understand what they mean?"

"No, I don't."

"It's a trap."

"For Mr. Mac?"

"Yes."

"I didn't know."

"Well, you did the right thing in tellin' me 'bout it. Stay here with Robb. I'll be back in not more than a couple of hours. Okay?"

"Okay, Jess."

She buttoned her jacket all the way up and hurried down the drive with the bag in her hand.

Theron waved goodbye to Jess and shivered in the December afternoon wind.

Doug stood alone beside the barn door as Mac, with his window halfway down, pulled up beside him."

"Glad you got my message; appreciate your comin'." Doug said.

"You said you wanted to tell me something about Jess," said Mac.

"Come into the barn."

"I'm not getting out of the car until you tell me what's going on."

Doug paused, then with a long wave of his hand said, "Come on in, Mac."

"I don't trust you, Doug."

"Okay, go home. I jus' thought you wanted to hep' her." He turned and walked into the barn.

Mac sat in the car for a minute and then, reluctantly, walked through the big wooden barn doors.

The hayloft window blasted a shaft of sunlight into Mac's face as Doug closed the doors behind him. Mac knew he was in trouble. With cupped hands over his eyes, he looked at the fourteen men surrounding him. Most of them squatted quietly on rows of makeshift benches, but some leaned against the barn walls and wooden posts. No one spoke while Doug dusted off the bottom of a rusty bucket, flipped it over, and sat at the far end of one of the rows.

Doug raised his hand and grunted, "I'm gonna start with a question. *Where is Viola?*"

"I'm not answering your questions, Doug." Mac said

as he turned toward the barn door. Three men blocked his way.

"Okay, Mac, then tell us where she's buried," said Doug.

Walking forward between the two lines of men, Mac thought over the jumble of words in his mind that he knew he couldn't say. Doug and his crew stared at him like a bobcat peeping into a chicken pen.

Mac gave them only a slight hint of what they wanted to hear. "We haven't seen her for months," Mac said. "Jess gave her some medicine and she left; don't know where she went."

Knowing I was lying and stonewalling, Doug boiled under his thick skin. He jumped up so fast his bucket fell over, then strutted to a spot beside the barn door and untied a hairy rope hanging from a pulley on the ridge beam. The glaring faces around the barn turned red. Mac tried in vain to explain more about Viola and make better excuses about why he didn't know where she was.

"What happened to Viola, Mac? I know she was there, I saw her wood cane by the front door. She wouldn't have left without it, and where'd your baby come from?"

"The baby's mine and Jess'," Mac said, regaining his composure.

"Yep. She already told me that, but you're not gonna get us to believe that little boy's not Viola's son."

The men grumbled.

Mac turned again toward the door to leave. The crowd jumped to their feet and spit out a blast of angry half-garbled venom.

"Say the word, Mac! Tell us what happened to her, tell us where she's buried, or tell us about the baby." Doug's high-pitched voice pierced the crowd's roar.

"Let me explain," Mac said, but by then nobody wanted to hear him. With orchestrated precision, two pairs of hands grabbed the back of his belt and shoulders, dragged him forward about fifteen feet, then placed him facedown on the ground. Another pair of hands locked his arms behind him and tied them together. A thick rope was threaded under each shoulder and around his chest, knotted on his back, and tied around his ankles. They fished Doug's hairy rope through the knot on his back and stepped away as Doug slowly hoisted Mac off the ground. Someone hurled his feet hard enough to start him spinning. Facing downward, all he saw at first was a ring of boots around him—brown and gray boots, scuffed and worn, swallowed by the cuffs of oversized coveralls and jeans, stained with red clay and manure. Doug pulled him higher. Mac looked down on the faces. Some were lit with joy, soaking in his fear, others were stretched tight with rage. After being lifted another ten feet closer to the roof, shaggy heads and long copper necks below him bounced to the rhythm of clapping hands and clogging feet, but a few men stood in dark silence and watched. Mike Cobb leaned against a post near the side of the barn.

The rope spun Mac toward the back of the room where he couldn't see the barn door opening or who had just walked in, but the men below came to a sudden quiet stop.

Mac recognized Jess' voice as she snapped, "Doug, what are you doin'?" Mac turned his head toward the door just as she looked up and saw him hangin' from the ridge beam.

"*Doug*! What the *hell* are you doin'?" She shouted louder.

"Tryin' to get your boyfriend to tell us the truth 'bout Viola and her baby," Doug said.

"Let him down," she said after marching to a spot a foot from Doug's face.

Mac stopped spinning. The rope started unwinding in the opposite direction. He looked at Jess below him. She kept her left hand tucked in her jacket pocket while she signaled with her right hand for someone to lower him to the ground.

She knelt, opened her pocket knife with her teeth, and cut him loose. The men circled and moved closer. Before they were within an arm's reach of her, she flew to her feet, jerked her left hand out of her jacket pocket and stretched her arm upward with a firm grasp around the necks of the two copperheads. She lifted the two snakes into the shaft of sunlight. The snakes' long bodies wrapped around and clung to her arm as if they were trained, obedient pets.

Holding her arm rigid and high, she lunged forward. The crowd ran backward and sideways. With their eyes fixed on the snakes, they gasped, fell over each other, as pent-up fears about Jess exploded in their minds.

In a clockwise motion, she walked around the barn, herding them out the wide door.

When the last man disappeared, she pulled a burlap bag from her right pocket and shoved the snakes in, headfirst, then whipped a string around the opening.

Mac was still sitting on the ground, too stunned to move.

She helped him to his feet and they both walked outside. A pickup truck skidded its way around the curve and down the driveway. A red dust cloud rose over the trees. A dozen men disappeared over the hill at the foot of

149

Stumpy Mountain. No sign of Doug.

Mac tried to get his mind around what had happened. How did Jess, with nothing but two snakes, run fourteen men out of the barn? Each of those men killed bigger snakes in their fields every summer, but he had never seen men, hardworking mountain men, with faces so terrified.

"Jess, was that witchcraft?" he asked.

She didn't answer at first, then said, "I really didn't do anythin'."

"So what made them panic like that?" I asked.

She looked back into the room and said, "When I first walked into the barn, they were all dancin' with their red faces bobbin' up and down and exhalin' the sweet smell of corn liquor. Their minds were so empty, anythin' imaginable could fly in. We'll never know what they saw when I pulled out the snakes—maybe dragons. Doesn't matter. All they really saw were their own fears and other things that didn't come from either one of us.

CHAPTER 21

JESS

The snow-covered mountain thawed into a million little streams long before buds appeared on the trees. I knew it was time to get rid of the two snakes. Kept 'em all winter, but they were nearly awake and I had to get rid of 'em.

The moment I picked up the burlap bag they started twistin'. Ornery critters. I placed an old hickory plank across the kitchen sink and mounted the bag at one end. I propped open the mouth of the bag with a soda bottle. Within seconds, the first snake appeared, flashed its tongue in all directions, then slithered its way onto the plank. In one quick chop with my meat knife, I popped its head off. The remainder of his body flipped and jerked which sent the second snake flyin' out with its head in attack position, mouth wide open exposin' its long white daggers. I stood perfectly still until it slithered away from me on the plank, then I hit it with the sharp blade across the back of its neck sendin' its head to the floor while its body twisted out its last death throes. I nailed the top ends of both bodies down to one side of the plank, stretched 'em along the length of the board, and nailed the tail ends. Then, with a sharp knife I slit both skins from top to bottom. By hookin' my

151

finger under the skin and around the meat, it easily slid it out in two long pieces. After pourin' salt over the skins, they were ready to hang on the side of the henhouse, in the sun.

With my heavy knife, I chopped the snake meat into pieces, picked out the big chunks and sealed 'em in a clean mason jar, and then put the jar in the freezer, saving it for fish bait. The small pieces I placed in another mason jar with holes punched in the top of the lid so it could be placed in the sun to dry the meat before grindin' the chucks and mixin' it with grain for chicken feed. Chickens go crazy for snake meat.

The heads aren't good for nothin' and they stay dangerous for a long time even without the bodies. If they're thrown out into the woods, anythin' that touched the sharp fangs would get a dose of the venom. I kept a D-handled shovel by the back door. It's about two feet long but heavy, solid, and sharp. I walked way past the upper garden where I found a good spot near the tree line. The hole needed to be deep enough so dogs or wild animals sniffin' around the woods wouldn't dig it up. The whole event only took about fifteen minutes but on my way back to the house, a gust of wind rattled the chicken pen door enough to knock over the wood latch. Six chickens got out and for about ten minutes or more they had a good run until I rounded 'em all up and stuck 'em back in their pen.

When I stepped into the kitchen, I knew right away someone had been there moments before. It was just a feelin', almost like a faint smell driftin' through the house.

I dashed into the bedroom to check on Robb. He was still sleepin' beside my bed, in the crib that Max had built for him.

I walked through the house lookin' for what had been disturbed or taken. The front door was slightly open. Some vials from the pantry were gone, a book from my shelf in the big room was gone, and both snakeskins stretched over a board were missin'. Another book from my desk titled *Leighis*, which means *Healin'*, was taken. It was Aunt Reese's oldest book, written in English and in the Celtic language. My aunt had a paperweight made of quartz that looked like a skull. I kept it on top of the old book, but it was gone, too.

Someone had been watchin' my house , waitin' for me to leave. Whoever it was took only items that pointed to the old arts, witchery, and the crafts my aunts practiced and taught. Someone was buildin' a case against me. For the first time in my life, I locked the front door.

The next day was Friday and I rehearsed all night what I had to say to Mac. When he arrived, I gave him coffee and a biscuit. He could tell I had somethin' to say and sipped his coffee slowly, waiting for me to start.

"You know Robb's not a little baby anymore and he'll be walkin' soon?" I said.

"Yes, but he's so eager, I bet he'll start running before he learns to walk."

"He's movin' all the time like a nest full of squirrels."

"You're right, but…what's on your mind?"

"I don't think we can take him to church no more."

"Okay, I can think of several reasons why we should stop going—at least for a while."

"You know, Doug's stirring' up too many people right now. He's got lots of people thinkin' we shouldn't be at their church services at all, 'cause of my family, and 'cause we're raisin' a baby and bringin' him there."

"You're right, but I don't know what else we can do about it."

"You understand, I'm worried 'bout Robb, not me or you."

"What are you thinking of doing besides stop going to church?" He knew I was leadin' up to something.

"I'm thinkin' we should get married," I said lookin' straight at him while I rested my fingers against my mouth to hide emotions I didn't know how to control.

He took a deep breath and looked away. "How do you think that would help?" he asked.

"'Cause it makes it all legal and everyhin', so they can stop thinkin' we're livin' in sin and all that stuff." For a long, uncomfortable minute, he thought about it, and I couldn't look at him. Robb called out from the bedroom givin' me a chance to run away and leave Mac by himself.

"So what do you think?" I asked when I returned.

"I also want to do what's best for Robb, but...also for us. I've been thinking about the same thing for a few months," he said.

"Well, is that a yes or a no?"

His face was red. He kissed me.

Preacher Ron agreed to officiate and help with some of the legal arrangements. We decided that it should take place in the Meetin' Hall. We invited no one, but we posted an announcement at the General Store that said anybody could come if they wanted to. Besides me and Mac and Robb, only Aunt Brusie, Tiny Todd, and Preacher Ron came. Mac didn't tell his family about it, but wanted to wait 'til the time felt right. I had never met his brothers or sisters-in-law and was in no hurry, since the two women were from Asheville.

Robb continued to sleep in his little bed in my room with me, and Mac continued to sleep on his spot on the couch. We didn't go to church for the next two years and I didn't see Doug at all durin' that time. I was told that since we got married, people weren't listenin' to him so much, but they also said he never stopped talkin' and bein' angry at me.

Jack Hemphill

CHAPTER 22

Theron stacked three containers of milk and one package of cheese in Mr. Cobb's refrigerator then looked at him, waiting to be paid.

"That's all I need today, Goat Man," said Cobb.

"Please, I'm supposed to get a dollar and twenty-five cents for today's delivery and the same for last week's, Mr. Cobb," said Theron.

Cobb opened a cabinet door, counted out exactly a dollar and twenty-five cents, and handed it to Theron.

"Thankyou kindly, Mr. Cobb, but I need last week's, too."

"Paid ya last week," said Cobb.

"Mr. Cobb, last week you asked for another week to pay me,z so I said okay."

"Nope, paid you."

Not knowing what to say next, Theron looked down.

"Tell ya what, Goat Man," said Cobb, "next week I'll buy the same amount of milk, but instead of one pack of cheese, I'll buy and pay for two packs—how 'bout that?"

"Okay, thankyou kindly, Mr. Cobb." Theron, thinking it was settled, shuffled out the door and stuffed the money into a sack on the cart. With a couple of taps on the goats, he turned the wagon around and headed toward the Todd house and Eugena.

Eugena cracked the front door for the third time that morning. Sun flashed across the dark livingroom floor. She listened for the clanging bells of Theron's wagon.

"He'll be along shortly, darling," said her mother.

"I know," said Eugena, shutting the door behind her and starting back to the kitchen.

"Why don't you see if he will help you pull up some carrots in the garden when he comes?"

Eugena smiled at the idea, then said, "I'm making a pie."

"I know. It already smells so good all over the house that the other children think we are having pie for lunch."

"No, Mama, it's for dessert."

"I know, Eugena."

"Call me when you hear bells, okay?"

Billy and Nanny clanged their way down the mountain, but Eugena was boiling water in the kitchen and couldn't hear their familiar sound. Mrs. Todd cracked the kitchen door wide enough to wave at Eugena and say, "I hear Theron comin'." Eugena immediately dumped a bowl of beans into the water and started stirring the pot so fast the wooden spoon clanged around the rim. Mrs. Todd said, "Why don't you let me finish the beans while you find the two garden buckets so you and Theron can go pull some carrots?"

When Mrs. Todd finished stirring the pot, she combed Eugena's hair, stopping twice to wet a few places and train her curls back into place, and keep them out of her face.

"Mrs. Todd. Mrs. Todd," called Theron as he opened the front door.

"Come on in," said Mrs. Todd, waving him into the

house.

"It's me. Theron."

"Of course, I know who you are, Theron. Come on in. You can put the packages in the refrigerator. Eugena's in there working on dinner."

Theron nodded to the two children playing on the floor. As he walked past Berry who was sitting in a soft chair, he nudged her lightly on the shoulder with one of his cheese packages and said, "Hi Berry. It's Theron."

"Hi, Theron," Berry said.

Theron walked into the kitchen and closed the door behind him. Five minutes later Eugena stepped out carrying a large steel bucket. Theron lumbered behind her carrying another bucket. Neither spoke. Outside, Eugena touched each of the goats on their heads as she walked by. Theron continued to follow her down the path into the long, curved garden. He place his bucket next to hers by the carrots.

With both knees on the ground, Eugena sank her chubby fingers into the soil and stroked it away from each plant far enough to wrap her right hand around the tip of the carrot while she pulled on the leaves with her left. Gently, each root slid out of the soil. She carefully wiped them clean before placing them in the bucket with all carrots pointed in the same direction. Every time she started digging a new plant, she looked up at Theron to be sure he was watching. As she leaned over the plants in the afternoon sun, her light-brown curls shined, while long strands that had escaped from the carefully placed hair pins fell across her face. Each time she looked up at him, he released a nervous laugh and moved the bucket a little closer.

When the carrot bucket was filled, they walked to the cucumber and squash patch and quickly filled the second bucket. Eugena picked up the squash bucket, shuffled it forward about fifteen feet, and plopped it back on the ground. Theron, seeing it was too heavy for her, picked it up along with the carrot bucket. They walked side by side back up the trail to the goat cart. Through a gap in the curtains, Mrs. Todd watched as Eugena gave each goat a carrot. The two animals gobbled down their snack with such passion it made Eugena and Theron laugh and they were still smiling as they came back into the house. After another half hour, Theron reluctantly tapped his goats to start the long walk home.

CHAPTER 23

McKENZIE

"My God, Mac, why didn't you show me these before now!" said Sidney Smith, editor for "The Great Smokey Magazine.

"I still have a long way to go," I answered.

"There must be over a hundred pictures here."

"More than two hundred."

"Well, the pictures are great, but where is the manuscript?"

"You just read it."

"That's it?"

"Well, that's all I've done on the actual article, but I'm keeping a log each day I'm with her. That's all of the article so far."

"If you're going to be a writer, you've got to *write!* Taking notes is not writing."

"It's going to take a while."

"Why?"

"Because she doesn't know I'm doing it."

"What's that got to do with it?"

"I think I should tell her."

"Okay, then *tell* her."

"That's what's going to take time."

Sidney closed the folder of pictures and stacked the notes on top.

"You've got a great idea here, great story Your pictures are dynamite—brilliant opportunity, but Mac, I'm not going to talk to you about this article again until you've got a completed manuscript. I want three thousand words and ten of the best pictures. Got it?"

"I understand."

"You've got personal feelings about her, don't you?"

"Well actually, I married her."

"You *what*?"

"Yep."

"I don't know, Mac. You might be too close."

"Well, it doesn't matter. I can't stop doing it."

"Okay, one question."

"What?"

"How are you going to know when the article is done?"

I didn't answer. We finished our coffee. He thanked me for showing the pictures and reminded me to let him know when I thought I had a finished manuscript. I watched his car disappear down my drive. I returned to the table in the barn, opened the photograph file, and re-sorted the pictures into groups—pictures of Jess, pictures of the Ridge People, pictures of their children and farms, and pictures of Robb. I couldn't even think of how I was going to tell her about what I'd been doing. One by one, I placed photos of Jess on the table, great magazine-worthy pictures of her working with vials, pulling herbs in the garden, walking the Ridge, holding and nursing Robb. But the ones I loved were the pictures of her just being Jess, early in the morning, or sitting on the rocker on the porch with her bare feet on the rail, or washing her hair. I had a couple dozen pictures of her laughing, chuckling, belly-laughing, and slapping-her-hand-on-the-table-laughing. She had a great laugh—infectious. Jess said she didn't care to have her picture taken at all so I had to steal pictures of her when she wasn't expecting it, but she was interested in seeing the enlarged prints and studied every one carefully. She never complained about how she looked. I know she was happy that someone cared enough to take her picture even if they were not always flattering shots. I'm sure she never thought of anyone else looking at them but us. I have to confess, I never let her see all of them.

Another year passed by and I realized I had no end in sight and I had long since been forgotten by the editor. Sidney Smith had asked how I would know when my writing was finished. I realized I had no idea. It was becoming clearer to me that the story of Jess and all she did, would take a full book. The story couldn't be told in a magazine article. I didn't know exactly what form it should take, but I saw something new every time I was with her and I never failed to record it in my log.

Jack Hemphill

CHAPTER 24

JESS

When Mac's car started down the drive, Robb waved good-bye one more time, then picked out one of the shovels from my shed and ran toward the river ahead of me.

"How 'bout carryin' the pail?" I said.

"Can I carry the shovel?" replied Robb.

"That shovel's as tall as you, Robb."

"I know," he said as he ran faster.

"Okay, I got the rest of the stuff."

We scooted down the hill to a compost pit covered in leaves.

"Best worm farm in Jefferson County, right here." I said.

"You got big ones?"

"Big as snakes."

"Wow, we gonna catch a whale!"

With a short pitchfork, I turned over four inches of rottin' leaves to reveal a deep black pit of decomposin' material shimmerin' with long red worms. Robb combed through the dark earth with both hands chasin' the biggest, longest worms and placed the slimy treasures in an empty tin can.

"Think we have enough?" I asked.

"I didn't find one long as a snake."

"Well, you found some as long as baby snakes, besides you don't want to scare away any fish."

"Yeah. Where we gonna go? "

"We're goin' back to my special spot."

"Great!"

"Well, I happen to know the fish there are hungry for long worms and since it looks like rain's gonna start any minute now, we can slip under the stone ledge and stay dry and keep on fishin'."

To get to my spot, we had to wade into the river far enough to walk around the first leg of the big rock. Beyond that, was a niche the size of a car carved into the stone — just enough room for both of us to sit on the lower ledge and spread out the gear.

"I wannta stick the first worm on the hook," said Robb.

"You sure?"

"Yep, gimme a fat red one."

Once we got the hooks baited and bobs set, I cast our lines twenty-five feet or so into an eddy beyond the rock. With Robb's feet dagglin' in the water, we sat side by side in quiet satisfaction watchin' the little red balls bobble in the waves.

Glancin' at Robb, I said, "You did a good job hookin' that worm. Last time you wouldn't touch it. What changed your mind?"

He thought for a moment before he said, "I got a story."

"A story? What is it?"

"'Okay, but you can't tell anybody."

"I won't tell. Cross my heart."

"I played like the worms aren't just worms. They're *magic* worms and don't mind the hook, but like to catch fish."

"Magic? What do you know about magic?"

"A little bit, but my friends say you know *all* about it."

"About magic?"

"Yes."

"Oh, really? What friends say that?"

"The kids I play with when we go walkin' on the ridge."

"You mean the children of my patients?"

"Yes."

"They tell you I do magic?"

"Yep, and spooky stuff. All of 'em say it and they think I know some magic, too."

"Well, Robb...anythin' people don't understand they'll call *magic* and maybe *spooky*. So maybe they jus' don't understand what I do for 'em."

"But you do some magic, right?"

"I don't call it that. I jus' do natural things."

"Whatcha mean, natural?"

"Well . . ." I paused for a minute. I always knew someday I would have this conversation with him, but I thought he would be a little older, not when he had just turned three. I closed my eyes and rolled my head back a little so he could see I was thinking. I didn't know why, but the first thin' that came to mind was a picture of our mama hens and their little flocks of biddies.

"Remember when I told you how baby chicks have to peck open their own shells when they hatch? The mama hen is always so happy they're comin' out. The first thing the biddies see is their mama. They know her because they felt her warmth every time she sat on the eggs. As soon as they get out, they run to her and snuggle under her wings and feel her warmness again. That's when the mama begins teachin' the little chicks everythin' 'bout how to grow up and how to be healthy, and safe, and happy. The chicks follow her everywhere."

"Why" Why do they follow her?"

"Because, it's natural. It's just what little chickies do."

I thought I had a bite and pulled my line in. "Well, we know they're out there. They stole my worm." I hooked another worm and tossed my line back into the water.

"Tell me more," he said.

"Well, do you remember 'bout three weeks ago before it was time to feed the chickens, I looked out my back window and noticed a bobcat outside the gate on the far side of the chicken pen, diggin' his paws under the fence. Looked hungry."

"Yes, I saw him. He looked mean."

"He *was* mean and the moment the mama chicken saw him she squawked and flapped her wings. Then, the little chickies hearin' their mother's call and seein' the big cat diggin' under the fence, ran under mama's outstretched wings as fast as their tiny waddle would let 'em. All six of 'em huddled under her. All I could see of 'em was their little yellow feet pattin' the ground tryin' to get closer to their mama.

"The hen settled over 'em, raised her head and fixed her stare on the bobcat. When the animal saw the chicken was not frightened, he hissed and curled his lips back to show his sharp milky teeth, but mama hen didn't move, not a feather, not a blink. Head stayed high and eyes still fixed on the cat. He slinked over the grass in a circle, looked back at the hen, did another circle, and turned his heard again toward the hen and displayed his hungry fangs.

"I picked up my rifle from above the fireplace and

looked out the back door. The bob cat made one more circle, looked at the hen one more time, then creeped back into the woods. The moment he was gone, the hen raised her wings and strutted around the chicken yard with her flock followin' her. They all saw how their mama, like magic, made the giant cat disappear."

Robb clapped his hands, then after watchin' rain ripplin' the water for a moment, he said, "But she didn't use any magic."

"That's what I'm tryin' to tell you, sweetie, there's *no magic*. All those things you've seen me do…don't come from magic or from me. It's jus' natural."

"Where's it comin' from?"

"I think you and I and all of us are jus' tryin' to snuggle under the wings of the same mama hen and let her take care of us."

Robb's bob disappeared under the surface and popped up so fast it bounced clean out of the water before it disappeared under the surface again.

"I got one, I got one!" he said.

"Pull the line. I'll help you bring him in."

We caught four fish that day. He caught three of 'em. It started to rain harder. We let all the fish go. Robb pulled 'em out of the bucket one at a time and watched 'em swim away. My favorite place to be in a rainstorm was right there in my special spot. The river came alive with a constant shower and wind. Rain gushin' down the mountain and over the rock ledge above our heads caused such a waterfall in front of us that the world disappeared. We were tucked so far under the shelf that we stayed dry. I put Robb on my lap and wrapped my big coat around both of us. From my knapsack, I pulled out a towel to wipe our hands, then gave Robb's his favorite lunch—ham sandwiches, and biscuits with gooseberry jam, boiled eggs, and brownies with apple juice to wash it all down.

The rain beatin' the river roared so loud we stopped talkin for a while, but he was enjoyin' his lunch so much we probably wouldn't have talked anyway. We kept each other warm under my big coat and I heard him laugh every time the wind blew the rain in a different direction, makin' new wave patterns in the water.

On the climb back home, the grass and wet leaves were slick and we had to walk slowly. He carried his rod in one hand and gripped my back pocket with his other hand. We were soaked and when we got home I put him in a hot bath and let him play the rest of the day in the house in his pajamas.

Around four o'clock he asked, "What's for dinner?"

"You're hungry already?"

"Yep, fishin' and runnin' in the rain is hard work."

He was right about fishin' and runnin' in the rain being hard work. After dinner, we were both ready for bed.

When Robb had turned three, Mac agreed we should convert the storage room into a bedroom for Robb. It was small, tucked between the kitchen and my room, but it made him feel more grown up.

"Tell you what. I'll let you have my big bed tonight and I'll sleep out on the couch. How's that sound?"

"Well," he said, then thought about it for a moment. "Why don't you sleep in my bed?"

"It's too short for me."

"But aren't you afraid to sleep out here?"

"No, of course not. Mac sleeps here and he loves it."

"I know, but when the lights are out, it's scary."

"I think I'll be okay, darlin'."

"Let me show you what's in my bag," he said as he ran into his room and returned, dragging his canvas tote all the way to the couch. With both hands, he reached into the bag, waited until he knew I was watchin', then with a big "rooooah!" he pulled out his stuffed tiger as big as a small dog, and held it in front of my face.

"Wow, I forgot all about it. Looks real with all those white teeth."

"Mac gave it to me."

"Yes, I know, at Christmas."

"I get it out and sleep with it sometimes, but since you're gonna be all by yourself out here on the couch tonight, you can sleep with him."

"Okay, he can protect me."

The rain came again for a while then tapered off before I saw a three-quarter moon peekin' through the night sky. Once Robb got in bed, it must have taken him one whole minute to fall sound asleep. I was bone-tired too, but it took me two hours to nod off. I always knew it would be hard for Robb to be my son, and I knew someday he'd be teased for bein' different, but I wasn't sure how long it would be before he was old enough for me to explain exactly what I do or how I do it. I was sorry he thought it was magic, and maybe that was the only way he could explain it to his friends, or maybe that's the only way they could understand it.

Ever since I was a young girl, most of the Ridge People thought I was a little strange. It never bothered me 'cause I *am* a little odd. Robb would learn to make no excuses for me or for himself, and eventually he would learn the price for being my son.

Jack Hemphill

CHAPTER 25

By the middle of October, the Saturday Stumpy Ridge Market was as busy as it had ever been. The usual people from Weavertown, Redbriar, and Marshall bought things they always liked to buy, but I saw more faces I never knew, looking at the displays and opening their wallets. The once-a-month event was held only in the spring, summer, and part of the fall so everyone talked more and learned more about each other on those Saturdays than all the other days in the year put together. Not everybody was interested in old remedies, but not everybody was interested in hooked rugs, or woven blankets, or clay pots, or ramps, or carved pipes, or any of the things sold at the market, but it didn't matter. The Ridge People sold and traded just as much as they needed. It was a time for men to share the exaggerated hunting tales saved for that special crowd, and it was a time for women to share exaggerated stories about each other. Any change was big news and on that Saturday, the big change was Dr. Clayton's opening a clinic in three small rooms behind the General Store under the Meeting Hall. The clinic would be open for the public only Fridays and Saturdays each week. The idea to have a clinic came from the Burns family, in an effort to take care of their employees at their three quarries. Medical expenses for all the quarry people were to be paid by the Burns family; everyone else that came to see Dr. Clayton would have to pay a standard fee for his services and for traditional medicine.

During that morning, those that knew Jess came by her spot under the big white oak to ask her whether the clinic opening bothered her.

"Not at all," she told them as convincingly as she could, but she knew they didn't believe her because it wasn't true and her friends could tell she was trying to put on a good face. It was not because she was afraid of Doctor Clayton, but because he was going to sell his medical care and prescribe his medicines to some of the families Jess and her ancestors had served for years. But Jess could not show any opposition to Clayton's new clinic.

Only three people in the world—Jess, Mac, and Doctor Clayton—knew what Clayton did to Viola, and only three people in the world knew Robb's birth certificate, signed by Clayton, was a fake. Because Jess wanted more than anything else to keep her child, she never talked about Clayton or about the birth certificate to anybody, especially after all the recent dust and noise stirred by Doug.

With his office at the base of the mountain, Clayton knew eventually he would see Jess and he wondered how he should act. Friendly? Cautious? Should he ignore her? He hoped he would not see her at all that first day, so he could hide his awkwardness at least a month longer until the next Stumpy Market Saturday. But that wish vanished when he saw Jess with her rug spread under the tree and all her ancient medications on display.

Clayton had printed flyers to hand out, telling about the Clinic and his medical services. Starting at the spot farthest from Jess, he worked his way up and down the rows, stopping at each table and blanket and handing out the announcements. Some people said they were glad he was there. Some just accepted the paper, but said nothing, and others were cautious, almost suspicious, and looked in Jess' direction when they realized what he was selling.

Clayton worked his way up the last aisle. Jess' spot was at the very top. He was surprised to see how many people were visiting that row and how many questions they had for Jess about remedies and healing. Most of them already had a knowledge of herbs and their uses. Some people asked directly for things like ginseng or yellow root. Others described their ailment and let Jess make recommendations. Clayton heard a little woman, not taller than five feet, asking Jess questions about treating her baby daughter.

"She's so unhappy, Jess," said the lady, "her rash keeps comin' back and she cries all night."

"Oh, poor little dove," replied Jess as she placed her hand over the woman's shoulder and looked at the girl squirming and whining in her mother's arms. "Here, darlin', take this bottle of powder and sprinkle it over all the places she needs it. See that blue car over there? My husband Mac lets me borrow it. You can change her in the back seat, put the powder on her, and then come right back and let's see how much better she's adoin'."

Jess talked with two other women and one man and sold a couple of bottles, but Clayton couldn't hear everything Jess was saying. He moved closer to Jess' spot keeping to the far side of the aisle and hiding behind people walking by.

Clayton heard the voice of the little woman returning

with her child. "Jess," said the woman, "She stopped crying straight away. What kind of powder is it?" she asked.

With his head down, Clayton ambled to a spot near Jess. He had his back turned, but was close enough to hear her clearly.

In a soft voice, Jess said, "It's a powder made from ground-up club moss spores. It cleans the rash, and soothes the condition right away, and keeps moisture off her skin to prevent a return of the problem."

"Thank you, Jess, how much do I owe you for this?"

"Keep the bottle, sweetie, you can pay whatever you can afford."

"I'm real low right now, Jess, but I want to pay you, but I jus' don't have much."

"Then jus' keep it and pay me next time. When you come back, all her rashes will be gone. You pay me then."

Doctor Clayton sat on a large root at the base of the big oak, right beside Jess, but out of her sight. He shuffled and stacked the jumble of flyers in his hand, then pretended to read them while listening to the Ridge People talking with Jess, thanking her, and buying her remedies.

Robb was allowed to play around the festival yard as long as he stayed in Jess' view. He sat against the oak and watched his mama with her customers. A big red ant crawled across his shoe. With a stick, he lifted the determined insect and placed it at the bottom of the tree, then followed it around the trunk until he met Clayton sitting on the opposite side. Robb joined him by sitting on an adjacent root.

"What's your name?" asked Robb.

"I'm Doctor Clayton," he answered quietly. "You must

be Robb."

"Uh huh," said Robb. "Howdja know?"

"Oh, well I knew your mother...I mean, I knew *Miss Shew*."

"What's your job, Mr. Doctor?"

"I help people get well."

"You're like my mama."

"I don't think so."

"How do you make people well?"

"With my treatments and medicines."

"Do you have a big garden to grow your medicine?"

"No, I get them from somebody that makes medicine for me."

Dr. Clayton leaned closer to Robb and said in a whisper, "Does your mother give you her medications when you're sick?"

"Oh yes, sometimes jus' a spoonful, and sometimes a cupful, and sometimes in my food."

"Tell me, Robb. Did any of it ever taste bitter?"

"What's bitter mean?"

"Did it taste bad?"

"Some of it feels like a lemon in my mouth?"

"Did some of it leave a bad feeling in your mouth or stomach?"

"Yes sir, stuff like ramps and pokeweed, but she gives me honey or sugar with it."

"Pokeweed?"

"Yep."

"Did you ever feel dizzy or like you wanted to throw up after you took it?"

"I did throw up once, but sometimes I get sleepy too, when she puts it in my food."

"You mean after taking her medication you felt like going to sleep?" He leaned forward to be sure he heard the answer.

"Yes sir…sometimes…but sometimes I feel that way when there's no medicine in it—I mean, I always get sleepy when I eat dinner."

"But, you get sleepy when she gives you medicine?"

"Yes, sir, sometimes."

"Well, thank you, Robb. That is interesting."

"Then you should get your medicines from my mama. She's right here," Robb said a little louder as he turned toward Jess.

"No, no, Robb. Don't bother her," but by then Robb was already scrambling around the big tree to tell Jess about the doctor.

Clayton stood and dusted off the seat of his pants and inched away. He couldn't resist one guilty glance back toward Jess. Their eyes met. Clayton jerked his head forward and attempted to walk away when he heard Jess' voice say, "Doctor Clayton."

"Hello, Jess," he reluctantly replied.

"Doctor Clayton," she said again to give him a chance to turn around.

"Heard you're openin' a clinic up here."

"Yes, just Fridays and Saturdays."

"Will you be givin' out medicine and shots and things like that?"

"Just to my patients."

"Got a lot of 'em up here?"

"Mostly quarry people. The Burns family pays for their employees."

"How 'bout the others?"

"We'll see."

By the end of the summer, the Burns family announced the stunning news that they had decided to close all three quarries and would pay for the medical care for only three more months.

"Mr. Doctor!" Robb yelled out when he saw Doctor Clayton drive up to Jess' porch. "Mama," he called, as he ran into the house to let Jess know she had company. She met him at the front door.

"Hello, Doctor," she said.

"Jess, we need to talk."

She opened the screen door and extended her hand for him to come into the house.

"Let's just stay out here," said Clayton.

"Robb, you need to pick up your things out here and take 'em into your room. We have to talk out here." Robb collected all his papers and toys. Jess put her coat on and waited until Robb closed the door.

"What in the world would you want to talk to me about, Doctor?" she said as she sat down in the rocking chair. Dr. Clayton remained standing.

"Jess, you know the Burns family have now shut down the quarries and this is the last week they are paying workers' medical bills."

"No, I didn't know it was this week."

"These people up here are still going to need *real* medical care," he rocked his feet forward and looked straight at her.

"Well, I assume you'll still give it to 'em," she said.

"Yes, that's why I'm here."

"What's it got to do with me?"

"I have convinced the hospital in Asheville to help fund

the clinic, but…" He leaned forward again and raised his hands, palms outward and said, "They know about you, Jess, and they won't fund the project as long as you are treating the same patients we hope to care for up here."

"What are you sayin'? They want me to stop treatin' my patients?" said Jess.

"That's about it…well, that's actually…that's *exactly* what they are saying."

"The Ridge People should decide that for themselves, don't ya think?"

"Jess, I don't think most of them know what modern medicine is. How are they going to decide?"

"They know when they're gettin' better and they know when they're healed."

"I have to agree with that, but sometimes they can feel better even when they're dying and don't know it."

"What's that mean?"

"I mean, I think some things you do could be harming your patients…and their children, and they are completely ignorant of it."

"Sounds like you been talkin' to Doug Helms."

"What makes you say that?"

"He's been tryin' to put me out of business for a few years now, but he can't do it."

"My conclusions are my own and the hospital's," said the doctor.

"My patients wouldn't agree with you or your hospital. Have the hospital people ever come up here and talked with these people themselves?"

"No, but I have."

"Well, that should settle it."

"I've talked to some of them and they've told me how

they have been healed and had suffering relieved, but the substance in some of your medication is so far outside modern sanitary standards that the hospital couldn't possibly let me treat people that are constantly exposed to it."

"To tell you the truth, Doctor, I don't know much about what you are callin' modern medicines other than my experience with the way you treated Viola."

Clayton froze for a moment, then said, "I wouldn't bring that into this conversation with me or with anyone else. I tried to save that poor woman's life after you exposed her to God only knows what!" He walked to the porch rail and looked over the valley toward Redbriar.

Jess said, "You can tell your Asheville hospital that I'm *not* gonna let you kill any more of my patients."

Clayton bounced his fist off the top of the rail, returned to his car, and without another word disappeared down the curved drive.

After stopping at the General Store, Dr. Clayton drove straight to Doug Helms' farm.

Jack Hemphill

CHAPTER 26

The front of Pastor Ron's house in Weavertown had four east facing windows. In his study, beneath the window, he had a shelf where he grew plants all year round — plants that would never survive the outside cold. He cared for them, trimmed them daily, tested the soil, and turned them to face the morning sun.

He was so absorbed in his work, he didn't see the four men march up to his house. Doug banged on the front door hard enough to say he meant business, but soft enough to be polite to a preacher.

"Doug, come in, come in everybody. Grab a seat in here," Ron said, leading them into his living room. "How can I help you?"

When the men found places to sit, they looked at Doug — undoubtedly the group's leader.

"Preacher Ron."

"Yes?"

"We are here to help *you*."

"That's wonderful. I can use all kinds of help. Can you build a new chicken pen?"

"I think you know why we're here," said Doug completely missing the preacher's joke.

"You probably want to talk about Jess Shew," said

Preacher Ron.

"We been puttin' up with what she's doin' on this mountains for years, and now that she's married to that guy from Asheville, she's talkin' 'bout comin' back to church with the boy."

"What's wrong with that?"

"She's got to be *banned* from the church."

"Banned? Why?"

"Cause it's not fair to the congregation and not good for the boy, neither."

"You think that's enough to ban her?"

"Reverend, she's committed crimes in the past, and she's doin' it now, and gonna do it in the future until she's stopped, and don't forget, that little boy's in the middle of it all."

"What crimes?"

"Remember Viola?"

"Yes, you told me she disappeared."

"Well, she disappeared alright. Jess killed her."

"How do you know?"

"She actually confessed to me that she killed Viola and buried her somewhere on the mountain."

"When did she say that?"

"Couple of years back, after Viola disappeared, Jess came ridin' up to my farm and sat on my cook's porch swing. I couldn't figure out anythin' I wanted to say to her, so I jus' listened."

"And she just blurted out that she killed Viola?"

"That's pretty much what she did."

"Why would she say that to you?"

"Preacher Ron, it's obvious. She knew I wouldn't buy what she'd been sayin' 'bout Viola, who hadn't been seen by nobody for a long time, just disappeared, then about the same time, Jess, the witch and midwife, pops up with a newborn baby."

"Doug, what did she actually say to you?"

"She told me she done killed her and told me she would do the same thing to me if I didn't stop talkin' 'bout her."

"And Viola had a baby?"

"Yep, she gave birth to Robb."

"Jess's Robb?"

"It was Viola's!"

"You have proof?"

"Jus' my word and Doctor Clayton's word."

"What's Doctor Clayton got to do with it?"

"Jess called him to come after Viola gave birth to Robb so she could get a birth certificate. 'Bout a month ago Dr. Clayton came to my farm to talk about Jess. He said that when Viola had given birth he was called by Jess to come to Stumpy and when he arrived at her place, the baby was already born healthy, but the mother was dead from somethin' Jess gave her to swallow, and he told me that Davis guy made him write Jess Shew's name and his own name as parents, on the birth certificate."

"The doctor will swear this is true?"

"Yes."

"Why haven't you contacted the sheriff?"

"I did — *we* did. We went to see him in his office, but he said the same thing you jus' said, 'Give me proof.'"

"Well, what *proof* do you have beside yours and the doctor's word?"

"We need you to help us get people to make statements about Jess and we need you to help us talk to the sheriff and get him to take us seriously."

"Doug, I agree with you about her. I've been over there to talk to her myself, but it did no good. She will not listen and she's been born into that kind of mystic stuff and she'll never get it out of her head. She's doing what her family always did, ya know? I do believe that little boy's worth saving. As for that Mac fellow, I don't know him, but he may be just as bad."

"I understand and I don't think Jess is going to be saved in any way. She and Davis need to go to prison for a while."

"But, what about Robb?" asked the preacher.

"I'm as concerned about that boy as anybody. He's got to be taken away from them and somebody else's got to be willin' to take care of him while they're locked up."

"Who would do that?"

"I told the sheriff that I would take care of him if they got sent away."

"Well, that's mighty generous of you, Doug."

"You know I can afford it and I got plenty of room."

Ron pushed his way out of the overstuffed chair and walked to the window. The morning sun reflected off the Redbriar River below, turning it into a shining red line carved around the mountain. He shook his head. "I'm going to have to think about this for a while."

"Preacher Ron, at least, for now, ban her! Keep her out of the services," said Doug, "Make sure everyone knows how dangerous she is or has become and, most of all, let's save that little baby boy. Don't he deserve a better chance than what she's gonna give him?"

"Every child on that mountain deserves a better chance than he's gettin', but everybody does their best."

"But their parents aren't murderers and witches."

"I'm gonna to pay her another visit," said the preacher.

"When?"

"Soon."

"By yourself?"

"Yes. Why? You think she's gonna do something to me?"

"Don't trust her, Reverend."

Jack Hemphill

CHAPTER 27

JESS

"Robb thinks he is old enough to sit in church," said Mac.

"He said that to you?" I asked.

"Yes."

"On his <u>own</u>, without you askin' him?"

"Okay. He said it after I asked him if he was old enough."

"What little boy's not gonna say he's old enough to do somethin'?"

"Well, I think he's old enough."

"How do you know?"

"Sometimes he sits on the couch with me for an hour or so. Doesn't fidget or squirm."

"Can he sit quietly and not talk for a whole hour?"

"I don't know, but don't you think we should try?"

Mac brought a new outfit for Robb to wear to church. Blue shorts with big blue buttons and suspenders and a separate white shirt and white shoes. Robb was so excited he jumped up and down and ran around the couch in the living room. I ironed my only dress, lavender blue with a white flower print, but I also wanted to wear my white summer hat with a wide brim which I only use on special occasions. Mac brought his jacket and tie.

Robb had dozens of questions 'bout what church was like and we explained it the best we could. We told him he would love the music and singin', but the preacher would do a lot of talkin' and he had to sit still and listen. He wanted to know how many other children would be there and I said I didn't know, but I was sure a few. I reminded him one more time he couldn't talk to them or play with 'em until the service was over.

There was a little space behind Robb's bedroom, a nook off the kitchen, where I had a tin bathtub with a drain line that ran through the floor. The tub filled the little room with just enough space left for me and Mac to take turns scrubbing Robb down with hot, soapy water. Robb loved his baths. I had to heat bathwater in several buckets, on the stove. One bucket for washin' and scrubbin' and two for rinsin'.

We waited until sunset Friday night to wash him down, and we had to explain that he needed to stay clean all day long on Saturday. That way Mac and I could bathe on Saturday night. This was the first time all three of us bathed on the same weekend. Mac split extra wood for the stove.

After Robb was put to bed on Saturday night, Mac took a bath and I helped rinse him off with the buckets of hot water. The fire in the stove had to be relit, and the all buckets of water had to be reheated before I could take my bath.

I was surprised how excited we were and rose early Sunday morning. We all sat in the front seat with Mac drivin' and Robb sittin' on my lap. Robb made up a song and sang it as we drove around to the east side of the mountain. A clear, cool breeze carried the sweet smell of new cut hay from Doug Helms' farm on the other side of the creek. The front door of the Meetin' Hall faced due west, greetin' the Ridge People as they paraded, in family clumps, down the mountain spine. Robb didn't mind women makin' over him and rufflin' his corn silk hair, but he scrunched up his eyes and cheeks every time he was kissed.

It was almost harvest time, and we all knew the hot days of summer were behind and looked forward to the refreshin' air of early fall.

Preacher Ron, in his usual suit with a bright white starched shirt and a deep wine- colored tie, was greetin' the crowd as they arrived at the front of the hall. He knew every name includin' the children. A few clumps of women had already gathered under the trees to get in some early gossip that just couldn't wait 'til after the service.

The preacher waved his hand when he saw me. He nodded to the couple talkin' with him, turned, and walked straight to us. Mac took Robb's hand.

"Jess, Robb, so glad to see you today," said preacher Ron.

"Glad we made it," I said.

"It's been a little while since I saw you, and little Robb has grown so."

"Yes, he's proud of his new clothes."

"Well, you're a big guy now, aren't you," he said wigglin' his bony index finger in Robb's ribs. Robb buried his head in the side of Mac's leg.

"Jess, it's good I got a chance to talk to you before church — with both of you about something." He looked at Mac, then back at me.

He moved closer and spoke softly. "You probably know a few people are still not happy about you coming to church," he said.

"Of course, but like I said before, we're not gonna let it bother us."

"Yes, good, but understand, I can't do anything about it...and even though it's been going on a few years, the attendance has dropped since all this thing started, and ..."

"This thing?" I said.

"I'm sorry, Jess, but you know what I mean."

"Have you talked to 'em?"

"Oh yes."

"And...?"

"And you know some feel you shouldn't be here worshiping with these people. I can't tell anyone to stop coming and you know Doug Helms owns this building and all."

"Preacher Ron, are you sayin' he's gonna to kick the whole congregation out in the cold because of me?"

"He didn't say exactly that."

"What did he say?"

"He expressed his concern."

"In other words, he told you to keep *us* from coming back," said Mac.

"I told him I can't do that." He stopped and waited for us to guess what was on his mind.

"Okay, I understand," I said, "We're supposed to decide on our own, to stay away. Right?"

"That would be very kind and unselfish of you both. But it would only be for a while."

"How long?"

"I don't know."

The preacher braced himself, waiting for my reply. His chin quivered as he looked around at the crowd standing in small groups, watching us to see how we were going to react.

Mac picked up Robb and held him in the crook of his left arm while he wrapped his right arm around my shoulders.

Preacher Ron turned and walked into the church and the crowd followed him, leaving us alone.

Jack Hemphill

CHAPTER 28

McKENZIE

Jess and I decided to spend the day at my farm. To Robb, going to the farm would be even better than going to church. We spent the night there. Jess said very little and I know how disappointed she was, so I kept the conversation focused on Robb who always loved the attention. Jess took one of the spare bedrooms in the farmhouse while Robb and I slept in the barn.

Eight o'clock was Robb's bedtime. After Jess tucked him in, she and I spent a little time talking over the day's events and what to do about it. I praised her for staying so cool that morning. She turned in early and I pulled out my latest notebook that was hidden in a locked drawer in the darkroom. After about an hour of scribbling down my thoughts, Robb called. He was sitting up in his bed.

"What's the matter, big guy?" I asked.

"Can't sleep, bad dream," he said through puckered lips.

"Bad dreams can't hurt anybody. You can forget all about it," I said as I brushed hair out of his face with my fingers. He looked down and said, "It was about Mama. Some people were not nice to her."

"Oh, Robb, you know lots of people *love* your mama."

"They do?"

"Yes, lots of people."

"Really?" he managed to push out a little smile.

"Oh yes, I've been watching her for a long time. Since before you were born."

"Why?"

"Because she is so interesting."

"Tell me."

I thought about it for a minute, then said, "Hold on, I'll be right back." In half a minute I returned to his room with my current notebook and my canvas bag with all the previous notebooks. "I'm going to tell you some things, if you promise to keep them secret—just between us. Okay?"

"Okay."

"You have to say 'I promise'."

"I promise."

"Not to tell anybody."

"Not to tell anybody."

"Okay. I'm so interested in your mama that I've written down everything she has done for the last four years, and I also have been writing about some things she has told me that happened on the mountain before I met her. Would you like me to read some of it and tell you some stories about her?"

"Yes." He sat up and fluffed his pillow against the headboard.

I pulled from my bag all eleven notebooks and put them on the bed beside him. "These are all my notes, all about Jess…I mean your mama, and some of it is about you too." Robb's eyes widened. "Let me look through them for a good story you would like." I thumbed through the notebooks for a few seconds before I said, "Oh yes, just the right one." I had been sitting at the end of his bed, but moved to a chair close to his pillow.

I started to read, "Jess is thin, but strong and very tall. She is pretty in her own way."

"What does that mean, *inner own way*?" He asked.

"It means she doesn't look like anybody else, but she is unique."

"What's *unick*?"

"Well, she's like nobody else. But maybe I should tell a story from memory." I put down the notebook and started over.

"Since you promised not to tell your mama and I'm showing you my notebooks and all the things I've written about her and you, I'll make *you* a promise. I'll tell you a story tonight and every time you come to the farm I'll tell you another one. Okay?"

"Okay."

"There are three things I want you to remember about your mother. She is the perfect mama, she loves you very much, and she is fearless."

"Fearless?"

"Yes."

"What does that mean?"

"It means she is not afraid of anyone or anything."

"I know."

"But there are a few people that don't like her, or us."

"Like the preacher?"

"I guess so, but others too."

"But why?"

"She's just different."

"Is that bad?"

"No. I think it's very good."

I put all the notebooks except the latest one back into the bag, turned out the light, and kissed Robb goodnight. I then told him some stories. It only took a few more minutes for him to fall asleep. He loved hearing about our family and especially stories about his childhood, but I had no way of knowing or foreseeing that most of his childhood would soon be taken from us.

CHAPTER 29

After closing and latching all the window shutters around the Meeting Hall, Preacher Ron walked to the big rock at the base of the ridge, climbed the steep part using his fingers and toes of his shoes, and stood at the top. From there he looked over the trees on both sides of the ridge. It was the end of November and everyone was still waiting for the killer winter promised by the woolly worms, but he knew his wait was nearly over as he shook his head at the feathery wisps flying northwest, high above the lower white and gray clouds stampeding like a herd of sheep heading due east. He looked up the ridge for the four women coming to talk about starting a crusade against Jess' anti-Christian practices, but there was no sight of anybody walking down the mountain, probably because it was noon and the sun had already been swallowed by the two layers of clouds. He returned to the Meeting Hall, and waited another hour. Two of the women arrived, both clutching the necks of their jackets against a cold, crisp wind.

"It's acomin'," said Martha.

"I know we jus' got here, Preacher, but this one's plowin' in fast, and we gotta get back home," said Mary. You best get on home, too, Preacher Ron."

"Okay, ladies, but soon as this thing blows out, we can meet here and start talking over what to do next about Jess Shew. Okay?"

They agreed. The two ladies turned to walk up the ridge while Ron started toward the parking lot. A cold gust of wind and a rolling shadow across the mountain were followed by a sharp flash of light and crack of thunder that rattled the earth under his feet.

It was Monday and Mac was packing to go back to his farm. He had just closed and locked his leather briefcase as Jess ran to the front door.

"Did you hear that, Mac?" she said. "I don't think you should go." She looked outside in all directions, then returned to Mac.

"Sorry, but I gotta get back to the farm. I'll be okay," said Mac.

"You know what thunder at the beginning of a winter storm means don't ya?" said Jess.

"No, but I would guess it means it's gonna be a bad one."

"More than that. It's gonna' be a deadly one and it's gonna be on us right behind that thunder. You're not gonna make it down the mountain."

"I'm all packed, Jess. I'll be going through Redbriar in a blink. Don't worry, I'll be back on Friday," he said as he bent over and ruffled Robb's hair. Robb waved as Mac picked up his bag and placed his hand on Jess' shoulder, gave her a quick goodbye kiss and said, "Don't worry, Jess, you know I'll be okay."

"I wish you wouldn't go, but I'll be watchin' for ya to come back." Within minutes after he left, Jess heard a soft hissing on the door and on the wood shutters.

She cracked the door to look out and received a blast of pure white diamond dust in her face. White waves were already flowing over the yard and everything in the world seemed to stand still, bracing itself for the woolly worm's prophecy. Jess glanced toward the drive, hoping Mac would already be returning, but she could barely see to the edge of her property.

Instinctively, she place another log on the fire and stoked the embers below. She snuggled into a heavy cotton blanket in the corner of the couch, hummed a melody from an old mountain hymn, then sang some made-up tunes. She heard a dull thump outside, listened for a moment, then continued singing until the door swung open.

"Mac!" she screamed. Robb ran and hugged his legs as if he had been gone a week.

"You were right, Jess. I must have been crazy to go out there."

"We knew you'd be back."

"Never saw a storm come on like this before! It was like a wall of feathers."

"Winter lightning. Never fails. Only thing you can do when it comes, is jus' get inside and wait it out."

"Well, here I am," he said as he sat on the couch.

Jess had tstarted a pot of ham soup early that morning and it had been simmering all day. The ham fragrance along with the soup beans, leeks, and string beans called "leather britches," mixing with the aroma of freshly-cooked cornbread, filled the little house. They had a good appetite that night, but went to bed early and slept like winter bears. There is something about powerful snowstorms, the silencing of all noise, the crisp chill, or maybe the isolation you know is coming that makes you curl up like a bug at night and go away into a long dreamless sleep.

Since Mac slept on the couch, it was his job to keep the fire going all night. He rose early. It was almost dawn, but it was time to put new logs on the fire. Jess always stored four cords of wood beside the back door in the winter, but kept a full cord in the house against the far end of the living room opposite the kitchen. The wind made a low constant whisper over the roof. Mac peeked out the front window through the shutters. Even though the roof covered the entire front porch, fine powder banked against the front of the house.

Jess kept a wide flat shovel by the back door. The dry snow made it easy to clear a path eighteen inches deep all the way down to brown stubs of grass. It had been snowing for twelve hours with no sign of ever stopping. Mac dug two trenches, one to the outhouse and one to the door of the chicken coop, built against the house to keep it warm. He checked on the hens and collected four eggs.

By the time he came back, Jess was fixing bacon and eggs with biscuits topped with gooseberry jam. Mac poured water into a kettle for tea.

"Robb's still asleep?" he asked.

"Yes, I can't believe it, he was so excited last night, and I'm sure when he wakes up, he'll be flyin' in here all stoked again."

"I'll put him to work shoveling."

"Any sign of it letting up out there?"

"No. The sky is gray and everything else is white. I can't see as far as the garden."

"Windy?"

"No, not windy, just constant white air moving like a slow river."

"We might be here awhile, but I got plenty of food. I always stock up in winter just in case."

"Mama!" shouted Robb as he ran into the living room.

"What's the matter Robb?" asked Jess.

"Look out the window! Can't see nothing.'"

"It's jus' snow, big boy. We're all gonna be in here for a few days," said Jess.

"Mac, too?"

"Yeah, I can't go anywhere until I find my car and I think I'm not going to see it for two or three days."

Robb ran to the front of the house and peeked out again, then ran to the back door.

"Let's get some breakfast, then Mac's gonna' to let you shovel snow out back."

Robb gobbled down his breakfast and had his boots, knit hat, and coat on before Jess could start her second cup of tea.

Mac let Robb help scoop a small path toward the garden, but in less than an hour, an inch of new snow had piled over the bottom of the trench. When Robb put the shovel down, Mac picked him up and tossed him into a snowdrift. He sank partially out of sight and gave off a squeal like a baby pig, followed by a burst of laughter as he tried to stand and make his way back to the trench. Mac stomped over to him and threw him into the snowdrift again. Then again and again. He never stopped squealing and laughing. Mac tired before Robb did and said it was time to thaw out on the rug in front of the fireplace.

This was their fifth winter together, but the first time Mac had stayed in Jess' house for more than three days. He tried not to let it show how much he was enjoying spending so much time with his family. Sometimes he forgot how old he was and found himself as giddy as Robb when they played in the snow, but every now and then he remembered the orchard and his responsibilities. One of Jess' neighbors, a half mile down the Stumpy Mountain Road, had a telephone, and twice Mac walked through the snow to call the Stinsons about farm business.

CHAPTER 30

McKENZIE

It turned out to be a storm like neither I, nor Jess, nor anyone had else ever seen. Within the first three days, deep drifts had overtaken the top of the chicken coop and the outhouse. I had to dig every day and sometimes twice a day just to maintain access. The snow stopped after the fourth day and it looked as if the sun would peek through, but the temperature dropped into such a hard freeze that the top three inches of snow crusted   over, making it more difficult to walk.

Jess had stored three smoked hams, thirty pounds of beans in burlap bags, twenty-one quarts of vegetables, ten pounds of cornmeal, and other staples. In her pantry, a thick solid oak door opened into a large deep-freeze closet built with three exterior walls protruding from the house, so in the winter, the closet stayed about the same temperature as the outside. We never questioned whether we had enough food and supplies, but snow returned every few days and by mid-January, my car was still buried up to its headlights. That's when we realized we were going to have to find some other food sources.

It took Jess and me a whole day to convert wood from an old crate in her storeroom into rectangular snowshoes.

Strapped to my ankles with strands of leather, they looked ridiculous, and clumsy, and I wasn't sure they would work. On top of three or four feet of white crusted snow, I toddled from the house to the riverbank like a child in diapers. The moment I stepped on the bank's steep slope, my feet shot out in front of me and I slid on my back across a band of gray ice into the river. I managed to keep my head and arms above the water as I fluttered and scrambled my way back to the bank. By the time I returned to the house some of the water on my back had started to freeze.

We drilled holes along the edges of the wood snowshoes and laced strands of rope across the bottom to give me traction. I tried another test trip the next day down the bank, then along the river and back to the house. My feet had perfect grip even on the icy river's edge. From the scraps of leftover crate and rope, I made Robb a pair of his own snowshoes. I watched his face as he crept along the snow. He could hardly believe that he was walking on top of snow deep enough to swallow him completely.

We shuffled our way downstream about fifty yards to a spot where the river took a turn to the right. The angle was serious enough for the flowing water to carve out a cove and create a deep slow-moving pool. The eight foot wide band of ice around the edge made the water in the pool's center appear black. I'm sure with my snowshoes, I could have walked several feet closer to the open water, but with Robb hanging on my side, I insisted we both stay on the bank.

Jess gave me a jar of bait she had made from snake meat. I threw several loose pieces into the pool to wake the fish. I knew they would be slow and sluggish that time of year and naturally interested in easy food. After about ten chunks of free food, thrown about twenty seconds apart, I tossed in my first line with a small weight and baited hook. Robb stood beside me holding the handle of an empty bucket with his eyes fixed on the water. Within seconds, the line tightened and vibrated. I eased the shiny brim over the edge and across the ice. Robb squealed and his big flat snowshoes clapped in the packed snow beneath his feet every time he jumped in the air. Twenty times in thirty minutes we pulled in fish. I unhooked them and dropped them into the pail, which had become too heavy for Robb to hold.

We didn't have to put water into the pail because the cold air quickly froze the newly caught fish. When we returned to the house, I removed Robb's snowshoes outside the door and gave him a fish that filled both his little hands. Immediately he dashed inside ahead of me. Jess showered him with *oooohs* and *wows*. The house already smelled like baked bread and soon it would smell like fried fish and baked bread. Over the next few weeks we pulled in as many fish as we needed, any day we wanted to.

Even though snow had not fallen for ten days, the sky was still a blanket of gray and the temperature remained well below freezing. The trench to the outhouse was still nearly three feet deep. We were out of goat's milk and knew Theron's animals wouldn't be able to make their rounds for a while. In good weather, the mile and a half walk to the goat farm on the back side of the mountain was an easy hike, but with two milk pails tied to my back and wooden snowshoes strapped to my feet, I didn't know whether I could make it there and back without staying overnight at the goat farm.

The hardest part was following the old trail which was completely covered by the storm. Two mountain streams along the way created little glaciers so slick that I had to remove my snowshoes and use a broken tree limb to help steady me as I inched my way across the fingers of ice. I rested at the final turn along the north side of the mountain. The open valley was almost all white. The side of Theron's barn and house were covered up to the windows with the rolling drifts.

A rough path had been carved out from the front door of his house to the barn with enough snow dug away to swing open the barn door. I found Theron sitting in the barn with his goats. Obviously, not expecting to see another person so soon, Theron let out a yelp when I walked in, scaring the herd of goats around him. They bleated and tried to run with no place to go. Some fell on the dirt floor as others ran over them until they were bunched against the far wall with their black and white faces pleading for mercy.

"Theron, it's just me, Mac," I said lifting my hands slightly.

"Oh goodness, Mac. Thought you was a ghost."

"Are you okay?"

He shook his head up and down, then back and forth. "I'm okay. I'm okay, but lost too many goats in the storms."

"I'm so sorry, how many did you lose?"

"A bunch."

"What happened?"

"Snow was so high they climbed over the fence and got away. Got these in here, but don't know where the others went. Still got to do the milkin' every day, can't deliver it though."

"Yes, of course." He squatted on a stool and pulled milk from the belly of the she-goat in front of him for another minute or two, then patted her on her side as he said, "All done, Polly." The animal returned to the other goats pressed against each other at the back of the barn. "I call her Polly," he said as he picked up the pail.

"What have you been doing with all the milk?"

"Got a place behind the barn, I dump it. It'll go down the hill when the snow melts."

"We could use some. I brought a couple of jugs."

"Got four buckets full by the door. Take 'em all."

"Thanks but I got to walk back in the snow. Just barely made it here with empty jugs. I'm sure two is all I can do."

"Well, take what ya want."

"Thanks," I said as I drew a five-dollar bill from my pocket.

"No. No money. I got to pour it all out if you don't come. Take it. Take it all."

"Have you been making cheese?"

"Yes, I got more cheese than I can store. Take some of that too."

"Can we put some cheese in one pail and milk in the other?"

"Yes, yes. That's good. That's good."

After watching me talk to Theron for a while, the goats started walking around the barn like I was just another wood post. Theron put eight chunks of cheese wrapped in cloth in my milk pail and carefully filled the other with fresh goat's milk then screwed the tops on tightly. He promised to come by Jess' house as soon as the snow melted enough for him to get out. I creased the five-dollar bill and slid it between a crack in the wood by the door, high enough so the goats couldn't eat it, but sticking far enough out of the wood for Theron to notice it in a day or so.

I needed to start back to be sure I got to Jess' before dark. I was right about how difficult it would be to plow over the banks of snow in my clumsy snowshoes while carrying two milk pails strapped across my back. Both pails were sealed, but the milk sloshed back and forth with every stride. Keeping my balance was twice as difficult as before.

I fell three times trying to cross the near-frozen streams. The third time, I slid on my back down the mountain slope thirty or forty feet, barely missing the trees. The drag of the milk pails slowed me enough to dig my feet in and stop. I wanted to follow the trail because it was the shortest way back , but after falling, I decided to go straight down to the toe of the mountain and walk beside the little river all the way around to Jess's property. Following the waggling river was probably twice as long, but definitely safer. I picked up my pace and carried a stick to whack the sides of the snowshoes every few hundred yards to knock off snow that continually caked on both top and bottom.

Rounding the last curve on the south side of the mountain, I realized the daylight was falling away and I still had a good mile to go. For the past hour, the wind had steadily increased. Snow clung to the trees keeping them from swaying and making their usual swooshing sound. It was odd to feel the air blasting my face so hard and cold enough to make it numb, yet the forest around me stood frozen in silence. Walking was difficult and slow and I was almost out of breath and hot under my coat, but my face was cold. As the light continued to disappear and the wind increased, I slowed down even more. With one bend in the river to go, a small light appeared at the top of the hill. I pictured Robb looking out the rear window of Jess' house watching for me, but I heard something that brought me to a complete stop as I sank slowly into the snow beneath my feet.

It was a woman's voice. Almost a whisper at first. It came with the wind and floated above my head. It filled the frozen, quiet forest. The long breathy note increased in strength, saturated the air, then diminished back into silence. After the sound stopped, I almost believed I had imagined it. I continued to make my way up the hill to Jess' house when I heard something else—not a growl, or moan—more like a hum so low I wasn't sure whether it was a sound I heard or a feeling that the Earth was vibrating. It increased, held its own, before fading way. It was the same sound, or voice, I had heard when I stood with Jess below her aunt's property on the other side of the mountain.

Fifty feet from the house, Robb's head was silhouetted in the rear window the way I imagined. He started flapping both hands the moment he saw me. The back door opened and he darted out two steps when I saw Jess' hand pull him back into the doorway and stuff a hat and coat on him. The snow trough from the back door to the outhouse was a foot deeper than the shallower channel I had dug toward the river, and Robb had to crawl over the high snow step before he could fly down the trench to meet me. With his arms wrapped around my neck and his legs around my waist, and with both milk pails still strapped to my back, my exhausted legs began to tremble. I kicked off the snowshoes and shuffled to the deeper trench.

"I'm going to put you down here, big guy, so I don't stumble."

Robb jumped into the snow and watched me unstrap the two pails. His eyes were fixed on everything I did until we heard the woman's voice rising again in the air. Robb turned away from me toward the mountain and the voice. We listened. I still couldn't believe anything could sound so sad and yet so beautiful at the same time. All day I had looked forward to being home and I know how anxious Robb was to see me. But for almost a minute we were so carried away by the mountain's voice, we forgot about each other. The song stopped. He jumped into the lower trail and started walking toward the mountain. I bent down and picked up the two pails and the snowshoes and looked at Jess who was standing in the back door. Instead of greeting me, she was watching Robb. I looked back. He was still walking into the wind flowing down the hill.

"Robb," I called. He didn't stop so I called again, "Robb!" He continued to walk. I said his name one more time even louder and he turned around.

"What was that?" he squealed out.

Jess said, "It's the mountain singin'. It does that sometimes when it's windy."

"But why?" asked Robb.

"I don't know. Maybe it's lonely. Maybe it wants us to sing somethin' back," said Jess.

"I don't know any songs."

"Just hum like your mama," I said.

He puckered his lips, took a breath, but all that came out was a little squeal and a burst of air that turned to white mist in the wind and blew away.

Both Jess and Robb were asleep by nine o'clock. I wrote

in my notebook for at least two hours that night, but I still wasn't sleepy. I couldn't stop thinking about how secluded Theron was. Some things just cling to the inside of your mind and won't go away. Living alone never seemed to bother him, but still, someone should have been checking on him.

The wind died down and there were no more voices. In the five years I had been coming to Stumpy Ridge, I don't think I heard the voices more than a dozen times, but whenever the wind blew, I stopped whatever I was doing and listened as if I needed to hear the mountain sing one more time.

Jack Hemphill

CHAPTER 31

McKENZIE

The first sunny day finally came in late February. We celebrated by taking a walk through the woods then along the river. All the trees dripped like spring rain. In soft spots in the snow, we sank up to our shins. After another week, only six inches covered the fields.

"Theron shoulda been here by now," Jess said as she looked out the back door.

"Hope he's okay."

"Probably busy with his goats."

"I know you're right, but we need to take a look anyway."

"Okay, we all could use a good long walk."

Robb was so excited, he marched halfway to the goat farm in front of us. I had to carry him the second half, with Robb on my shoulders and his legs straddling my neck. I noticed the barn door was open and no sign of Theron. A few goats were in the yard drinking from a stream of melted snow trickling past the barn door.

Without a word, Jess started running toward the barn and we followed, slushing through the gray mush as fast as we could. The goats inside scattered away from us as we walked in. After nervous pawing and bleating, they slowly closed around us. They were hungry.

The loft was still half full of alfalfa hay. I climbed the ladder and tossed bails to the floor below. Working my way around the edge of the loft, I tossed about a dozen bales. That's when I found Theron, facedown in the hay. My first instinct was to call Jess who immediately flew up the ladder and knelt beside him. At her direction, I made a bed of hay and stacked bales around him creating a little nest. Jess sat with her back against the bundles and pulled Theron against her chest and cuddled him in her arms.

"Bring me some milk in a cup or bowl," she said.

I dashed back to the lower level. Robb was sitting at the bottom of the ladder watching the animals devouring the hay. That's when I remembered the she-goats needed to be milked. I found a clean ceramic bowl beside a sink in the barn. After flipping over a pail to use as a stool, I pulled a she goat beside me and squeezed out a bowl full of milk, then asked Robb to follow me up to the loft. At the top, I gave him the bowl of milk and told him to find Jess and give it to her. He scurried off while I returned to the first floor to continue milking the goats. As I sat on my makeshift stool, I listened to the splash of milk hitting the dry bottom of the bucket at my feet, and I heard Jess in the loft singing a soft, slow melody.

When I climbed back to the loft, Jess had ripped off a strip of her blouse and folded it into a neat point to drip the fresh milk into Theron's mouth. Robb was watching from his own little hay nest he had created beside her.

I found some food and blankets in the house and we all spent the night in the loft. Jess hummed and whispered things into Theron's ear continually. I was beginning to recognize some of the melodies, but I had no idea what she was saying to him. Every few hours, she stopped long enough to give him a few more drops from the bowl. Robb and I dozed off, but when the morning sun came, Theron opened his eyes. Jess told him we were going to try to get him to his own bed. He nodded slightly. We waited a few more hours as he gained more strength. He was able to hold onto me as I carried him over my shoulder down the ladder. The goats could smell Theron the whole time he was in the loft and even though they couldn't see him, they stayed calm knowing he was still nearby.

I laid him on the dirt floor long enough to catch my breath. I nodded for Jess and Robb to come down. Seeing Theron carried down the ladder over my shoulder made the herd nervous. Once again, they pressed themselves against each other near the far wall.

"We need to get him out of here right away," I said. "Robb, Jess, open the door."

I slid my right arm under his back and left arm behind his knees, but before I lifted him, I was rammed by a goat on my left shoulder so hard it knocked me to the ground. My right arm was still under Theron. One of the goat's horns barely missed my chest. The other horn tore my shirt as it plowed across the skin behind my shoulder.

I heard Theron cough out a word or two to the goat. I did not understand what he said, but as soon as he spoke, the goat took several steps backward and watched me roll to my knees and lift Theron.

Jess opened the barn door as I pushed my way through the herd into the yard. Jess tried to keep them in, but they were far too quick for her and they hopped out into the snow. Robb ran back and forth like a sheepdog trying to corral a couple of small animals. I was able to get ahead of the herd crowding around me all the way to the house. Some of the snow banks against the house and fence were still as deep as the goats' knees. I put Theron in his bed and Jess covered him with wool blankets. When I walked out of Theron's house, the goats, who by then had lost his scent, started crying with their perfectly pathetic voices that goats do so well.

Theron had taken care of every one of them since the day they were born. He was there to hold them at birth, teach them to come to the sound of his voice, milk them when they needed it, feed them every day, talk to them in the night, and keep them warm in the barn. He was as much a part of their lives as their mothers. Every time he put them into the barn at night, he called each one by the name he had given them at birth. They knew his every move, but something was very wrong, and they were afraid. The big male goats were the first to complain and stomp in protest around the yard. Then the whole tribe joined in a slow, circular march smashing down the snow piles as they widened the circle. Jess immediately ran to get Robb away from the herd. She managed to slip through the pack and pick him up with one hand then tramp back across the yard into the house. The goats continued to cry until one by one, they returned to the barn.

The next day, I took Robb home. Jess stayed with Theron. After a week, Theron was strong enough to take care of himself and his herd, and Jess came back home. Every few days after that, for a couple of weeks, I walked back to Theron's ranch and assisted him with his chores.

Looking back on that day, I remember that the moment Jess saw Theron on the loft floor, she knew exactly what to do. After it was all over, I thought she would tell me what was wrong with him, but all she said was, "He was burning hot when we found him on the loft floor. I held him that night and he cooled." That was a typical explanation from her. I had learned to never ask about her patients' illnesses and never ask how they were healed.

The winter was the worst in that part of the Appalachian Mountains that anybody could remember. It put the Preacher's efforts against Jess on hold, but the long isolation was almost over and somewhere inside, I knew he was anxious to start again.

Somewhere around 2:00 a.m.,x I knelt on the hearth and stoked the pile of embers, added two logs, and stoked again. The dry wood ignited right away. When I stood and turned, I saw Jess standing behind me.

"Jess! You startled me," I said.

"Couldn't sleep," she said.

"I couldn't either. Little chilly. "

I picked up my blanket and sat on the couch. Jess sat down beside me.

"Why couldn't you sleep?" I asked.

"'Cause it's the end of a long winter, I guess."

"It *was* long."

"I know you mus' be anxious to get back to your farm."

"I'm sure I got a ton of work to do, and Stinson's going to need money to pay workers. Even in an orchard, there's work to be done in the winter."

"You know, Robb enjoyed having you here."

I nodded, then said, "I actually hate to leave."

"It doesn't really matter how long the winter was—I loved every day of it…'cause you were here." She looked at me and slid her hand over mine.

I thought I was a writer, a man of words, but I couldn't

think of what to say or do other than what I felt, so I pulled her close and kissed her lips. She kissed back and wrapped her arms around me. For the first time, I felt her warmth against my chest. We held each other until daybreak.

Jess started breakfast. The smell of sliced ham frying in a pan brought Robb bounding out of his room. She served the ham with scrambled eggs, jam, grits, and fresh milk.

I dug my car out of the slush that morning and drove to the General Store for supplies. Spent most of the day with Jess and Robb and then returned to my farm. It took a good two weeks to catch up on my business, but as soon as I did, I returned to my family on the mountain.

CHAPTER 32

McKENZIE

On the way to Jess, I drove by the General Store and collected messages and mail for her. It would take her two days after that to prepare all the requests and pack them or bottle them for delivery. Because we knew it would take twice the time to climb down and back up the snow-covered trails, we decided to make two trips on separate days, so we would carry only half the items each day.

Before we started delivering, we checked on Aunt Brusie who was glad to see us and never mentioned the long winter even though she must have been completely isolated for weeks. She understood why we couldn't stay and kissed us good-bye. Jess chose to walk only the top half of the ridge that day.

As I expected, the mountain trails were slippery, but every family was glad to see us come. They all wanted to talk and we had to explain why we couldn't stay long.

The last house we visited was John Curley Todd's house. I was sure we had not received any requests for medicine from the Todds, but Jess wanted to visit them anyway.

Bare trees stood defiantly piercing the white blanket covering the hills. The snow had almost melted from John

Curley Todd's roof. Icicles hung in varying lengths like organ pipes. Gray smoke streamed from the chimney and hovered above the house. The last hundred yards were the steepest and slowest for us. Some layers of ice were floating on streams of thawing snow. We held onto branches and rocks as we eased our way down.

Mudhound caught our scent and announced our arrival ten minutes before we knocked on their door.

"Well, hello, Jess, and hello, Mac!" said Mrs. Todd.

"Brought you a few things, Mrs. Todd," said Jess.

"Aren't you nice to climb all the way down here to see us? John Curley's gone around the other side of the mountain to check on things. He'll be sorry he missed you."

"How's he been?" asked Jess.

"Good. Real good all winter."

Eugena ran out of the kitchen and threw her arms around Jess.

"Hello, my Eugena," said Jess.

Eugena kissed her.

We took off our coats and boots and warmed by the fire.

"Brought you some herb tea," said Jess, pulling a jar out of her bag.

"Eugena, make some hot water for tea," said Mrs. Todd. Jess gave the jar to Eugena who dashed off to the kitchen.

Berry sat on the couch beside her mother. "Where are all your brothers and sisters?" Jess asked Berry.

"They all outside playin' or workin'," said Berry.

"Have you played in the snow this winter?" asked Jess.

"Only a little, but Mama's afraid I might fall off the

mountain."

"Oh, I'm sorry."

"It's okay. My Daddy took me for some walks."

"Tell me about it," said Jess. Berry took a long breath and talked about the snow for five minutes. You never think about how many ways there are to feel somethin' as simple as snow and how many subtle sounds it makes while kickin' your feet through it, until you hear about it from a blind child.

Eugena returned with three cups of tea and one cup of milk and a plate of cookies. Jess told her about all the families she had visited that morning and how they were recovering from the weather. Mrs. Todd stepped into the bedroom and returned with a pile of blankets, sweaters, and doilies the girls had made during all the cooped up weeks.

"Kept 'em busy all winter," said Mrs. Todd.

"How did you keep the boys busy?"

"John Curley got 'em digging out around the house. Hard work. After dinner at night they jus' lay on the floor, by the fire, made bad jokes, told stories until bedtime."

Tell me, how's that little Robb doin'?" Mrs. Todd asked.

"He's five years old now, but a good boy. He and Mac did some shovelin' around the house like your boys. He's back at home right now. Theron's stayin' with him."

Eugena joined us and sat beside her little sister.

Jess leaned toward Mrs. Todd and said, "Have you heard any more from Doug?"

"Before the big winter storm blew in, he and Preacher Ron, and a bunch of other people, mostly from the other side of the mountain, were all set to start up somethin' against you two."

"They've been talkin' 'bout me for the last five years. What else could they say?"

"I heard some of 'em buzzin' with the preacher and Doug at the back of the General Store."

"What'd they say?"

"They were all excited about Dr. Clayton."

"What about him?"

"From what I heard, he's joinin' 'em and they said something about the doctor gettin' the sheriff involved, but that's all I know."

Jess closed her eyes and shook her head.

"I have an idea," said Jess. "Why don't I take Berry for a little walk?"

"I don't know about that, Jess," said Mrs. Todd.

"Oh, it would be good for her. Just around the yard once or twice," Jess said.

Mrs. Todd looked at Berry who was holding in a secret smile.

"Just around the house, Berry." said Mrs. Todd.

"Yes, ma'am," Berry said.

"Well..." Mrs. Todd hesitated.

"Oh, please, Mama, we can't go far," said Berry.

"Bundle up good."

Jess picked up her bag, took something from inside it, and slipped it into her pocket at the same time she whispered something in Berry's ear. Then Jess helped her with her coat and boots. Mrs. Todd reminded them again that they needed to come right back.

They held hands as they crept through the front doorway. The door closed behind them and Mrs. Todd sat back on the couch.

"Good cookies," I said.

"Thank you," said Mrs. Todd., "My mama's recipe."

Mrs. Todd tilted her head to one side and craned her neck trying to see Jess and Berry out the window.

"They're fortunate to have a mother like you, Mrs. Todd," I said. I noticed how nervous Mrs. Todd was, so I walked to the window overlooking the side yard.

"I still worry 'bout her." said Mrs. Todd.

"I understand. She's a sweet girl."

She finished her tea and continued to glance out the side window then walked to the front window. "Oh, here they come now," she said.

Jess knelt inside the doorway and gave Berry a hug which Berry returned with both arms around Jess's neck. Jess kissed her, whispered in her ear, stood and said, "Mrs. Todd we have to go, but please tell John Curley we're sorry we missed him."

"Well, you're dears for comin', and come back soon," said Mrs. Todd.

"We will."

Jess kissed Mrs. Todd good-bye, picked up her coat and bag, and walked out the door in front of me. Mudhound appeared from nowhere and followed me across the yard until I caught up with Jess at the gate.

"What's your hurry, Jess?"

"Sorry, I just thought it was time to go."

We made the first turn and looped back to a point above the Todd house. I heard a scream coming from the house below and I turned to go back.

"It's okay," Jess said, holding my elbow and patting my arm to assure me. Another long scream, muffled by the snow around us, rose up the hill. The front door opened and Mrs. Todd appeared, and cupped her hands around her mouth, and called for Jess three times. Jess pulled me away from the edge of the trail far enough so Mrs. Todd couldn't see us.

"Jess, tell me! What's going on?"

"I will," she said, but continued to climb the mountain. Halfway around the next turn and well out-of-sight, Jess stopped and leaned against a rock.

I stood in front of her and said, "Now, Jess, *tell* me! Tell me what's going on down there."

In spite of the pools of tears filling her eyes, she couldn't hold back the smile that quivered her lips. She placed her hand on my arm as she said, "I put a blue silk ribbon in Berry's hand. It was my Granma's and I always thought it was the most beautiful thing I owned, and I instructed her to keep it and show it to her mama as soon as she got home."

"But why? What would be the point?" Jess turned her head, trying to hide the oncoming emotional avalanche. She bowed and leaned into me. I wrapped both arms around her as she let out a high-pitched squeal that burst wide open into a cry and a scream that started over with each breath, and ended in quiet laughter. She squeezed me tighter and buried her head farther into my shoulder.

She finally became still, and silent, and pulled back against the rock. Her face was soaked and shined with a smile so wide her eyes nearly closed.

"Jess, I still don't understand it!"

"I don't think I can explain."

"But you gotta tell me *something*."

She stopped smiling, relaxed, and looked at me with expectant eyes, as if she were waiting for me to understand.

"Jess!...Can she *see*?" I asked.

"Yes!" she said containing her emotion. She looked back at the Todd house for a moment, then said, "I don't know how to explain it. I watch for it, listen for it, and the more I do, the sooner it happens."

"How long have you known it was going to happen?"

"All winter."

"But you didn't see her this winter."

"I didn't see her, but it doesn't matter. I felt it commin'."

"Why did you leave so fast and not answer Mrs. Todd?"

"'Cause I wanted her to hear it all from Berry and if I stayed there, I knew I would cry."

"Well, you cried anyway."

"I know, but I didn't want 'em to see me."

She rested the back of her head against the rock. Her face was still wet and shiny. I watched her, hoping she would say more, but she had given me as much as she could, or would, at that time.

We walked up to the ridge and then down toward the General Store. We were both quiet, but I felt her joy, and it was a moment that neither of us wanted to spoil with more words. Eventually, I would appreciate how important that day was and how much it would affect our lives.

Jack Hemphill

CHAPTER 33

The spring and summer were filled with continuous talk about the worst winter anybody could remember. Everybody had a story of surviving and every household spent the next six months rebuilding, or replanting, or recovering.

Theron returned to the ridge to make his usual rounds, but with only half the milk and cheese as before. He never found the lost goats, but continued with what he had left. Fortunately Billy, and Nanny were among those saved. As always, his first stop was at the General Store, where he unloaded half his containers to be sold. Before climbing the ridge, he took his goats down to the nearby stream for watering. It was a quarter mile out of his way, but they needed it before their long pull up the mountain. The cold winter had been followed by a cool summer and had already brought clear blue skies and flocks of birds preparing for a new winter. He untethered the two goats and let them walk through the stream and drink as much as they wanted. He watched them walk slowly upstream, take a few sips of water, stick their noses in the air as if they smelled something irresistible, slosh a little farther into the shadows, then start the pattern over again with a drink of water followed by sniffing the air and so on.

Theron leaned against a tree on the bank and watched wispy clouds float by. When he thought it was time to call the goats, he stood and called their names, "Billy, Nanny." No sign of them. He squinted his eyes to see deep into the shadows covering the stream. "Billy, Nanny, come." He walked up and down the north side of the riverbank, crossed the stream and ran through an open gate into the flat pasture where Doug Helms once grazed his cattle. The only tree planted in the middle of the field was Mac's apple tree with a fresh crop of red fruit scattered on the ground. The goats were so busy gobbling up the apples that they paid no attention to Theron calling their names. He finally pulled them away from the feast with a rope he tied around their necks.

Each week for the remainder of that September and into October, Theron's goats eagerly returned to the pile of apples in Doug's field and devoured them like rare delicious meals. After the tree gave up its last apples in mid-October, Billy and Nanny enjoyed grazing in Doug's wide pasture filled with sweet alfalfa. But their weekly trips extended deep into fall and the tasty stalks began to droop and wither. In the first week of November, Theron walked with his goats into the pasture not expecting to stay long because all the apples were gone and the alfalfa season was almost past. He noticed the goats' heads were again held high, sniffing the air. Once inside the fence, the goats ran ahead of Theron, crested the small hill, and disappeared out of sight. When Theron reached the open pasture, the goats were feeding on several bales of alfalfa and a basket of apples laid near the tree.

Theron stopped, looked to the top of the hill, then over the tree line to the big cattle barn. He put both hands behind his head and locked his fingers while he scanned everything again from the edges of the pasture to the barn. He let them eat for a while longer before looping a rope around their heads and guiding them back to work.

The next week Theron walked in front of the goats through the gate and up the hill. The same meal was placed under the tree. The following week he found the same thing, but only alfalfa bales. Theron sat on the ground and watched them graze. The earth rumbled a little before the roar of an engine made Theron spring to his feet and watch Doug Helms' truck bouncing down the hill. He parked behind the apple tree.

"Damnedest thing I ever saw," said Doug as he climbed out of the car. "Imagine an apple tree growing in the middle of an old pasture like that…all by itself."

"Howya doin,' Mister Doug?" Theron managed to mumble out as he stood like a soldier at attention waiting for the discipline of his sergeant's size eleven boot.

"Couple of fine lookin' animals you got there, Theron."

"Yep."

"How many you got?"

"Used to have a lot, but lost a bunch in the winter, ya know?"

"Heard 'bout it. Sorry. Bad break."

"Gonna try to build it back up."

"Couldn't get 'em in your barn when the storm came?"

"Well, it's not really big enough to keep that many for that long, but lots of 'em got away over and through the old fences."

"Whatya feed your herd over the winter?"

"I had some hay in the barn and some jugs of molasses."

"Whatya feedin' them now?"

"Anything they'll eat."

Doug reached over and ran his hand across Billy's side and belly, then did the same to Nanny.

"Got an idea, Theron."

"Okay."

"Bring 'em up here. All of 'em. This used to be a pasture for grazin' cows. Got lots of stuff still growin' and I still cut and store it all in the barn, but I end up giving it away. It's more than enough for your herd all winter, and even if we have another storm like last winter, I got enough room and enough alfalfa in that barn up there to last 'til spring for three times as many goats as you got."

"I thankya kindly, Mister Doug, but I can't afford to pay you nothing."

"Already got the hay and the barn. It's not gonna cost me nothin' if you come."

Theron looked down at his feet as he kicked a clod of dirt with the heel of his boot.

"Think about it, Theron, I'll take my truck to your place and we'll bring 'em up here a few at a time. They can stay as long as you like, or jus' 'til they get back healthy."

Theron nodded and kicked another clod.

"I'll see you here next week, okay?"

"Okay, Mister Doug."

Theron had to herd his goats four or five at a time from his farm along the trail below Jess' house to Stumpy Ridge Road where Doug parked his pickup truck. It took them all day to transfer the entire stock. They let the animals graze for a few hours on Doug's land before Theron led them into the barn. The previous day, Theron had moved most of his personal things including his cat, Pickles, from his farm to the caretaker's house behind the Doug's barn.

It only took the goats a few days to get used to their new home and the enormous pasture.

"Theron," Doug called as he stepped through the barn door and waved his hand.

"Yes, Mister Doug," said Theron.

"Let me show you somethin'."

Theron dropped his buckets and followed him to a low spot at the bottom of the pasture where several goats were drinking from muddy pools.

"When I had cattle, I installed a pump in that old box over there which sucked water about a hundred and fifty feet up the hill. That's how they got their water every day, as long as the pump worked. When it didn't work they came down here and drank from these here mud holes."

"That was good they had another place to get water."

"Yes, but it's too dirty. What I always wanted to do was dig out a pond down here and let the creek flow through it."

"That's a good idea."

"Yes, but the only problem is that the reason this is a mud hole is because it's a foot of soil on top of solid rock that runs from here to the creek. The water's got no place to go. What I would have to do is blast out a wide and deep trench in the rock from the upper part of the creek, and then long and wide enough to make a good drinking pool right here. The trench would continue all the way back to the creek on the lower side. That way the pool would fill and always be runnin' with fresh water."

"Are you gonna do that for the goats, Mister Doug?"

"Yes. Two big problems you can help me with. When we're blasting, you have to keep the animals in the barn. It'll take some days so you're gonna have to keep them happy up there for a while."

"Yes, Mister Doug." He looked over the field a minute trying to picture the construction.

Doug said, "We gonna have to pull up part of the fence in two places, and we can't let the goats come down here until the fence is back up. So you're also gonna have to find a way to keep them watered and away from the fence during all that time. Think you can do that?"

"Yes."

"Any questions?"

"Whatcha gonna blast it with, Mister Doug?"

"I thought about doin' this a long time ago. I've got more crates of dynamite than I'll ever need, tucked under the back left corner of the barn. I bought it jus' for this purpose, but never got to use it."

Theron looked around at the creek, the fence, and the pasture, then said, "It's gonna scare the goats, but they gonna love the water. When can we start, Mister Doug?"

"Tomorrow. But, Theron, we're business partners now. Why don't you just call me *Doug*?"

"What does that mean, 'business partners'?"

Doug waved for Theron to follow him to the front of the barn. Years before then, he had placed two old log chairs there so he could sit and watch his cattle grazing in the pasture. As they sat down, Doug continued, "It means I'm helping you with your business and you help me."

"I jus' sell milk and cheese."

"I know. That's your business."

"Okay, but how do I hep *you*?" said Theron.

"Well . . ." he rolled his head back, closed his eyes momentarily, then said, "I'm helpin' you keep your goats healthy and you're helpin' me sell your milk and cheese in my store, so I make a little money, too."

"I understand, Mister Doug."

"Call me just Doug."

Theron nodded as his cat, Pickles, jumped into his lap.

Doug watched him stroking her head for a full minute, then looked back over the pasture and said, "I'm glad to have someone livin' on the farm again."

The blasting took ten days. Theron thought it probably scared the Ridge People more than the goats. After three more days, the fence was replaced and the goats were released into the pasture. Every one of them ran immediately to the new pool, drank, and walked in the cool mountain stream. There was plenty of alfalfa hay and, on cold nights, Doug's barn was more than adequate to keep them warm. Theron finished moving everything he owned to the caretaker's house behind the barn.

Jack Hemphill

CHAPTER 34

Theron had just finished all his chores and gotten all the goats safely put away for the night when Doug called out, "Theron, we're gonna have dinner about a half hour late tonight

"Okay, Doug, but how come?" he replied,

"'Cause I finally got a new cook. She moved into the cook's house this afternoon, so it'll be pretty nearly 7:00 before it's ready."

"Okay, Doug, that'll be fine."

"If you get there a little early, you can help set the food on the table. I may be a couple of minutes late."

Theron arrived at Doug's house by 6:45 and called out for him. No reply, so he went straight to the kitchen. The new cook was carefully pouring hot gravy into a bowl. He didn't speak to her until she had finished. "Hi, I'm Theron." he said.

The new cook snapped around as if she were startled.

"Eugena!" he said when he saw her face.

"Hi, Theron. I knew you were comin'."

"How did you get here?" he said.

"Mister Doug brought me."

"I thought you were livin' with your grandmamma now."

"I did, but she done died and I was goin' back to my mother's when Mister Doug told her how much you both needed me over here, so he's paying me and gave me my own little house."

"Well . . ." He grinned with embarrassment, but just stood and stared awhile then said, "I'll get to eat your food."

"Yes, and I'll get to eat with you."

"Well . . ." he shook his head. "I'm supposed to help you carry stuff to the table."

"Sure, why don't you carry this gravy bowl if you can do it real careful."

The table was all set, all the plates and food in bowls carefully placed. The house was filled with roast beef and cabbage fragrance when Doug walked in.

"Well, if it tastes as good as it smells, then I did a good thing to bring you down here, Eugena. Don't you think so Theron?"

"Oh yes, I already knew she's a good cook," said Theron.

"You two have known each other for a long time."

"Yes, I know her whole family, except her grandmamma who's dead now," said Theron.

"I'm sure your grandmamma was lucky to have you cook for her," said Doug.

Eugena nodded yes.

"Eugena, you gonna cook breakfast too?" asked Theron.

"She'll cook breakfast and dinner for you and me and we will still eat right here in my house, but she will cook lunch for us and all three of the workers, and I'll carry the lunch down to the table in the barn. But, in the winter, I'll still bring it down there for the other workers, but you and I and Eugena will eat it in your house."

They spent the rest of the meal talking about the food and the chores Theron and Eugena would need to do the following day. Doug was used to buying food for the farmworkers and always had it delivered to the General Store for him to pick up.

"Eugena, you know how to make desserts?" asked Doug.

"Mama showed me how to make cake and Dad made icecream sometimes, but we only had it for special things like birthdays."

"Can you make cookies?" asked Doug.

"Oh yes, but you gonna have to buy me more sugar and butter," said Eugena.

Okay, we'll have cookies after every dinner and cake on special occasions and I'll get the store to order some ice-cream," said Doug.

After dinner, they carried the dishes into the kitchen. Doug excused himself and said, "I'll let you two clean up the kitchen and dishes. Eugena, you might want to show Theron your porch swing."

Doug left. Theron and Eugena slowly washed dishes, wrapped and put away leftovers, then walked together back to the cook's house so she could show him her swing. They watched the sunset.

Jack Hemphill

CHAPTER 35

JESS

When we were on the farm, Robb liked to sleep in the big barn and Mac stayed with him. I had a beautiful room in the house with a big soft bed, carpet, and curtains. I had my own bathroom with a door that opened right into the bedroom. It was so comfortable, I was afraid I would oversleep the next mornin' when Mac's family was comin' in to meet me. I was usually awake by four or five, but I was so excited about meetin' the family that I got up around three-thirty . After I put on my pants and shirt and started toward the door, I saw my reflection in the oval mirror in the corner of the room. I didn't have a full mirror anywhere in my own house, so it had been a long time since I saw what I looked like, except for Mac's pictures of me.

I won't say I was either happy or disappointed with my image in the mirror, but I didn't think I was ugly, just not hard to look at. My hair was as light as the fur of an alpine goat and twice as curly. I never really cared if it was long or short. I just wanted it kept out of my face. I found a comb in my bag and stroked my hair forward until the kinks were out, then I combed it back. It was stiffer than before and stuck out all over my head. Mac would think it looked like a dandelion done gone to seed.

After another ruffle through my bag, I found my scarf, deep green with a white band of small flowers stitched around the perimeter. I brushed all my hair back away from my face and tied the scarf over my forehead and behind my neck. My hair shot behind me like an explosion of straw. Finally, I pulled the scarf off and retied it with my hair in a large, fat ponytail.

I took another good long look in the mirror and decided my flannel shirt was too baggy. I had only brought two shirts, both flannel. I looked in the closet and found a rack of clothes. They must have been left there by Mac or one of his brothers. I took off my flannel and picked out a long-sleeve light-blue shirt. It hung down as far as my thighs in the front and back and made me look taller and maybe a little prettier.

I threw my comb back into my mushroom-54colored canvas bag. It landed with a pop against something solid and hollow. Six months I had ignored the little white box hidin' at the back of my bag. I saw it every time I put somethin' in there, but I made myself ignore it, almost afraid to think about it. I had bought the little box the previous winter at the General Store. First time the store ever had it for sale, but when I got it home, I tucked it away out of sight and never told anybody about it.

There was a table and lamp by the bed. I took the box from my bag and placed it on the table and sat on the bed, looked at the box for a moment, then opened and tilted it until a small skinny bottle fell out. I turned it upright in the light hoping I still liked the color. Pale pink. Of all the women in my family, I can't remember a single one who ever wore fingernail polish. I never even saw no one put it on. I thought both of Mac's sisters- in-law would be wearin' it.

I was surprised and even pleased to find a little brush at the end of the stick in the bottle. My right hand trembled slightly as I stroked the color across each fingernail on my left hand. I discovered it's impossible to put on just a little bit. It ends up in pink blobs and it doesn't look right until each nail is completely covered. Takes forever for that stuff to dry. Blowin' it didn't seem to do any good. I walked around the room shakin' my hands, stoppin' for a moment to blow over each nail, and finally walkin' to the big oval mirror and held out my hands. They didn't look normal at all, like I had just gotten over some long illness, but maybe that's what Mac's sisters-in-law like. How would I ever know?

I felt like takin' a long walk. When I slipped my white sweater over my head, my fingernails stuck to the wooly inside. I pulled the sweater off. My hands looked like the paws of a wolf. I pulled off as much of the white fur from my nails as I could, put my sweater back on, and went out for my walk in slacks and long light-blue shirt.

Jack Hemphill

CHAPTER 36

McKENZIE

My favorite time of day is when the eastern sky begins to glow, but still more night than day. As usual, I slipped down the trail and followed the river. Deer like to drink from the stream in the cool dawning hours. Quiet. They felt safe. A shallow stretch near the bend was always a good place to look for the herd. The wind in my face and the water's gurgle over the rocks was enough to hide me. But instead of seeing the herd standing in the water, I saw someone sitting on the big rock just before the bend. In the mist and predawn glow, it was a shining image, almost part of the mist and almost part of the rock.

I eased back into the woods and walked a short distance before slinking back to the river a little closer to the person. I leaned against a tree to steady my camera, snapped two or three photos, and then watched for a while. The figure was so graceful it had to be a woman.

She glided into the water, slowly walking downstream. I stood motionless as she moved by me. That's when I realized it was Jess.

After she waded to the bank and disappeared into the woods, I returned downstream to the trail. I sat on a rock for a while before going back up to the house. Dawn was burning its way over the hills. By the time I got there, Jess was already in the kitchen side of the barn, whipping eggs in a bowl. Ham crackled in a frying pan on the stove.

"Jess, you're up early."

"So are you," she said.

"But I always get up early when I'm home. I like exploring the woods with my camera."

"I took a walk in the woods this morning, too. Where were you?"

"Looking for another beautiful sunrise."

"How was it?" she asked.

"Cool and quiet. How about you? See anything interesting?"

"Yes," she said as she poured the bowl of eggs into the hot frying pan, sending up a cloud of steam and a loud rushing noise. I didn't hear the rest of her sentence. If she said anything about seeing me, it was lost in the sizzle. Beautiful images of her floating in the damp, cool air above the river still filled my mind. But I couldn't tell her I watched her, and couldn't let her suspect how many pictures I took of her that morning, and I couldn't let her know how many pictures I had taken of her over the past few years any more than I could let her read the thousands of notes and descriptions of her I had recorded. I still couldn't imagine talking to her about it.

Robb smelled the bacon and came running. The coffee, the eggs, and the bacon were all done at the same time and she pulled from the oven a pan of cornbread reheated from yesterday's supper. After breakfast, Jess and I had second cups of coffee while Robb hustled off to explore the barn.

"I'm still a little nervous about meeting your family,"

she said.

"They're just like me — orchard boys."

"But, they run a business in Asheville, and married Asheville women."

"I know, and I guess the truth is that in a lot of ways they are very different from me, but they'll love you and Robb."

"I'm sure they'll love Robb."

"Jess, don't fret over them. You'll be fine and you know they're bringing plenty of food and all you have to do is fix drinks and dessert and I told you we're going to eat right here on these old tables, and the kids will eat on the wood floor in the loft."

"What will the wives wear?"

"Better get used to their names. Lola is married to Tom and Katie is married to Ham, and they'll probably be wearing summer cotton print dresses, nothing fancy."

"You know I only have one dress, and I save it for Sunday."

"Wear your pants and blouse. Just whatever you would in Stumpy Ridge."

"I'm afraid I'm gonna to look too . . ."

"No! You are not going to look *too* anything. Don't worry about their clothes, their hair, or their perfume. You'll look fine. I love that light-blue shirt. Never saw you in it before."

"I found it in the closet."

"Well, good! Keep it. Just tuck it in and it'll look great. I've never seen your hair like that either."

"Does it look like a broom stickin' out the back of my head?"

"No. Looks great." It did look great to me, but maybe

I still had the picture of the part angel, part ghost I had seen in the mist by the river. "I love the way you look right now."

CHAPTER 37

Jess' stomach tightened when she heard the braks on Tom's car squeal to a stop and the thud of two doors as he and his wife slid out of their car in the driveway in front of the old house. Tom and Lola carried baskets and trays. Jess looked around for Mac who was still in the loft putting old blankets on the floor for the boys to sit on. She picked up a dish towel to hide her fuzzy fingernails.

"Well, hello, you must be Jess." said Lola.

"Yes," she said as she wiped her hands on the towel and walked to meet them.

"I'm Lola and this is Tom."

Lola wore a blue cotton skirt, a white blouse with a white sweater. She had a black belt around her tiny waist, and wore dark red lipstick to match her painted fingernails.

Jess nodded and motioned with her head saying, "We're gonna eat on these here tables pushed together, so if you jus' wanna put everythin' down there, I'm sure that would be okay."

"Where's Mac?" asked Tom.

"Up here," said Mac. "Be right down."

The silence that filled the next thirty seconds was desperately awkward, and Lola, who usually couldn't stop talking, didn't know what to think about Jess. "So,

Jess, I don't think Mac ever told me how you two met," said Lola.

"Well, we met at the Stumpy Ridge Market, but I really didn't pay much attention to him until later when I shot him."

"Shot him?"

"Yeah, and it took me several days to nurse him back together. I sort of got to know him then, but that was five or so years ago and I guess I'm still gettin' to know him.

"And you two have a son?"

"Yes, we have a five-year old son named Robb."

"You must have gotten to know Mac pretty well!"

"Yes, well…Robb's playin' out back. He'll be back in a minute."

"Tom, Lola, thanks for coming," Mac said, stepping down from the loft ladder in time to save Jess.

"How've you been?" said Tom.

"Jess was just telling us about how you two met," said Lola.

"It's an interesting story, but have you met Robb yet?"

"Looking forward to it," said Lola.

"Tom, let's go out back and let me show you the new well Stinson dug for me," said Mac. "We'll let the ladies get to know each other." Jess aimed a stare at Mac that said, "Please, don't leave me alone," but it was too late. Tom was already headed out the door. Lola moved close to Jess and they sat down at the long table covered with an oil cloth. "So, Jess, tell me more," she said in a chummy tone as she patted her hand on the table.

"Mac stays with us about three days a week, mostly on the weekends."

"So Robb doesn't see his dad during the week?" Lola

asked.

"Sometimes he brings him down here for a while in the summer. Robb loves the farm and this big old barn."

"All little boys love barns. So why not move down here. What keeps you two up there on Stump Mountain?"

"Oh, no, it's *Stumpy, Stumpy Ridge, not...Stump Mountain.*"

"Sorry."

"I have my work up there. Didn't Mac tell you?"

"No, not exactly. He said you grow herbs used in medicine or something like that."

"As far as I know, my aunt and I are the last two Celtic medicine women in these here mountains."

"You heal people?"

"Yes."

"Now did you actually say you shot Mac?"

"I shot at him. The truth is I shot at the rock under his feet and he fell, bustin' open his head. So I had to nurse him back for a few days."

"Yes, of course, but why did you shoot at him?"

"He was spyin' on me. Couldn't see who it was, but thought he was some kind of prowler."

"Did he have his camera with him?"

"Yes."

"And so you gave him some of your remedies?"

"Yes, and other treatments. Like I said, it took a few days."

"You did say that."

"I have more patients than I know what to do with. I didn't need any more, but he jus' kind of plopped into my yard like a fallen bird."

"So he was unconscious when you did your stuff on

him."

"Had to carry him into my house, stretch him out on my couch and get his clothes off. Had to feed him like a baby at first. That's what you have to do for people who bang their heads. But why does it worry you that he was unconscious?"

"Oh, I just can't picture him getting involved with that kind of stuff, you know, old Celtic remedies, unless he was unconscious, you know what I mean? Or unless he was writing one of his articles."

"Writin' what?"

The door banged against the inside wall as Robb flew into the house. "Mama, two kids got out of a car in front of the barn!" He pointed out the window.

"Yes, Robb they're your cousins." Jess turned Robb around to face Lola. "This is my Robb."

Mac and Tom returned through the back door at the same time Ham and Katie and their two children walked in the front door.

"Hey, Mac, Hey, Tom, Hey, Lola, and — oh! You must be Jess and little Robb!" said Katie who couldn't wait to put her basket down and give Jess a hug and Robb a kiss on his cheek. Robb glanced back at Jess who returned a little smile as if to say, "It's okay, some people just do that."

"Robb, you gotta meet my kids," said Katie as she took him by the hand. Her daughter, Suzy, gave him a hug and her son, Gill, gave him a slight wave. "Why don't y'all go outside for a little while until we call you for lunch?" Gill ran toward the back door and Suzy took Robb's hand. Again, he looked at his mama for approval.

The women started setting the tables, reheating things in the oven, cutting bread, and spreading mayonnaise, and all the things necessary for a family feast. Jess immediately liked Katie who kept every moment filled with enough conversation and laughter to wash away much of Jess' hopeless awkwardness. By the end of the day, Jess almost felt as if she were part of the family. Gill and Suzy played made-up children's games with Robb in the loft, in the orchard, and every part of the barn. When it was time to go, Robb walked with them back to the car. Jess hugged and kissed Katie good-bye then returned to the barn to help Lola wash out her salad bowls and cookie sheets.

"Robb is a real fine boy. I'm happy for Mac," said Lola, "You two ever talk about getting married?"

I didn't know Mac had not told them we were married. I said, "In a way, we're kinda like already married. We both love our son, and we care for each other in ways I never thought about before I met him."

"For Robb's sake, you might want to make it legal, you know?"

"Well, to us it's legal."

"I don't remember seeing Mac so happy except when he's writing," said Lola. "

"What does he write about?"

"He's been talkin' 'bout some articles, but I think he needs to write a full-length book. Maybe you will be his inspiration someday."

"Oh no, not me. I don't think I could be that."

Jack Hemphill

CHAPTER 38

Chief Deputy Buchanan watched as the two sheriff's cars wheeled up to the south portico of the Jefferson County Courthouse in Redbriar. Another deputy in a light brown, severely starched, and perfectly creased uniform hopped out of the car and opened the back door to let Jess out before escorting her into the courthouse. A second car pulled in behind and went through the same routine, except it was Mac being escorted into the courthouse.

Mac was taken to a small room at the back of the ground floor while Jess was taken to a conference room where the sheriff was waiting with Doctor Clayton and Doug Helms.

"Miss Shew, take a seat in the chair at the end of the table."

"Your deputy said I was comin' here to be questioned and not under arrest. Is that right?" asked Jess.

"Correct," said Sheriff Turner before opening a folder of papers and a notebook. "As you can see, we have Mr. Helms and Doctor Clayton with us here who have agreed to be part of this interrogation."

"Why?" asked Jess, "Why them?"

"Okay, let me tell you why they are here and why you are here, Miss Shew."

"A complaint has been turned over to me accusing you

and Mr. McKenzie Davis of unlawful conduct. Formal charges have not been filed and you are free to go if you choose, but I have to tell you, if you so choose, I will have the formal charges in the judge's hand before you get back to Stumpy. This is an informal hearing requested by me as a way of saving you two and the county a lot of wasted time and money. These two gentlemen, with another man who is a preacher, have provided us with affidavits as to your alleged illegal behavior and practices and I am giving you a chance to respond to allegations before I take further actions. Do you understand?"

"No, I don't understand, and where's Mac?"

"What part do you not understand?"

"Where's Mac?"

"He is in another interrogation room, telling his side of the story, so what you tell me and what he says to my deputy better match. Now do you understand?"

"What exactly am I bein' accused of?"

The sheriff read from a paper on the table. "Miss Shew, you are accused of practicing witchcraft, which in itself is not a crime in this state, but practicing it as a form of medical treatment without a license is a serious crime. I'm going to summarize a few statements included in this file and I'm going to ask you to confirm, or deny, or explain them. At the end of the interrogation, I alone will decide to arrest you both or let you go. Are you going to cooperate and answer our questions?"

"Yes."

Sheriff Turner placed a Bible in front of her and asked her to swear to tell the truth. Jess took the oath and Sheriff Turner started his interrogation. "I have a document in my hand labeled *EXHIBIT ONE*. This is a partial list of potions you have been selling and distributing to your patients. I will read a few and I want you to give me a brief answer of what they are supposed to do."

After he read the list to Jess, she said, "Sheriff, they heal. Ask my patients." A stenographer scribbled down her response.

"I also have an affidavit signed by fourteen men who accuse you of attacking them with witchcraft. It is marked EXHIBIT TWO. According to the statement, you placed a spell on them causing them to be partially paralyzed and stumble to the ground while you whipped them with a dangerous weapon, namely, two live copperheads that you held by the tails. This event took place in Doug Helms' barn on December 1st, 1948. Do you have an explanation?"

"Since Mr. Helms is sittin' right here, why don't you ask him how come I was in that barn with fourteen men who had hung Mac from the rafters by a rope, and why I had to lower him and cut him loose while your fourteen witnesses looked on?"

"Miss Shew, I will ask him those questions at another time, but you must answer my question first in as few words as you can. Do you have an explanation for the accusation of an attack against these men?"

"I think I just did, Sheriff. Doug Helms and the other men were tryin' to kill Mac who is my best friend and the legal father of my boy. I saved his life!"

"How do you explain the snakes?"

"The statement that you read said it was December 1st. You ever seen a copperhead in December?"

"*You're* supposed to answer the questions, Miss Shew, not me."

"You know snakes are half asleep that time of year.

Not exactly *dangerous weapons*," Jess said staring straight at Doug, then continued, "I'm tall, and strong, and maybe I could beat the tar out of one, or two, or three of 'em, but fourteen?"

The sheriff turned to another page. "Did you or did you not cast a spell on Mike Cobb in October three years before that, causing him to fall off a pile of rocks and suffer bodily injury?

"Did Cobb explain why any sober man would try to stand on that pile of loose, shaky rocks on the side of Stumpy Mountain?"

"You have to answer the question."

"I just did. Anybody dumb enough to stand on that pile of rubble can't complain or blame me when he falls."

"Jess," the sheriff moved a little closer and spoke in a deliberate voice, "Do you give medication to *minors*?"

"I've provided medication for the children at the request of their parents for years."

"Jess...what I mean is, do you give your healing herb stuff to children?"

"No, I sell it to their parents."

"You are a parent. Do you give it to *your* child?"

"Of course, I love my son."

"You give him your potions?"

"Yes, of course."

"Where is he now?"

"At my house with one of your deputies watchin' him."

"Gentlemen," the sheriff turned his head to Helms and Clayton, "any questions you want to ask?"

Doctor Clayton spoke up immediately, "Jess...Miss Shew, have you ever given your boy or the parents of any other child, remedies containing cockleburs, or bloodroot, or pokeweed?"

"Yes, but all those things have been used for soothin' and healin' for hundreds of years."

"Did you know they can be extremely poisonous?"

"Yes, everybody knows that. Cocklebur can be poisonous if not boiled hard before it's used. I learned that as a child, but I take care to boil it hard, and we never use anythin' but the green berries of pokeweed, cooked twice."

"Has anyone ever tested your cockleburs or analyzed anything you've done?"

"Yes, my patients."

"But you people don't know the long term effects of your treatments, do you?"

"Of course, *we people* do. We care for them their whole lives. Doctor Clayton, we heal 'em. We're there for the women when they cry in pain. The moment their children are born, we feel the little hearts beatin' in our hands. We patch up the men when they bleed. We know what makes 'em laugh. We know what they love and what they fear. We celebrate with them when they are healed. And finally, when it's time for 'em to die, we kiss their cheeks, and warm them in our arms until they're gone."

Dr. Clayton sat back. Sheriff Turner waited a moment for him to speak, then turned to Doug and said, "Mr. Helms, any question you want to add?"

"Yes, just one." He clasped his hands and leaned his elbows on the table and said, "What happened to Viola, Jess?"

"I've already answered that question to you in person." she replied

"First of all," said the sheriff, "who is Viola, and

second, Jess, like I said, this is not a formal hearing, even though you took an oath, but I think you should answer Mr. Helms' question so I can hear it and decide whether it's relevant or not."

"Viola was a patient of mine who came to my house for some help. She disappeared and nobody knows what happened to her."

"What do you mean by, 'help?" asked the sheriff.

"Treatment. She stayed for a few days, gave birth, and left. She was weak from labor, but she still left."

"And where did she go?" asked Doug.

"Don't know, but she had a brother in Florida. She said she'd be back and said, 'If anythin' happens to me, don't let the father of my baby ever get his hands on my child.'"

"Did she say who the father was?" asked the sheriff.

Jess looked at Doug, closed her eyes, took a deep breath and said, "She told me his name. Don't remember it, but I wrote it down somewhere. I'm sure I can find it if I have to."

Doug, who had not taken his eyes off her since she walked into the room, looked down at the dark lines etched across the back of his leather hands, then turned his head and gazed out the window.

Down the narrow hallway, Mac sat with Chief Deputy Buchanan on one side of him and another deputy on the other. A recording secretary scribbled constantly at the far end of the table.

"Mr. Davis," said Buchanan as he read from a paper on the table, "Let me tell you why you are here."

"Yes, that would be nice."

"A complaint has been turned over to us accusing you and Jess Shew of unlawful conduct. Formal charges have not been filed and you are free to go if you choose, but I have to tell you, if you so choose, the formal charges will be in the judge's hand before you get back to Stumpy Ridge. Even though you have taken an oath on the Bible, this is an informal hearing requested by the sheriff as a way of saving you two and the county a lot of wasted time and money. We have three affidavits describing your alleged illegal behavior and practices and we are giving you a chance to respond to allegations before taking further actions. Do you understand?"

"Fire away, Deputy," Mac said.

The deputy read, "You and Miss Shew are being accused of practicing witchcraft, which in itself is not a crime in this state, but practicing it as a form of medical treatment without a license is a serious crime." He put his paper down for a moment and said, "I have to tell you that your answers today will determine whether the sheriff will decide to arrest you or let you go, so I recommend you take what we ask seriously and think carefully about what you say. If you lie to us, you will be arrested for obstruction of justice. Understand?"

"Like I said, deputy, *fire away*."

He gave him a suspicious glare, picked up his paper again, and read, "*EXHIBIT ONE.* This exhibit is a partial list of potions you and Miss Shew have been selling and distributing to your patients. I will read a few and I want you to give me a short answer as to what they are supposed to do."

Mac leaned toward him and glanced at the list and said, "You think I'm supposed to know what all those things do?"

The deputy snapped back, "I will be asking the

questions and you are to give me your short, concise answers. Understand?"

Mac extended his hand forward, palm up and said, "I don't know the answer to your question."

The deputy slid the list in front of him. Mac glanced down the list of things on the page and said, "I still can't tell you what any one of those things is supposed to do."

Buchanan flipped the page. "EXHIBIT TWO," he said with an official voice. "This is an affidavit signed by fourteen men. It says you were present when Jess cast a spell on them causing them to be partially paralyzed and stumble to the ground while she whipped them with two live copperheads that she kept in her coat. This incident took place in Doug Helms' barn on December 1st, 1948. What can you tell me about this incident?"

"All fourteen men signed that?"

"Tell me what you know."

"I can tell you this. I've known her more than five years. We share a child together. She has never cast a spell on anything. Are these the best questions you can dream up?"

"Okay, Mr. Davis. Let's get to it. Have you or Miss Shew ever given medication to a minor who is not your child or have you or Miss Shew ever given medical treatment to the son you two 'share together'?"

Mac let his head fall back slightly and closed his eyes and said, "Just what crime did you say we are accused of?"

"Practicing medicine without a license."

"I don't know the answer to your question," he said without emotion.

With each answer, the scratching of the stenographer's

pen became louder. As required, his answers were brief, but she never stopped scribbling.

Chief Deputy Buchanan turned to his last page, placed it on the table and said, "Did you ever meet a woman named Viola?"

"Yes."

"When, where, and how?"

"We were both patients of Jess."

"Where?"

"At her house."

"What did Miss Shew treat you for?"

"A head injury."

Did she give you medication?"

"Yes."

"What did she treat Viola for?"

"She was pregnant."

"Did she give her medication?"

"Yes."

"How long were you both there?"

"Several days."

"She treated patients at her house for several days?"

"Yes," Mac said and looked at the stenographer, but before she could start writing his single word answer, Chief Deputy Buchanan fired back.

"That, Mr. Davis, would be a *clinic* and without question, a medical clinic."

Mac knew then he was finished. The deputy had what he wanted and escorted Mac to a room where Jess was waiting.

"The sheriff will be with you in a few minutes," said Buchanan. He left and closed the door. Didn't lock it, but waited in the hall. Jess stood and they embraced without speaking.

After a minute Jess said, "Do you think Robb is okay?"

"Robb's tough. I just hope the deputy they left with him survives," Mac said. She smiled and nodded.

After only ten minutes, Buchanan opened the door and swung it against the corridor wall.

"They're ready for you," he said, stepping back and gesturing with his hand.

Mac followed Jess, and Buchanan followed both of them. Another deputy was standing outside the door at the end of the hall. They were ushered into a room to a table with six chairs. There were also chairs around the walls. The sheriff sat at one end of the table and three people sat along one long side. Mac and Jess sat on the other long side with three deputies standing behind them. Against the wall at the end of the room, sat Doctor Clayton and Doug Helms. A stack of typed papers had been placed in front of both Jess and Mac.

When they were seated, Sheriff Turner said, "We have discussed the evidence among the staff and with our attorney, Mr. Simmons, who is sitting in front of you and will explain the situation." He nodded to Simmons who read from documents in his hands.

"After reviewing the current evidence, affidavits, and your collective statements given to the county today, it has been concluded that there is more than substantial documentation to issue an arrest warrant for both of you. The deputies behind you have been instructed to escort you immediately to the county jail next door, unless you agree to certain conditions." He flipped the paper over, revealing another document that looked more official. It had a seal at the top and signature lines at the bottom.

Simmons looked over the official paper for a moment, wiggling a fountain pen between his fingers. He dropped the pen deliberately on the table and said, "Miss Shew... may I call you Jess?"

"To tell you the truth, Mr. Simmons, I would prefer to be called by my married name, Mrs. Davis," she replied softly.

"Very well, Mrs. . . . . Davis, what I have in front of me is a statement that you will be asked to sign. There will be a similar one for Mr. Davis to sign. Essentially it says that you hereby agree to stop all illegal practice of medicine, dispensing of all drugs and potions to both adults and minors, and providing medical advice and treatment. You will also agree to give up the practice of casting spells, incantations, hypnotism, or anything that would give the appearance of witchcraft. You will agree to surrender all medicines, concoctions, potions, as well as all equipment, and recipes or formulas from which your potions are made.

"Mr. Davis, you will agree to cease providing assistance to the illegal practice and stop any further delivering of medication to other people.

"We are aware that you two have a child and are concerned about his welfare. Mrs. Davis and Mr. Davis, I have been an attorney for three decades. I have seen a thousand cases. And I can tell you from experience based, on the evidence against you supporting very serious felony charges, that if you don't agree to these simple terms, you will both go to prison and that six-year old boy will become a ward of the state and his childhood will be over long before you get out."

He put the papers down and continued, "The

documents in front of you are in quadruplicate. Read them and sign all four copies, but you have the right to refuse. If you refuse, stand, empty your pockets onto the table, and place your hands behind your back."

They read in silence. Jess held the document close to her chest and read slowly. Mac noticed the slight tremor in her fingers rippling the paper. When they finished reading, she said, "I would like to talk this over with Mr. Davis."

Simmons looked at Sheriff Turner.

"We'll leave the room, except Chief Deputy Buchannan. You have ten minutes," said the sheriff.

"We would appreciate it if the Major would stand outside the door," Mac said. The sheriff nodded and they all left the room. Neither Doug nor the doctor looked at us as they walked by.

"Mac, if we sign it, whatta we do next?" she said. "I don't really know how to do anythin' but what I've done since I was a young girl."

"Except, be a good mom," Mac said in a whisper, trying to ignore the pounding inside his chest.

"I'll never let 'em have him. You know that." She shoved the papers away from her, closed her eyes, and intertwined her fingers so hard the tips turned red and the knuckles turned white. After a minute or so, she pulled the papers close and signed them.

CHAPTER 39

October air is always cool and dry, especially at five in the morning. That's when the rooster starts crowing. Great Aunt Brusie rose from bed wearing her long white gown and started her tasks right away. She had several more days of chicken feed left in the burlap bag, but decided to let them have the whole bag that morning. The little flock must have known something was different and fluttered around her feet as she spread handfuls of the yellow feed across the chicken yard.

After watching the excitement for a moment, she returned to her work desk in the living room and started rewriting her will. It was similar to the one she had made years before with one fundamental difference. In the first will, all her possessions and land were to be given to her closest living relatives, Jess and Theron, jointly. The only change she made that morning was to divide her estate into two equal parts. She drew a line on an old land survey of the property, showing Jess' inheritance included the house, at the top of Stumpy Ridge, and the land surrounding the top twenty acres on the north side of the mountain, including the family cemetery. The part being given to Theron took in the entire north face of the mountain below the rim, all the caves, and forty acres of

267

farmland on the south side of the mountain. She drew the lines with a pencil and used a ruler wherever she needed a straight line. With a pen, she signed the will and the survey. She then signed her name in the family Bible on the first page just below her mother's name and placed two dates beside her name, October 15, 1877, and October 15, 1952.

She carefully folded the will, the deed, and the survey in the long direction through the center, and slid them into the middle of the family Bible. She wrote a short letter to her neighbor with instructions on how to take care of her chickens and another long letter explaining everything to Jess.

Still in her white gown, she cleaned the whole house, stopped at four o'clock, and dragged a rush bottom rocker across the room to a spot by the west window. A puffy cloud floated by. She watched it turn yellow, red, then maroon. As the sky gave up all color and light, the last ember in the fireplace gave up its last spark.

Great Aunt Brusie climbed into her bed, smoothed her white gown, spread her long white hair across the pillow, twined her fingers together across her chest, closed her eyes, smiled, and stopped breathing.

CHAPTER 40

McKENZIE

Stumpy Mountain Road was winding and slow, but that morning it seemed slower than ever because I was an hour late. Robb waited for me on the porch every Friday morning and I was always there by ten. His smile, and wave, and eyes as wide as pie pans were hopelessly addictive and I didn't want to disappoint him.

The road followed the river, and my turn into Jess' drive was at the last big curve before the bridge. I knew something was wrong before I rounded the bend. Her house is too far buried in the woods to be visible from the road, but I had that should-have-been-there-an-hour-ago feeling.

Two large dump trucks, a small truck with a gray tarp over the back, and three official sheriff's vehicles filled her drive. I maneuvered my car into the grass beyond the porch and ran into the house. One of the deputies dressed in brown was in the kitchen filling cardboard boxes with Jess' vials and bottles and another deputy was in her storage room dumping all the contents of her herb jars into cloth totes. Both were so busy they didn't even notice me as I walked all the way through the house and out the back door. Three other men were digging up everything in both the upper garden by the house and in the lower garden near the river. Steel trash cans with tightly secured lids lined the back of the house.

No sign of Jess and Robb. I walked around the house to the end of the front porch, leaned on the rail to see as far as I could into the other side of the yard, then looked up. Jess and Robb were sitting on top of the long, high rock outcropping. They were sitting close to the same spot where I spied on her, the day I fell. They didn't see me at first. I walked into the yard and waved both hands over my head. Robb jumped up and waved back. Jess signaled for me to join them. As I ran back through the house, I recognized the two men as the deputies that drove us to the sheriff's interrogation exactly a week earlier. The deputy in the kitchen yelled at me as I flew out the back door. I couldn't hear what he said and had no desire to find out.

Robb greeted me with a big hug as if I could make everything all better. I sat beside Jess. "They're taking it all, Jess."

"I know. I couldn't watch," she said.

"Then don't stay here. Let's go down and get a few things for you and Robb and go back to my farm for the weekend or as long as you want." Robb and I waited for a response as she watched a man in a jumpsuit below us lifting barrels into the dump truck. Each barrel was filled with things she had grown for her patients, but all of it was going to be dumped where it would rot away or be devoured by scavengers and worms.

She didn't answer but stood and took Robb's hand. I followed them back down the rock. She said nothing to the men in the house still plowing through her books and private notes, putting some in a wood box and some in another trash can. She left enough feed and water for the chickens to last a week. The deputies never even saw us drive away.

Jess let Robb sit in the front seat beside me while she sat in the back. Robb was sure I had accomplished my mission as hero and saved them from the bad guys. I watched Jess in the car mirror just as I did that day we met. She planted her elbows on her knees and covered her face with both hands. With each sob, her shoulders heaved and head shook, but she never made a sound and didn't know I was watching.

We stayed a week at my farm before returning to Jess' house. I was right. They had taken everything that related to her healing practice and much more. Almost all her books, everything she cooked with, all containers, her personal notes, her list of patients and record of deliveries, the records of who had paid in money, who had paid in barter, and who still owed her money. Her gardens were nothing but churned earth. They had taken all the chickens and even the snakeskins hanging on the fence. Jess expressed no emotion as she packed the remaining personal items and clothing. We locked up the house and headed back to my farm with a full carload. We made one more trip to get some of her favorite furniture before the snow came that year.

Jess and I moved into the same bedroom she had been using on weekends for the previous three summers at my farm. We set up all Robb's belongings in a bedroom adjacent to us, but one weekend each month, he slept in his little room in the barn and I slept in my old barn bedroom beside him.

By the next spring, she sold her house to an old couple from Black Mountain. They had been friends of her family for years and wanted to live a little closer to Redbriar. We moved some of her furniture to her aunt's house. When the warm weather returned, we spent our weekends on my farm, but the rest of the week we lived at Aunt Brusie's house at the top of the ridge.

CHAPTER 41

McKENZIE

Robb looked back one more time at the old brick school house and the crowd of children on the playground.

"What do you think?" I asked.

"It's kinda big," said Robb.

"I know, but you'll meet some new friends there and your mama and I will be right down the road."

He nodded. As we drove off the school drive onto the main road, Robb pulled his feet onto the car seat, wrapped his arms around his knees, and looked out the window. He was quiet most of the way back.

"I know you love the house on the ridge. So does your mama, but you know what, you won't have to go to that school until after the whole summer is over, and we're all going to live up at Aunt Brusie's house until then. We'll move back down to the farm while you are in school, but we'll still spend the weekends in the mountain house until school lets out in the spring. Then, we'll stay at the ridge again for the whole summer. How does that sound?"

"Okay," he said, with a little more cheer in his voice.

"Also, this summer, you and I are going to explore the caves under Stumpy Ridge," I said.

"We will?"

"Yes! I've wanted to do that for a long time and never had anybody to go with me, but now you've turned six. You're big enough to explore caves." His eyes widened as he nodded in agreement.

We returned to the General Store parking lot and walked to the Ridge house expecting to see Jess on the front porch waiting for us. She was not in the house so Robb and I walked down the path to the family graveyard. Robb ran ahead of me through the rhododendron and found Jess kneeling by a basket of asters and daffodils. She was so busy cutting stems and placing flowers on the graves that she didn't see us at first.

"Hey, there's my little soldier!" said Jess as Robb ran to her. "How did it look?"

"Okay, I guess," said Robb.

"Just okay?"

"Well, maybe a little scary."

"There'll be lots of other kids just like you there. Don't worry."

He shrugged, looked back up the hill, then asked, "Can I go down to the Todds' house and play with Berry and the kids for a while?"

"Sure," she said. Robb waved as he ran past me.

I knelt beside her and gathered cut stems into a pile while she finished tying a string around a bundle of daffodils. She was wearing her garden boots, brown pants, and the light-blue shirt I had bought for her. She looked pretty, but she was struggling. Six months had passed since her aunt died and the sheriff took her treasures. She pretended that it was just another turn on the path, but she was sinking deeper into herself. She was trying to stay above it, but it had all ended so quickly for her.

"Robb isn't too sure about going to that school," she said.

"He'll be fine. While we were there, we watched a bunch of older kids playing — probably fifth or six graders. I'm sure they looked big to him. But, you're right, when he starts there next fall and sees other kids his own age, he'll feel better."

Jess nodded and moved the basket of flowers to the next grave. She didn't say a word or look at me for a long while. I knew she wouldn't talk any more about it until she was ready, so I didn't push. I said to her, "Can I help?"

"No, only one left to do."

"Aunt Brusie's?"

"Yep."

"I miss her, too," I said. The name on the rough granite had not yet been carved so Jess placed the flowers in the middle of the stone.

"I wish I had known her better," I continued. "I'm sure I'll never meet anyone like her again." Jess stopped for a moment, closed her eyes, and gave a slight shake of her head in silent agreement.

Her eyes bounced off me before returning to her work. That was her way of telling me she wasn't ready to discuss it. I waited a few more minutes, but I couldn't help feeling she needed to talk about it a little.

"It just seems to me...I mean, don't you think...when she died, we lost more than just your aunt?" I said.

She didn't look at me. It was May and grass was already trying to grow over the fresh earth on the grave. Jess sat on the ground, leaned back, and rested her head on part of the mound. She looked up through the trees at the churning gray-white clouds as they rolled over us. I sat down in the grass, waiting for her to speak. For a while, I watched the clouds and the still, endless blue beyond them.

"Jess, look around at what's happening." I finally said. She looked at me, then back to the clouds. "This is 1953. Don't you see how things are changing now, since the war? You know it's not going to stop and nothing is going back like it was. Maybe all that has happened to us was inevitable." I let her think about it for a minute then said, "You know Dr. Clayton is going to keep his clinic and the people of this mountain, all the Ridge People, will eventually go to him. What choice do they have now? He'll probably open one in Weavertown, too. In addition to that, Redbriar will someday soon get their own hospital. Sooner or later, somebody's going to figure out how to build a big highway through these mountains."

She rolled toward me and said, "You think Dr. Clayton can ever do what I've done for them?" She spoke so softly, I could barely hear her above the sound of the trees.

"No, he can't and never will, but, your practice...I don't think it will ever come back because, like I said, everything is...I think it all died with your aunt."

She lay back again.

"What's next?" she asked.

"We'll spend the summer here on the ridge and the winter at my farm. It's all going to be new to Robb. Let's see what happens." She nodded and thought about it for a while. She reached over and placed her hand over mine. We intertwined fingers and listened to the trees.

CHAPTER 42

McKENZIE

We knew it was going to be an exciting day and we could hardly wait until late afternoon. The clouds were thick and layered with different tones of gray. Occasional shafts of sunlight ran over us and around the mountain. The trees moved in rhythm with a strong, steady wind. Robb held my hand, but his eyes were wide and constantly looked in all directions.

Part of the climb to the cave's mouth included shuffling across a long, narrow, white, wet ledge with a thirty-foot drop-off below. Robb walked in front of me, shuffling his feet a few inches at a time while holding tightly to the rock wall beside him. I kept my hand firmly locked around the back of his belt.

We pushed our way through thick clumps of trees until we came to a clearing and a stone cliff that rose to a platform about twenty feet high. Beyond that, another hundred yards away, were two huge layers of rock that collided millions of years ago forcing both layers to rise out of the mountain forming a long, narrow gap between them. Still following every detail of Jess' instructions, we descended into a steep tunnel, a hidden cavern inside the mountain. Robb walked on his own, part of the way, but the wind rushing over the gap in the mountain above us and the darkness of the cave below frightened him.

"Hold my hand," he said.

"How about a ride on my back," I said.

"Okay," he said slowly, but bravely.

We climbed down as far as we could, and sat on the rock floor until our eyes adjusted to the dark. It was a flat space forty feet below the top of the mountain. We were in a crevice about a hundred feet long between the two layers of stone. The lower stone, the surface we sat on, had a dry gully formed long ago by water running to a dark shaft in the cave's floor.

I said to Robb, "Jess warned me about getting too close to that big hole." I looked at him to see if he was listening. "Hear that, Robb?" I said, tapping him on the top of his head.

"Yes," he said so softly, I knew his mind was trying to take it all in.

"All we have to do now is wait a little while."

"How long?" asked Robb.

"I don't know," I said. "We just have to wait." Robb climbed off his rock and sat beside me on the floor. After fifteen minutes, we heard the wind whipping the leaves on the mountain high above us.

Cold air rushed from the dark cavern below. The wind came and went away, then returned for a longer blast, only to recede and return again and again, until the rising air was so strong we felt our hair flapping above our heads. The earth's vibration beneath us became a long deep moaning sound. The low voice filled our heads. The winds increased. After a moment of silence, the sound jumped two octaves. The high voice didn't sound as sad as it did when I stood by the river in midwinter, but it was much more frightening.

We felt we were in the mouth of a giant beast as he sucked in and wailed out over and over again a long howling cry. Both of Robb's hands gripped my fingers so tightly they shook. I smiled at him pretending I wasn't afraid. I took a deep breath and joined the voice with the loudest scream I could throw out. Robb laughed.

"You, too!" I yelled. Robb's shoulders rose to his ears as he filled his chest and waited for the next roar of wind. Together we yelled back with all we had, at the sound and wind rushing over us. We were no match for the mountain, but each time we did it, Robb laughed harder until he was laughing so hard he couldn't catch his breath long enough to yell. We stayed in the cave not more than twenty or thirty minutes, but it seemed like all day. The voices slowly weakened until the only thing left was the whisper of air still rising to the sky and falling back into the endless hole below us. Exhausted, we pretended our voices had killed the dragon.

As a final victory gesture, I threw a stone into the dark hole. Robb picked up a small rock and did the same, but it landed on the hard floor at the edge of the shaft. He started to go after it, but I stopped him.

"I think we should head back," I said as I glanced up to the blue opening above.

I looked back. Robb was gone.

"Robb!" I screamed, running to the edge of the hole and saw nothing but emptiness below me with just enough light at the bottom, to see the shaft curve downward and out of sight.

I screamed his name again. It was useless. I sat on the

edge and lowered my legs, feeling for a rock or ledge to start my descent. The inside of the shaft was smooth with no place to get a toe-hold.

I scrambled out of the cave and inched my way down the mountain's rock face calling Robb's name every few minutes. It took thirty minutes to climb halfway down to a ledge protruding from the mountain about seven feet. I heard something below. I lowered my head and listened.

Goat bells rang in the distance. I called Theron's name, but the clanging faded away.

After another fifteen minutes, I was at the bottom, in a cluster of rhododendron. I pushed my way through the thick foliage until I arrived at a small clearing against the mountain. A pattern of wagon tracks crisscrossed the ground, maneuvering its way through an opening in the bushy trees. At the base of the mountain was a long thin opening in the rock. I slid inside. It was dark. A scattering of straw was being sucked through the opening across my feet and up the empty shaft. No sign of Robb. I cried out one more desperate gasp then squeezed, facedown, through the opening back into the light. Four red drops on the dull granite below me were already starting to dry. My fingers trembled as I touched them.

I heard my voice screaming his name. It was useless. I found more blood in the yard and even more by the cart tracks, but none beyond that. I bolted through the rhododendron to the trail that leads northeast around the back side of the mountain. The trail was steep and rocky and I was exhausted. I fell twice. My shin was bleeding, but the throbbing in my leg was easy to ignore. The painful part was the fear for Robb that tore through my mind like a Sherman tank.

The best I could determine, Theron had a forty-five minute head start on me and as long as he was on the rough trail I was probably gaining on him and his goat wagon, but I knew, however, that when he rolled onto Stumpy Ridge Road, he would take off much faster. I didn't know what direction he would go from there.

By the time I reached the parking lot beside the General Store, my legs felt like granite slabs and my mind was so numb I almost didn't see the crowd gathering outside the old building.

"Mac!" someone shouted. I looked up and saw Mrs. Todd running across the lot toward me. "Mac, over here. Theron brought him in. Come!" she yelled, waving her hands.

I followed her to a door on the side of the General Store displaying Doctor Clayton's sign. Clumps of people watched me run by, but their faces were pale blurs and their voices were muffled. Mrs. Todd stayed outside while I pushed through the door into a corridor with another door directly across a hall. A sign by the door said *Doctor Clayton*. When I walked in, he was leaning over his desk, but he dropped his pen and rushed straight toward me.

"Mac, wait," he said putting his hand on my chest.

"Where's Robb?"

"I put him in the other room and Theron's in there now, but, Mac, I got to tell you...I did all I could. It was *too late!*"

I tried to move around him. He stepped in my way again. "I don't think you should go in right now," he said softly.

"Get out of my way," I said.

"Mac, wait," he said again as I shoved my way past him.

The first thing I saw when I walked into the examination room was a door open to the outside and an empty examining table in the middle of the room. He was gone. Doctor Clayton followed me into the room, then ran out the open door calling Theron's name. When he returned he said, "Theron took him."

"Took him! Where?"

"I don't know, but he had his goat cart out there and it's gone, they're both gone."

I walked to the door and placed my hand on the smooth wood frame. Clayton went back into his office leaving me alone. The sunlight shot into my eyes and washed across the floor. For the first time, my knees trembled. They started to buckle, but I caught myself and spun into a chair and listened to the silence until Clayton returned with a piece of paper folded with two neat creases. "Mac, you need to find where Theron has taken him. And, sooner or later you will need this paper," he said handing it to me like a secret message. I opened it and read the two words on the top. It was a death certificate. I crumpled the paper and shoved it into my pocket.

I tried to think where Theron would go. The only thing that popped into my mind was the barn at Doug Helms' farm. Forgetting my knees, I darted out the door and started toward the farm. Before I reached the creek, I heard Jess' voice. She was running from the General Store toward me.

"Where is he?" she shrieked.

"Theron took him somewhere. I'm going to check the barn." We crossed the creek and pasture as fast as we could. Goats scattered. We ran through the barn and then to Theron's little house. No sign of him or his cart. "We should check Doug's house," I said.

"Maybe he went to my house on the ridge," Jess said, "I'll run up there."

"Okay." We took off in two directions. As I ran up the hill to the farmhouse, I remembered Theron sometimes left the cart behind his house. I returned and walked through the barn and slid open the rear door. The cart was there. I slid the barn door shut and leaned against it. Again, my knees started trembling. I walked slowly back through the barn. Before I got to the door, I heard a humming sound like bees in the loft. I stopped and lowered my head. The sound continued. As fast as I was able, I ran down the hill and called Jess who had not yet crossed the creek. I waved for her to return and we both hurried back to the barn.

"Walk in and listen quietly," I said. After we stood in the barn for a moment. We heard something, we climbed to the loft, and followed the sound all the way down one long side and across the short end. In the far corner, in a little nest of hay, Theron sat with his arms wrapped around Robb, humming, and rocking. Beside him was a porcelain bowl of milk with a piece of cloth tied in a knot draped across the edge.

Theron knew we were there, but didn't look at us and didn't stop humming. Jess knelt by his side and looked at Robb whose head drooped forward and his eyes were fixed, staring at nothing. Jess stroked Theron's head until he stopped humming, then she turned to Robb and whispered his name. We waited for some kind of response. Nothing happened. She spoke his name a little louder. I sat straddling a bale of hay beside her. With my elbows planted on my knees, I leaned closer hoping to see a change, any change. His face remained frozen.

I knew the look. I had seen it too many times in the war on too many young faces of soldiers who would never come back. But I couldn't tell her.

She waited an endless moment, then said, "Robb, look at me."

We watched in vain.

She said his name again.

His eyes shifted to her. Not a gaze into the distance, but focused on her face.

"Hello darlin'," she said softly.

He blinked.

With my help, we made another nest of hay for Jess. As she settled into it, she reached out and Theron placed Robb in her embrace. With Robb's back against her chest, her warm arms surrounded him. She whispered in his ear then sang little songs and hymns, and rocked him gently, pausing every few hours, whispering again.

Long before dawn, Jess said to Theron, "Bring your wagon around to the front of the barn."

Theron scurried off immediately. I carried Robb down the ladder with Jess ahead of me to steady my legs. With Theron's help, we managed to move him into the goat cart and take him up the ridge to Aunt Brusie's house, without being seen by anyone on the mountain.

Jess made a bed with blankets and pillows on the floor by the living-room couch, placed Robb in the middle, and covered him like we used to do when he was a baby. We let Theron go back to his house for rest.

She placed another blanket and pillow on the floor so she could lie beside him. I sat on the couch. Neither of us felt like talking even though we were wide awake. The thought of sleep never crossed our minds. Jess placed her right hand on Robb's left shoulder and patted it every few minutes.

Sometime early in the morning she took a break and I sat on the floor beside him. Robb slept, but occasionally opened his eyes for a few minutes then drifted away.

Jess returned with two large cups of tea. I sat back on the couch and sipped for a while. "I'm going to get some air," I said as I walked to the front porch into the early September morning. Bright, clear stars were scattered across the black sky. I sat on the top step and finished my tea. It kept me warm, for a while but cold slowly seeped into my skin.

Somewhere between guilt and grief is a river. I let it flood my mind until I shivered all over. I stared into the dark, looking for something to bring me back—to bring *my boy* back. I didn't move. Again, pictures of those poor souls that fell, dying in snow, deep in the Belgium forest, haunted me. Their last living act was to cast their gaze into the sky—like a final prayer—hoping for something from the infinite. But yesterday it was my son that fell and hope wasn't enough. I wished I had fallen instead of him. I wanted him back, and hope wasn't nearly enough.

I looked up again, then closed my eyes. Don't know how long. It would be another hour before sunrise, but somehow I stopped shivering and I was warm again. The black above began to glow a deep gray, then blue-gray, then peach-gray.

I picked up my cup and walked back to the couch. Jess stood and said she was going to try to give Robb some nourishment. I knelt by him until she returned from the kitchen with a bowl of milk, a spoon, and a couple of pillows.

"If you lift his head and shoulders, I'll prop him up with the pillows and try to spoon- feed him." she said.

Robb swallowed the milk a few drops at a time until the bowl was empty. Jess wiped his chin and face. Robb watched her the whole time except for a few shifts of his eyes to me.

"I think we'll leave the extra pillows under his head for a while," she said.

She touched the tip of his nose with her finger and said, "Mama will be right back." She then picked up the bowl, spoon, and towel. He watched her walk away to the kitchen. The moment she was out of sight, he said softly, but clearly, "Mama."

I shot to my feet and started to call Jess, but she had heard his voice and was already dashing back.

She sat on the floor and talked to him, sang songs and hymns. By noon, we opened the windows and let warm September winds blow through the house. Robb's face no longer looked frozen. With his brown eyes, big and moist, he watched Jess like any child who naturally loved his mother.

CHAPTER 43

JESS

It only took a few days before most Stumpy Mountain people knew about Robb. Many came right away, askin' what they could do to help. At first, I intended to let 'em see him only for a few minutes, but everybody wanted to help and they all found different ways to do it. Mac spent as much time with us as he could, but I would have been alone with Robb most the time if it weren't for the women that volunteered to stay with him a little while each day to give me some rest. For the next three years, almost everyone we knew on Stumpy Ridge helped us.

Whenever I had a chance to take a break, I curled up in my chair beside the rail at the end of the porch. I remember a day in late August. Light from the afternoon sun peeked through the trees. I was enjoyin' the warmth on my face as I sipped a long cup of tea. I heard someone kickin' stones down the trail to my house. When he came into view I squinted to see who it was, but the sun was behind him and I didn't recognize him until he reached the bottom of the hill and walked toward me.

"Oh, hello, Jess," Doug said as he walked up the steps. "Didn't see you over there."

"Hello, Doug," I said reluctantly.

He walked across the porch and sat in the empty chair beside me. "It's been a while," he said. "I know I'm the last person you expected to see up here."

"Three years," I said.

"Excuse me?"

"It's been just over three years since I saw you, but what brings you up here now?"

"Jess," he scratched a three-day-old stubble on his chin. "I would like to see him."

"Robb?"

"Of course."

"Why, after all this time?"

"Because three years ago I was told he was dead, then I was told he was not quite dead, then told he was startin' to recover but would never, in any way, be normal again, then people started sayin' he has made remarkable progress. I would like to see him, and would appreciate it if you would let me have a minute with him."

"Why were you not interested in seein' him when you thought he wasn't goin' to be normal?"

"I did want to see him, but I knew that whole mess with the fall and everythin' must have been killin' you, and you didn't need dealin' with me then and besides, Theron came to see you almost every day and he always told me how Robb was doin'."

"Well, I'm glad Theron did that. I know he's helped you a lot."

"Yes, Theron's been like a son. Know what I mean?"

I didn't answer.

"You know what I mean?" He asked again a little louder, then continued, "Since I was never able to keep my son."

"You're talkin' about Douglas?" Referring to Doug's first son.

This time he was the one who didn't answer.

"You know Douglas' death wasn't my fault?" I said.

We both looked away for a minute before he spoke, "Do you think Robb will remember me?"

"No. He can't remember anythin' before the fall. He was like a newborn child after it happened. Had to learn everythin' all over.

"What do you mean?"

"I mean everythin', even little things like how to talk, how to eat, how to walk."

"He lost it all?"

"Yes. He will never remember the first six years of his life or anybody he knew back then."

"What'd you do for him?" Doug asked.

"Lots of Ridge People been helpin' us."

"How did you get them to do it?"

"I didn't ask nobody to do nothin'. They just came."

"Who?"

"Half the Ridge has been here."

"Like who?"

"Well, more women than men, of course, but Eli Williams was one of the first to start comin' and he always brought Boney, his dog. The Berryhill brothers came and brought roots, and herbs, and vegetables."

"But how'd they help?"

"Well, Mrs. Hollars and her son Albert were the first ones to start comin' regularly."

"Yeah, I know the Hollars and their boy."

"Well, she always brought somethin' cooked, but Albert always brought his cat named Gray in a knap sack.

Albert and Gray were born on the same day, so they pretty much think they're brothers or somethin', so he carries his little pet everywhere. Anyway, Albert and Gray always made Robb laugh every time they came and it helped him open up."

"How? By gettin' him to laugh?"

"When Albert first sat on Robb's bed and let his cat out of the sack, Gray immediately sniffed Robb's hands then gave him an approvin' lick with his sandpaper tongue. That was the first time we heard Robb laugh. Also, the first time Robb moved his arm and hand was to touch Gray's soft fur. I think Robb loved seein' how much the cat enjoyed playin' with him. He continued movin' his hands and arms by constantly pettin' the little critter. Every time he stopped strokin' her, she nudged her nose under his hand to get him to start all over again. After a few months, Robb was laughin' more every day, even on days when Albert and Gray weren't there.

"So it was one inch at a time," said Doug.

"Yes, and I'll tell ya 'bout somebody else that helped Robb. It was Berry Todd. You remember her?"

"Of course, I know John Curley and Tiny and I heard all about Berry getting' her sight back."

"Berry spent a lot of time with him. Probably more than anybody else. She and her mother came every week. Later Berry started comin' all by herself. She made up some simple games for 'em to play. After about a year or so, she brought crayons and paper. With hand over hand she showed him how to hold the crayons and draw lines on paper. When he first started drawin' on his own, his little sketches made no sense to me, but they did to him. I think he knew exactly what he was trying to say. Sometimes he watched her draw. She pinned his pictures and hers on the walls, eventually fillin' all four sides of the room."

Doug turned his chair toward me and scooted a little closer.

I said, "Berry is two years older than Robb and she's teachin' him arithmetic that she's learnin' in school right now."

"Can he read?" asked Doug.

"It took a while — a long while. Like I said, Mac couldn't be here ever' day, but when he was here, he read to Robb almost continually. I read to him too. Mac wrote down little words for him to learn. We started with his name, and now he is learnin' to read children's books.

"Can he walk?"

"Sometimes when I was alone with Robb, I lifted him from his bed and supported him with my arms around his chest and his waist. I walked around the house with his feet barely touchin' the floor and he pretended he was walkin'. After six months, he stood on his own and after another six months he took his first new steps on his own.

"Who else came to help?"

"The two Crowder girls came with their mother to bring corn and other food. Later, the girls brought their guitars and harmonica and played music. Both girls clogged in rhythm while they strummed and blew their instruments. After a few months, Robb learned to stand beside them, bounce his knees, and half stomp his feet. He loves to walk now and is learnin' to clog and even run."

Doug put his hand on the arm of my chair and said, "Jess, I want to see him."

I had a lot more to tell him about Robb, but I don't think he could listen anymore.

"Okay," I said, "Let me go in and get him."

"No, Jess. I want to see him in his own room," said Doug.

"Doug, I'll tell you somethin'. I'm goin' in to talk to him. I'll tell him that someone he met a long time ago has come to see him, and I'll tell him you want to see his room. I'll find out if that's what he wants to do. Then I'll figger out if I think it's good for him, and I'll come back here and tell you if I'm gonna let you see him or not."

Doug nodded.

When I returned after talkin' to Robb, I gave Doug five minutes in his room with the understandin' that I would be at the door watchin' and listenin'. Doug surprised me by agreein' without argument. Robb was sketchin when Doug walked in and introduced himself and asked about his drawin's on the walls. Robb enjoyed explainin' each one. I was proud of him. After exactly five minutes, Doug said good-bye and said how much he enjoyed meetin' him. Robb waved good-bye.

Back on the porch Doug said, "Jess, he's a fine boy." He looked up at the ridge for a moment, then continued, "I see Dr. Clayton once a week at the clinic. He told me he comes by here every few months or so to check on Robb."

"Yes, the doctor comes here maybe four times a year, but he just looks at Robb, and talks to him like you did, doesn't treat him or nothin'," I said.

"Last Friday the doctor said to me that he watched Robb go from beyond hopeless to where he is now, and he said that he had no medical explanation for it, and I've got to tell you I'm as confused as Clayton, but I'm glad you finally did whatever the hell it is you do."

I had to close my eyes and take a breath before I said,

"You know back when you brought your little Douglas to me, I was very young and had a lot to learn?"

"Yep, but you're out of all that potion stuff now. The sheriff made sure of it, right? But, whatever it is you're doin' now, keep it up."

"Doug," I said closin' my eyes again, "I'm just an ignorant woman who somehow felt touched by heaven, don't ya see?"

"Well, I can only tell ya I was never touched by heaven or anythin' else."

"Everybody is, even old goats like you. Most people jus' don't realize it yet or don't wanna admit it."

Robb walked out of the house onto the porch and said, "Goin' down to the brook. Okay, Mama?"

"Okay, sweetheart," said Jess.

"Nice to meet you, Mr. Helms," he said with a little wave.

Doug watched him walk down the steps, around the house, and out of sight. Doug continued to look into the yard, as if Robb would reappear any moment. Finally, his head drooped. He was quiet for a long while. I left him alone until he turned in my direction, but didn't look at me. He said *good-bye*. His voice was soft, almost a whisper, like rustling of dry leaves. By then the sun was behind the ridge, and we were completely in its shadow.

Leaning over the rail on the west side of the porch, I watched him climb the hill. Also from there, I could see down the mountain and Robb strollin' toward the brook. He picked up a stick and scratched the ground as he walked along. He then stuck the stick into a hole in a tree trunk, rattled it back and forth, probably lookin' for critters. After a few more steps, he found somethin' on the ground and pulled it close to his face, examined it for at least a minute before shoving it into his pocket, and then skipped through a thicket, down to the brook, out of sight.

I thought about his accident three years earlier and the distance he had come. I glanced one more time toward Robb and resisted the temptation to slip down the hill and check on him, but I realized that what Doug had seen that day was a normal, complete nine year old boy and that everyone on the mountain knew about Robb's recovery and, although they didn't know it, Stumpy Ridge would never be the same.

At the top of the trail, Doug stopped and leaned forward as if he were talkin' to someone, then disappeared over the ridge. In the shadows, I saw a figure, much smaller than Doug, walkin' away from him toward our house, but I couldn't tell who it was until she reached the final curve. When Berry saw me, she waved and ran the rest of the way to the porch.

"Hi, Berry, come sit beside me for a while. Robb's down at the creek, but he'll back before long," I said.

"I really came to see *you*, Miss Jess."

"Good, I always love our visits."

"It's my dog, Mudhound. Somethin's wrong with him."

"Oh, I'm sorry, darlin'. What's the matter?"

"He just sits in the yard all day and won't go nowhere and won't even bark when people come to see us. Not eatin' much either."

"He's always been such a lively dog. Can't imagine him not barkin'."

"I'm sure you know just what I should do."

"Yes, come sit by me."

She pulled a chair close to the arm of my rocker, and opened wide her bluebell eyes, and said, "Tell me about healin'."

"What kind of healin'?"

"The way *you* do it."

"You know I don't do potions, herb medicines, and stuff like that anymore?"

"Yes, I know."

"Okay, then what do you want to know about healin'?"

"I wanna know everythin' about it."

Berry sat still as a picture — waitin'. She had a confident look on her face, not beggin', just knowin' I had an answer.

"Healin' is a gift that comes to everybody. It shines inside us," I said, "just a gentle glow at first, constantly comin' into our mind. Maybe right now we can't see it all, but, sweetheart, learn to trust it. Trust it like a child trusts its mother. It may come to us so softly we don't notice it at first, but it grows brighter and when we feel it, it has more power than we can ever imagine."

She wrapped both hands around the arm of my chair and said, "How does it feel?"

"Have you ever gotten up early in the mornin' and somehow you just knew it was gonna to be a great day, or somethin' good was gonna to happen that day?"

"Yes, now and then."

"And on those days, what happened?"

"They were great days!"

"So what do you think did that?"

"The glow?"

"What else could it be? Have you ever been afraid and, for no reason, you suddenly found yourself brave? Or, have you ever searched everywhere for somethin' lost but couldn't find it until the idea to search for it in an unexpected place came, and there it was — where did those thoughts come from?"

"Yes, that's happened to me lots of times. How did you know?"

"'Cause, it happens to everybody. It's always there, even when we don't realize it. Like I said, it's a gift. And it's one we don't ever lose; we jus' lose sight of it, but there's always somethin' shinin' in us that will bring everythin' back into memory. Maybe it seems to come out of nowhere, or maybe it appears to us in completely unexpected ways."

"Even to Robb?"

"Yes, to Robb, too. There's somethin' goin' on in our lives besides ourselves, somethin' controllin' all of us. When we surrender to it, and look for it, we feel its touch as soft as a baby's kiss, but it's a bitter potion for some people. I think that's why all children are easier to heal than adults, and women are usually easier to heal than men. I've watched stubborn old men with minor ailments fade away and die quickly while others, with more serious conditions, but more trustin', recover in a day."

"But how can that help Mudhound?"

"When you're with him and you're happy, what does he do?"

"Wags his tail. Runs around me."

"And, when you're sad, what does he do?"

"Hangs his head."

"You don't have to tell him that you're happy or sad. He just feels your thoughts, right?"

"Yes. He always knows how I feel before I say anything to him."

"So how does he know? He's just a dog."

She shook her head.

"Mudhound sees, feels, and hears your thoughts as clearly as if you told 'em to him, so he sees himself the way you hold him in your mind, so look beyond what your *eyes* are seein' and watch for things shinin' in you like a gift. Let 'em change your thoughts of him, and see what happens."

"But why don't we see 'em all the time?"

"We *do* see 'em, but most people just don't realize what they are and don't pay no attention…Now you know what to do. Okay?"

"Okay."

"Go back and look for things in him—things you thought were lost, or things you thought you never saw before, and I want you to come back tomorrow and tell me about it."

"That's it?"

"That's where you start."

The next day was Friday and by late morning I sat on the front steps waitin' for Mac to come. I don't think I ever told him how much I missed him when he was gone, and his face always told me how glad he was to be back.

Berry and Robb dashed down the trail followed by Mudhound who barked and greeted me with a lick on my hand. Berry gave me a hug and a kiss. She looked at Mudhound and, with a wide smile, she looked back at me. That was her way of sayin' he was himself again, and I knew she didn't want to talk about it in front of Robb. All three ran down to the creek together.

Jack Hemphill

CHAPTER 44

From the middle of November into March, it was too cold for Eugena and Theron to do their usual after dinner porch swinging. But the other eight months of the year, they spent at least two hours at the end of each day, quietly swinging together with the ropes giving off a sound like a purring cat. By 7:30 the mountain range that stretches between the Redbriar River and Tennessee casts its giant shadow across Doug's farm.

Even in July, the air cools rapidly after sunset. Eugena kept a blanket draped over the back of the swing giving them an excuse to wrap together under her quilt, enjoy the smell of the air, and swing slowly. Sometimes, on cold nights, they moved close and pulled the blanket over their heads just far enough to peek out into the dark.

One Saturday night in late July, Eugena cooked beef and potatoes. All three of them ate too much, but loved every bit of it. After dinner, Doug returned to his house, as usual, to let them be alone, but not long after the sunset, he marched up her porch steps."

"Theron. You feel the air?"

"Yes."

"Do you feel the water in it?"

"Water?"

"You know, moisture, like rain."

"Can't say I do, Doug."

"Well, I do, and what that means is we gonna have a doozy belchin' at us by morning."

"What's a doozy?"

"I mean there's gonna be lots of lightning and thunder popping all around here."

"Don't worry, I keep the goats calm."

"No, it's not that. I'll want you to do somethin' with me early in the mornin'."

"In the rain?"

"Yes, I will need to pick you up at the barn around four o'clock. This kind of storm always throws out lots of lightning and thunder right before dawn."

"Is this what we talked about the other day?"

"Yes. You still okay with it?"

"I'm okay, Doug."

Theron was already waiting as Doug's pickup pulled beside the caretaker's house. The black sky was already throwing white sparks in the distance. Three times the two men walked into the barn and carried large wooden crates to the back of his truck. Doug drove the truck all the way around to the parking lot behind the General Store while Theron led his two goats and cart across the stream and up the hill to a spot behind Doug's truck. Doug lit a lamp. They transferred the crates from the truck to the wagon then guided the goats from the parking lot down the rough trail along the north side of the mountain. Rain started blowing against their backs. Every time lightning flashed, Theron looked behind at the thick sheets of rain chasing them down the hill. The goats complained constantly, but Theron walked beside them reassuring them all the way to the bottom of the mountain and through the cluster of laurel.

Thunder continued to roll around them like it was looking for a place to strike. Twice it hit the mountain and shook the earth under their feet. So much water was running down the mountain's stone face, that they had trouble finding the narrow mouth of the cave. Doug slid in first and pulled the crates one at a time behind him while Theron pushed them with his feet on the outside. The wooden containers barely fit through the slit. Doug placed the containers side by side on the floor of the cave while Theron held the lamp. It shimmered light up the long shaft above them.

Doug said, "Your dad once told me he took you here many times when you were little. I know how special this place is to you. I'm gonna ask you again. Are you okay with what we are gonna to do?"

Theron looked up into the shaft and said, "I haven't been here since Robb fell. I know my daddy's not here. He wouldn't let him fall like that." He scrambled up the shaft to the ledge, pulled something from under a rock, climbed back to his place beside Doug, then handed him the picture of his parents.

Doug moved the photo close to the lamp and said, "They were good friends. What do you think they would say about what we're doin'?"

Theron nodded slowly, thoughtfully, then said, "'Where I'm sittin' right now is where I found Robb… when he fell…facedown, not breathin' or nothin'.'"

Doug gave the picture back to Theron and said, "Did you know that this is also the same spot I found my son Douglas many years ago, after *he* fell?"

"No, I didn't know that."

"He was unconscious, but still breathin'. I took him immediately to Jess, and she held him for an hour, and he died in her arms."

"No, I didn't know that."

"Turn the goats around and get them on the trail, well beyond the bushes. I'm gonna light the long fuse and meet you out there and then we need to get as far away from this cave as fast as we can."

Theron found the goats hiding from the storm with their heads buried in the laurel thicket. He talked them out of the bush and led them to the trail on a spot where he could wait for Doug. Rain dripped from his nose, chin, and eyebrows. He stood between both goats with his arms around their necks. All three shivered together.

Doug laced the long fuse around the sticks of dynamite. The wind whipping into the tunnel was immediately sucked up the shaft with such force he had to hold the fuse tip and the match close to his chest to light it.

Theron lowered his head and shook rain from his long hair. A low moan rose from the mouth of the cave and joined the sound of the driving storm and rumbling thunder. Doug slipped out of the cave, ran through the laurel, grabbed the harness, and said, "Let's go, let's go!"

The stone trail had become a small river rushing against their feet. Theron walked in front pulling the goats while Doug pushed the cart. The cave's voice suddenly jumped two octaves. Another bolt of lightning hit the mountain. The dynamite exploded with a shock wave so powerful it knocked both men to the ground. The earth shook like it was collapsing under their feet. The goats charged up hill and ran off the trail overturning the cart, dragging both goats into a gully. Theron and Doug ran down and unhooked their harnesses. Theron guided the animals back to the trail as Doug righted the cart and pulled it back up to the trail. Another deep rumble rolled under the mountain. Theron had to grab the cart and drag his feet to keep the goats from running off again.

It took them another hour to get back to the farm. They had just enough time to dry off and change their clothes before breakfast.

Theron said as he was walking into Doug's house, "I don't think I can eat breakfast this morning, Doug."

Doug patted his back and said, "If you don't go into breakfast, Eugena's goin' to worry about you and she'll come lookin' for you. What would you tell her?"

"I don't rightly know."

"Theron, you understand we can't tell anybody about what we did?"

"No, I don't understand."

"I know you were never afraid of the sound or the caves, but most of the people around here *were* afraid, and lots of them thought it was some kind of curse and if they knew what we did, they might be more afraid of what's gonna happen next. Those voices were always part of Stumpy Ridge and now they're gone. Jus' wait. The fears will go away in time."

"Did we do somethin' wrong?"

"No, the caves belonged to you. You could do whatever you wanted. It was right to do it. It's safer now, but we jus' can't talk about it. Give 'em time. They'll get used to it being different. More Ridge People will walk all the way up to the summit now."

"The what?"

"You know the top — the stump — it also belongs to you now, but you can let them use it. Tell them they can all use it."

"Maybe it's all blown up."

"It's gonna be different, I know. The explosion was bigger than I thought it would be. It was supposed to sound like another lightning strike on the mountain and look like the caves just collapsed — just died."

"It scared me and scared my goats."

"The stump will be better than ever. Just wait. "

"Okay."

"Then I think you should come to breakfast and pretend it's just another day."

"Okay."

All Eugena talked about that morning was the storm. Theron and Doug nodded to give her a little comfort, but didn't talk about it. Theron helped her remove the dishes and then he was off to do his usual chores.

The storm had already awakened Mac before the lightning hit the top of the mountain and the dynamite exploded in the cave. Robb and Jess came running out of their rooms. They looked out all the windows around the house, but only saw a little glow of dawn shining through the pounding rain.

"What was that?" asked Jess.

"I saw a flash and the earth felt like it was coming apart. Can't explain it. Never felt anything like it," Mac said.

"When it stops raining, let's go see what happened," said Robb.

"You're not going anywhere near the top of that mountain!" said Jess.

"I'll be fine, Mama. We're just going to see what

happened from a distance."

"I'll tell you what," said Mac, "we'll both go, but wait 'til the rain lets up. We'll just run up to the top of the ridge and we can look around from there." He nodded to Jess and said, "Be right back in no time."

They waited two more hours before going outside. The storm had moved south toward Asheville and the rain turned into a fine mist. They climbed to the ridge and then up the big stone outcropping at the top. Two other men were already standing on the summit and several dozen below them were making their way up the ridge. Part of the plateau had collapsed and the cave was no more than a rubble-filled scar carved down the north end of the mountain.

They knew right away it was gone and no one would ever see it again. No one after that morning would ever hear the voices, and the legends would remain memories only in the minds of the Ridge People.

As promised, Mac and Rob inspected the mountain for only a minute, then started back. To be sure they were safe, Jess had secretly followed as far as the ridge and was waiting for them at the top of the trail. All three walked home together.

The explosion that collapsed the north face of the mountain left shattered limestone and granite rocks piled from the base to the rim. Over the next few years, rainwater washing over the north side of the mountain deposited soil in the voids and cracks between the rocks. Thick moss grew out of the newly-deposited earth, eventually covering the stones and turning that part of the north face deep green. Grass, vines, and small plants grew out of the moss. Wild violets and wild roses sunk their roots around the rocks and covered the end of Stumpy Ridge.

Asheville grew at a steady pace and stretched her arms into most of the county, including all the property surrounding the Davis farm, but none of the three brothers wanted to sell any part of it. New highways cut their way past Asheville and dug deep into the mountains. Since it was impossible to construct a road of any kind on the Stumpy Ridge spine, the mountain remained one of the few secluded places in the county. Jess never asked anyone to climb the rocky trail to her house, but she always welcomed every visitor that was willing to hike the two-mile journey. In spite of the long, steep walk, people came to her almost daily to ask for advice, comfort, and healing. To give her time to meet with visitors and patients, Mac took care of the house and the property whenever he could, including cleaning, gardening, feeding the chickens, and anything else Jess needed.

CHAPTER 45

ROBB

When I was nine, my parents enrolled me in the elementary school in Asheville. They had spent years preparing me for that day. After extensive testing, I was allowed to enter the third grade, skipping the first two. I stayed at the head of my class for the rest of my school years and no one was surprised when, at the end of my senior year in high school, I received a scholarship to college. Four years later, I had a Bachelor's degree in literature from Wake Forest. During those years, I managed to go home about once a month to see my parents and Berry, who still lived with her parents. I joined the Army and after Officers Candidate School, I served two years at Fort Bragg, but my last year I was a signal officer with the 101st Airborne Division in Phu Bai, Vietnam. Just like my father, I wanted to serve my country and I know he was proud of me. Berry wrote to me every day I was there. For some reason, her letters made me feel safe.

Sometimes Berry enclosed a wild rose pressed between the pages. She spent a lot of time with my mother and wrote down little stories about what she was doing and what was going on around the ridge. As soon as I returned home, we were married in Dad's old barn.

Dad's brother, Uncle Tom, had three children and each of them had two of their own. Uncle Ham had five children and eight grandchildren. Berry and I had two fine girls. Altogether we had a clan of forty-two people.

We all gathered at the family farm for every holiday, but occasionally Berry and I took our children to celebrate with her sister, Eugena, at the Helms farm. Of course, Theron and Doug were part of those celebrations, and Eugena cooked the feasts, but eventually, as our children grew, they wanted to be with their cousins *every* holiday at our farm. So, with the family's permission, we invited Eugena, Theron, and Doug to join us.

For the first couple of years, Doug wouldn't come, but Eugena and Theron finally persuaded him, making a total of forty-five people at our family celebrations. I never told Doug that I knew he was my real birth father. It was best for both of us to let it stay a secret.

I was just a boy the last time I saw Doctor Clayton, but I was told he eventually closed his clinic on the ridge and opened one in Redbriar. Because of its success, a new hospital was built there with Doctor Clayton as the head physician. He wrote to Mama for years after that, asking about her healing work, and she was happy to reply. Preacher Ron left the mountain about the same time as Dr. Clayton. I never heard anything about him again.

I started writing professionally as soon as I got out of the Army. We had a house in Asheville, but Berry and I also had our own room in the farmhouse and stayed there as much as possible. I always wrote better at the farm.

I knew Berry thought of my mama as her second mother, and Berry had always been special to Mama. It didn't bother me at all that Mama shared things with her that she never discussed with me. Mama was the unquestioned center of the Davis family and we always made sure she had a chair in the middle of the group. Whenever the grandchildren celebrated birthdays, they always wanted to have their picture taken with her.

I guess my parents were what you would call *quiet people*, but when she got started, Mama could talk Dad's ear off. He was smart enough to let her continue without interrupting until she was finished. When his turn came, his comments were usually short and to the point.

Sometimes when Dad and I were alone, he spoke so slowly with such a deliberate but soft voice, I was compelled to listen and remember every word. Right before my first child was born, Dad and I spent the morning together in the barn. Even though the weather had not yet turned cold, we started a roaring blaze in the barn fireplace. He wanted me to help him burn old documents. His face was serious that morning which told me he had something important to talk about.

Two stacks of boxes sat on the floor. The larger one I knew very well. It contained all his notebooks about his life with Mama and me. Dad never told Mama about the notebooks and I understand why. Those books were the only secrets he ever kept from her. But she was aware of them and understood how important they were to Dad. So she never let on that she knew.

More than ten years of his thoughts and observations, and everything about my childhood from the time I was born to the time I was enrolled into public school in Asheville, were contained in those books. Twice during the previous year, he asked me to read them over as many times as it took to know every word by heart.

The last thing Dad said before we burned them was that when they were gone, they would be *my* memories as much as they were his. He said they were his gift to me and I could do with them whatever I wanted. Some of the old notebooks were so dry, they blazed white hot the moment they were shoved into the fireplace. They burned continually until completely gone, leaving almost no ash and only a small ghost of white smoke.

The second box was filled with pictures taken during the war in Germany and France, but they weren't pictures of the war or of the countryside. They were photographs of the fallen soldiers. I told him I had never seen them, but that wasn't true. Everything my Dad did in his life and everything he stored away in the barn always fascinated and haunted me, and I had explored all his secrets many years before, including photos of those poor dying souls lying in the snow in Belgium's Ardennes Forest.

Dad said he had one more thing to give me before we burned the pictures and it would be my decision what to do with it. He pulled a key from his pocket and unlocked a drawer in his desk. From the drawer, he retrieved a small brown envelope and handed it to me. I sat on the floor between the box of photos and the fireplace and unsealed the envelope letting a single piece of paper slide into my hand. It was wrinkled and slightly tattered, but the words were clear. It was my *Death Certificate* signed by Dr. Clayton twenty-four years earlier. Neither of us spoke as I read the document, and without hesitation I shoved it into the box to be burned along with the pictures. We placed the box in the middle of the red embers. The cardboard container immediately burned away leaving the pile of pictures and the certificate exposed to the growing heat. They curled, turned brown, then charred black before exploding into a flame that left nothing but thick dark smoke floating effortlessly up the chimney.

Dad and I never again discussed the pictures we burned that morning and I believe he finally put them out of his mind. I knew exactly how Dad felt and what he thought. Fresh in my memory were the same faces bearing the same fixed stare on too many soldiers I saw in the A Shau Valley, Khe Sanh, Quang Tri, and Phu Bai, Viet Nam.

Long after I returned from military service, people still asked if I recalled anything before my fall when I was six years old. Except for my father's notes, I still knew nothing then about my life before the accident. But the first thing I remember after the accident, was my mother's voice calling my name, waking me out of darkness, and the first thing I saw was her face looking down on me. It was like being awakened from the dead.

When I was in combat, I grieved for every soldier I saw lying on the ground. I grieved for them, but I believe, like me, each of them, after falling, heard a voice calling him to open his eyes and see a mother's smiling face looking down on him.

As of today, I've written twelve books and forty-five articles — all published and widely read. Six of the books were classified as post-Revolutionary War and pre-Civil War historical fiction, four were novels about the great migrations of Scots-Irish into Appalachia and the preservation of their culture for almost two centuries, and one book was about the people of Vietnam. My latest book, however, is the story of my family, inspired by Dad's extensive notes about us.

Not long after I started writing it, the early years of my

childhood began to come back as my own recollections. As I continued writing the book, all lost memories of my childhood and my family returned.

To protect the privacy of the Ridge People, I changed their names and the name of the mountain. Out of respect for my mother and father, I had the book classified and published as *fiction,* even though the things they did for me, the things they did for the Ridge People, and the ways they showed their perfect love for each other are recorded exactly the way I remember them.